DOOMSDAY: Minutemen

The Doomsday Series

Book Four

by

Bobby Akart

Copyright Information

Other Works by Amazon Top 50 Author, Bobby Akart

The Doomsday Series
Apocalypse
Haven
Anarchy
Minutemen
Civil War

The Yellowstone Series
Hellfire
Inferno
Fallout
Survival

The Lone Star Series
Axis of Evil
Beyond Borders
Lines in the Sand
Texas Strong
Fifth Column
Suicide Six

The Pandemic Series
Beginnings
The Innocents
Level 6
Quietus

DEDICATIONS

For many years, I have lived by the following premise:

Because you never know when the day before is the day before, prepare for tomorrow.

My friends, I study and write about the threats we face, not only to both entertain and inform you, but because I am constantly learning how to prepare for the benefit of my family as well. There is nothing more important on this planet than my darling wife, Dani, and our two girls, Bullie and Boom. One day, doomsday will come, and I'll be damned if I'm gonna let it stand in the way of our life together.

The Doomsday series is dedicated to the love and support of my family. I will always protect you from anything that threatens us.

ACKNOWLEDGEMENTS

Writing a book that is both informative and entertaining requires a tremendous team effort. Writing is the easy part. For their efforts in making the Doomsday series a reality, I would like to thank Hristo Argirov Kovatliev for his incredible cover art, Pauline Nolet for her editorial prowess, Stef Mcdaid for making this manuscript decipherable in so many formats, Chris Abernathy for his memorable performance in narrating this novel, and the Team—Denise, Joe, Jim, and Shirley—whose advice, friendship and attention to detail is priceless.

In addition, my loyal readers who interact with me on social media know that Dani and I have been fans of the television reality show *Big Brother* since it began broadcasting on CBS in the summer of 2000. The program was one of the greatest social experiments ever imagined. Each season, more than a dozen contestants compete for a half-million-dollar cash prize.

During the months-long airing of the program, the houseguests are isolated from the outside world, but we, the viewers, get to watch their every move via more than a hundred cameras and microphones. The opportunity to study how people interact under these unusual stressful circumstances has allowed me to create diverse and interesting characters for you, dear readers.

Over the years, we've been fortunate to meet several of the past *Big Brother* contestants, and this year, for the second time (the first being our friend Judd Daugherty, who was a doctor in the Boston Brahmin series), I've actually written four of them into the characters through the use of their first name and unique character attributes.

During the airing of season twenty during the summer of 2018, early on in the show, an alliance formed between a group of six who controlled the game from start to finish. You can imagine the high fives Dani and I exchanged when they named their alliance *Level 6*, the title of book three in my Pandemic series released in the summer of 2017.

To season twenty winner, Kaycee Clark; our favorite *showmance* of all time, Angela Rummans and Tyler Crispen; and to one of the funniest, most real people I've ever seen on television, "JC" Mounduix—thank you for inspiring the Rankin family in the Doomsday series!

Thank you all!
Choose Freedom and Godspeed, Patriots!

ABOUT THE AUTHOR

Bobby Akart

Author Bobby Akart has been ranked by Amazon as #55 in its Top 100 list of most popular, bestselling authors. He has achieved recognition as the #1 bestselling Horror Author, #2 bestselling Science Fiction Author, #3 bestselling Religion & Spirituality Author, #6 bestselling Action & Adventure Author, and #7 bestselling Historical Author.

He has written over twenty-six international bestsellers, in nearly fifty fiction and nonfiction genres, including the chart-busting Yellowstone series, the reader-favorite Lone Star series, the critically acclaimed Boston Brahmin series, the bestselling Blackout series, the frighteningly realistic Pandemic series, his highly cited nonfiction Prepping for Tomorrow series, and his latest project—the Doomsday series, seen by many as the horrifying future of our nation if we can't find a way to come together.

His novel *Yellowstone: Fallout* reached the Top 50 on the Amazon bestsellers list and earned him two Kindle All-Star awards for most pages read in a month and most pages read as an author. The Yellowstone series vaulted him to the #1 best selling horror author on Amazon, and the #2 best selling science fiction author.

Bobby has provided his readers a diverse range of topics that are both informative and entertaining. His attention to detail and impeccable research have allowed him to capture the imaginations of his readers through his fictional works and bring them valuable knowledge through his nonfiction books.

Author's Introduction to the Doomsday Series

November 8, 2018

Are we on the brink of destroying ourselves?

Some argue that our nation is deeply divided, with each side condemning the other as the enemy of America. By way of example, one can point to the events leading up to the Civil War in the latter part of the 1850s, right up until the first cannon fire rained upon Fort Sumter in Charleston, South Carolina. It's happened before, and it could happen again.

The war of words has intensified over the last several decades, and now deranged people on the fringe of society have taken matters into their own hands. Ranging from pipe-bomb packages mailed to political leaders and supporters, to a gunman shooting congressmen at a softball practice, words are being replaced with deadly, violent acts.

To be sure, we've experienced violence and intense social strife in this country as a result of political differences. The Civil War was one example. The assassination of Martin Luther King Jr., followed by the raging street battles over civil rights and the Vietnam War, is another.

This moment in America's history feels worse because we are growing much more divisive. Our shared values are being forgotten, and a breakdown is occurring between us and our government, and between us and the office of the presidency.

Our ability to find common ground is gradually disappearing. We shout at the television or quit watching altogether. Social media has become anything but *social*. We unfollow friends or write things in a post that we'd never dream of saying to someone's face.

Friends and family avoid one another at gatherings because they fear political discussions will result in an uncomfortable, even hostile exchange. Many in our nation no longer look at their fellow Americans as being from a different race or religion but, rather, as supporting one political party or another.

This is where America is today, and it is far different from the months leading up to the Civil War. Liberal historians label the conflict as a battle over slavery, while conservative historians tend to argue the issue was over states' rights. At the time, the only thing agreed upon was the field of battle—farms and open country from Pennsylvania to Georgia.

Today, there are many battlefronts. Media—news, entertainment, and social—is a major battlefield. The halls of Congress and within the inner workings of governments at all levels is another. Between everyday Americans—based upon class warfare, cultural distinctions, and race-religion-gender—highlighting our differences pervades every aspect of our lives.

Make no mistake, on both sides of the political spectrum, a new generation of leaders has emerged who've made fueling our divisions their political modus operandi. I remember the bipartisan efforts of Ronald Reagan and Tip O'Neill in the eighties. Also, Bill Clinton and Newt Gingrich in the mid-nineties. The turn of the century hasn't provided us the types of bipartisan working relationships that those leaders of the recent past have generated.

So, here we are at each other's throats. What stops the political rancor and division? The answer to this question results in even more partisan arguments and finger-pointing.

Which leads me to the purpose of the Doomsday series. The term *doomsday* evokes images of the end of times, the day the world ends, or a time when something terrible or dangerous will happen. Sounds dramatic, but everything is relative.

I've repeated this often, and I will again for those who haven't heard it.

All empires collapse eventually. Their reign ends when they are either defeated by a larger and more powerful enemy, or when their financing runs out. America will be no exception.

Now, couple this theory with the words often attributed to President Abraham Lincoln in an 1838 speech interpreted as follows:

America will never be destroyed from the outside. If we falter and lose our freedoms, it will be because we destroyed ourselves.

The Doomsday series depicts an America hell-bent upon destroying itself. It is a dystopian look at what will happen if we don't find a way to deescalate the attacks upon one another. Both sides will shoulder the blame for what will happen when the war of words becomes increasingly more violent to the point where one side brings out the *big guns.*

That's when an ideological battle will result in the bloodshed of innocent Americans caught in the crossfire. Truly, for the future of our nation, doomsday would be upon us.

Thank you for reading with an open mind and not through the lens of political glasses. I hope we can come together for the sake of our families and our nation. God bless America.

PREVIOUSLY IN THE DOOMSDAY SERIES

Dramatis Personae

PRIMARY CHARACTERS

George Trowbridge — A wealthy, powerful Washington insider. Lives on his estate in East Haven, Connecticut. Yale graduate. Suffers from kidney failure. Father of Meredith Cortland.

The Sheltons — Tom is retired from the United States Navy and is a former commander at Joint Base Charleston. Married to his wife of forty years, Donna. They have two daughters. Tommie, single, is with Naval Intelligence and stationed on a spy ship in the Persian Gulf. Their oldest daughter, Willa, is married with two young children. The family lives north of Las Vegas. Willa is a captain at Creech Air Force Base, where she serves as a drone pilot. Tom and Donna reside in downtown Charleston.

The Rankin Family — Formerly of Hilton Head, South Carolina, now residing in Richmond, Virginia. Dr. Angela Rankin is a critical care physician at Virginia Commonwealth Medical Center in Richmond. Her husband, Tyler, is a firefighter and a trained emergency medical technician. He was formerly a lifeguard. They have two children. Their daughter, Kaycee, age eleven, nearly died in a helicopter crash as a child. Their youngest child, J.C., age eight, loves history and is a devoted student of America's founding.

The Cortland Family — Michael *Cort* Cortland is chief of staff to a prominent United States Senator from Alabama. His wife, Meredith, is a teacher and the daughter of George Trowbridge. The couple met while they attended Yale University. They have one child, twelve-year-old daughter Hannah. They live in Cort's hometown of Mobile, Alabama. They have an English bulldog named after Yale's mascot, Handsome Dan.

The Hightower Family — Will Hightower is retired from the Philadelphia Police Department and in his mid-forties. After he left Philly SWAT, he got divorced from his wife, Karen. He moved to Atlanta to work for Mercedes-Benz security, only seeing his children—Ethan, age fifteen, and daughter Skylar, age eleven—periodically. Will also has a second job as *Delta*.

Hayden Blount — Born in North Carolina, but now resides in the Washington, DC, area. She is an attorney with a powerful law firm that represents the president in front of the Supreme Court. She formerly clerked for Justice Samuel Alito, a Yale graduate. Single, she lives alone with her Maine coon cat, Prowler.

Ryan and Blair Smart, Chubby and the Roo — Former residents of Florida, and now founders of the Haven, a prepper community built on the former location of the Hunger Games movie set in Henry River Mill Village, North Carolina, just west of Charlotte. The Smarts, together with their two English Bulldog sisters, Chubby and the Roo, now reside at Haven House within the community and have surrounded them with like minded thinkers as they prepare for the coming collapse.

György Schwartz and his son, Jonathan — The Schwartz family name was synonymous with high-flying financial deals, currency manipulations, and wealth. One of the thirty richest and most powerful men in the world hadn't come easy, but once attained, it allowed him to engage in shrewd financial arrangements and political machinations. They live on the Schwartz Estate in Katonah, New York, just across the Connecticut state line.

SECONDARY CHARACTERS

Alpha, Bravo, Charlie — The Haven needed a security team, but these individuals needed to have other skills that contributed to the daily operations and development of the community. The Smart's first hire was Alpha. Ex-military with an expertise in building primitive, log structures, he was a perfect fit and became the head of the security detail which included recruits Bravo and Charlie. Will Hightower, who was referred to as Delta at the Haven, was also a member of the team.

Echo — real name, Justin Echols, and his wife, Charlotte, were the oldest members of the Haven until the Sheltons arrived. Although not a member of the security team, Echo was part of the Haven's hierarchy. He and Charlotte were former farmers who had an expertise in sustainable living and caring for livestock. Their role as providers to the Haven community was invaluable.

X-Ray — real name, Eugene O'Reilly, was the newest member of the Haven community, having arrived on the afternoon of New Year's Eve. Bearing the same name as the famous character on the *M*A*S*H* television show, his grandfather provided him the nickname X-Ray, and it fit his perfectly. A science nerd growing up, X-Ray was especially adept at all things electronic or associated with the internet. His elaborate Faraday Cages and computer setups seemed to be a perfect fit for the Haven.

Book One: *Doomsday: Apocalypse*

It was the beginning of great internal strife, neighbor versus neighbor, warrior versus warrior. The fuse was lit with a simple message, understood by a select few, but impacting the lives of all Americans. It read:

On the day of the feast of Saint Sylvester,
Tear down locked,
Green light burning.
Love, MM

And so it begins …

In *Doomsday: Apocalypse*, all events occur on New Year's Eve

New York City

It was New Year's Eve, and New York City was the center of the annual celebration's universe. Over a million people had crowded into Times Square to bid a collective farewell to the old year and to express hope and joy for the year ahead.

There were some, however, who had other plans for the night's festivities. A clandestine meeting atop the newly constructed One World Trade Center, ground zero for the most heinous terrorist attack on the United States in history, revealed that another attack was afoot. One that sprang from a meeting in a remote farmhouse in Maryland and was perpetrated by a shadowy group.

In New York, Tom and Donna Shelton, retirees from Charleston, South Carolina, belatedly celebrated their fortieth anniversary atop the Hyatt Centric Hotel overlooking Times Square. Caught up in the moment, they made the fateful decision to join the revelers on the streets for a once-in-a-lifetime opportunity to be part of the famous ball drop and countdown to New Year's.

However, terror reared its ugly head as a squadron of quadcopter drones descended upon Midtown Manhattan, detonating bombs over Times Square and other major landmarks in the city. Chaos ensued and the Sheltons found themselves fighting for their lives.

After an injury to Donna, the couple made their way back to their hotel room, where they thought they were safe. However, Tom received a mysterious text, one that he was afraid to reveal to his wife. It came from a sender whom he considered a part of his distant past. It was an ominous warning that weighed heavily on his mind.

The text message read:

The real danger on the ocean, as well as the land, is people.
Fare thee well and Godspeed, Patriot!
MM

Six Flags Great Adventure, New Jersey

Dr. Angela Rankin and her husband, Tyler, were in the second leg of their educational vacation with their two children, Kaycee and J.C., although the New Year's Eve portion of the trip was supposed to be the fun part. They had arrived at Six Flags Great Adventure, the self-proclaimed scariest theme park on the planet.

Following a trip to Boston to visit historic sites related to our nation's founding, they were headed home to Richmond, Virginia, with planned stops in Philadelphia and Washington to see more landmarks. The planned stop at Six Flags was to be a highlight of the trip for the kids.

The night was full of thrills and chills as they rode one roller coaster after another. Young J.C., their son, wanted to save the *wildest, gut-wrenchingest* roller coaster for last—Kingda Ka. The tallest roller coaster in America, Kingda Ka, in just a matter of seconds, shot its coaster up a four-hundred-fifty-six-foot track until the riders reached the top, where they were suspended for a moment, only to be sent down the other side. Except on New Year's Eve, some of them never made it down, on the coaster, that is.

When the Rankin family hit the top of the Kingda Ka ride, an electromagnetic pulse attack struck the area around Philadelphia, which included a part of the Mid-Atlantic states stretching from Wilmington, Delaware, into northern New Jersey. The devastating EMP destroyed electronics, power grids, and the computers used to operate modern vehicles.

It also brought Kingda Ka to a standstill with the Rankins and others suspended facedown at the apex of the ride. At first, the riders avoided panicking. To be sure, they were all frightened, but they felt safe thanks to Tyler's reassurances, and they waited to be rescued.

However, one man became impatient and felt sure he and his wife could make their way to safety. On his four-seat coaster car, with the assistance of a college-age man, they broke loose the safety bar in order to crawl out of the coaster. This turned out to be a bad idea. The young man immediately flew head over heels, four hundred feet to his death.

The man who came up with the self-rescue plan and his wife attempted to shimmy down a support post to a safety platform within Kingda Ka but lost their grip. Both of them plunged to their deaths.

Safety personnel finally arrived on the scene, and they began the arduous task of rescuing the remaining passengers, leaving the Rankins for last since they were at the front of the string of coaster cars. Unfortunately, as the safety bar was lifted, J.C. fell out of the car, only to be retrained by a safety harness that had been affixed to his body.

Despite the fact that he was suspended twenty feet below the coaster, held by only a rope, the family worked together to hoist him to safety and an eventual rescue. But their night was not done.

The Rankins made their way to the parking lot, where their 1974 Bronco awaited them. Tyler pulled Angela aside, retrieved his handgun that was hidden under the chassis of the truck, and explained. The EMP had disabled almost all of the vehicles around them. Thousands of people were milling about. Most likely, they had the only operating vehicle for miles. And the moment they started it, everyone would either want a ride or would want to take their truck. When they decided to leave, it would be mayhem. So they waited for the most opportune time—daylight.

Mobile, Alabama

Michael Cortland split his time between his home in Mobile—with wife, Meredith, and daughter, Hannah—and Washington, DC, where he served as the chief of staff to powerful United States Senator Hugh McNeil. Congress had remained in session during what would ordinarily be the Christmas recess due to the political wranglings concerning the President of the United States and attempts to have him removed from office. But that was not the reason Cort, as he was called by his friends and family, was taking the late evening flight home.

He had been summoned by his father-in-law, George Trowbridge, to his East Haven, Connecticut, estate. Trowbridge was considered one of the most powerful people in Washington despite the fact he'd never held public office. Cort was the son Trowbridge never had, and as a result, he had been taken under the patriarch's wing and groomed for great things.

The conversation was a difficult one, as the old man was bedridden and permanently connected to dialysis. However, as they conversed, Cort was left with these ominous words:

Either you control destiny, or destiny controls you.

Cort was consumed by what his father-in-law meant as he waited for a connecting flight from Atlanta, Georgia, to Mobile, Alabama. The flight that should have been routine was anything but. On final approach to Mobile, the plane suffered a total blackout of power. Nothing worked on board the aircraft, including battery backups, warning lights, or communications.

The pilots made every effort to ditch the plane in the Gulf of Mexico, but the impact on the water caused the fuselage to break in two before it sank towards the sandy bottom of the gulf.

Cort leapt into action to help save his surrounding passengers, including an important Alabama congressman from the other side of the aisle. His Good Samaritan efforts almost killed him. He almost drowned on that evening and was fortunate to be rescued and delivered to the emergency room in Mobile.

After a visit from Meredith and Hannah, Cort began to assess the devastating events around the country and then hearkened back to the words of his father-in-law regarding destiny. Deep down, he knew there was a connection.

Atlanta, Georgia

On the surface, Will Hightower appeared to be a man down on his luck although some might argue that he'd made his own bed, now he had to sleep in it, as the saying goes.

Will's life had changed dramatically in the course of two years since a single inartful use of words during a stressful situation caused his family's world to come crashing down. He had been a respected member of Philly SWAT, one of the most renowned special weapons and tactics teams in the nation. Until one night he lost that respect.

During the investigation and media firestorm, his ex-wife, Karen, turned to the arms of another man, one of his partners. His son, Ethan, and daughter, Skylar, were berated in school and alienated from him by their mother. And Will made the decision to leave Philadelphia to provide his family a respite from the continuous attacks from the media and groups who demanded Will be removed from the police force.

With a new start in Atlanta as part of the security team at Mercedes-Benz Stadium, Will looked forward to a new life in a new city, where his children could visit far away from his past. Ethan and Skylar arrived in Atlanta for a long New Year's weekend that was to begin with a concert, featuring Beyoncé and Jay-Z, at the stadium.

A poor choice by his son landed the kids on the field level of the concert in front of the stage, and then the lights went out. Saboteurs had infiltrated the stadium and caused all power to be disconnected. The thousands of concertgoers panicked, and the kids were in peril.

Will was able to find an injured Ethan and frightened Skylar. He whisked them away to the safety of his home; however, their evening was not over. Will was able to pick up on the tragic events occurring around the country. The collapse he'd feared was on the brink of occurring manifested itself.

Then he received a text. Four simple words that meant so much to his future and the safety of his children. It read:

Time to come home. H.

He'd been asked to come home. But not in the sense most would think. His home was not back in Philadelphia with an ex-wife who'd made his life miserable. It was in another place that he'd become a part of since he left the City of Brotherly Love.

It was time for him to go to the Haven, where he was simply known as Delta.

Washington, DC

Hayden Blount was young, attractive, and a brilliant attorney. She also represented the President of the United States as he fought to protect his presidency. After winning reelection, the president came under attack again, but this time, it was from his own side of the aisle.

Making history, his vice president and members of his cabinet invoked a little-known clause of the Twenty-Fifth Amendment to the Constitution to remove him from office because they deemed him unfit for the job.

Using Hayden's law firm to represent him, the president counterpunched by firing all of the signers of the letter and installing a new cabinet. This created chaos within Washington, and many considered the machinations to have created a constitutional crisis.

The matter was now before the Supreme Court, where Hayden once clerked, and she was putting the final touches on a brief that had to be filed before midnight on New Year's Eve. After a conversation with the senior partner who spearheaded the president's representation, and a brief appearance at the firm's year-end soiree, Hayden left for home.

Trouble seemed to be on the horizon for the young woman when she got stuck on the building's elevator for a brief time. After enduring two drunken carousers, the elevator was fixed, and she happily headed for the subway trains, which carried people around metropolitan Washington, DC.

She was headed south of the city toward Congress Heights when suddenly, just as the train was at its lowest point in a tunnel under the Anacostia River, the lights went out, and so did all power to the train.

A carefully orchestrated cyber attack had been used to shut down all transportation in Washington, DC, including the trains, public buses, and the airports. The city was brought to a standstill, and Hayden was stuck in the subway, in the dark, with a predator stalking her.

She got away from the man who would do her harm, using her survival skills and Krav Maga training. Then she helped some women and children to safety by climbing up a ladder and through a ventilation duct.

Once at home with her beloved Maine coon cat, Prowler, Hayden began to learn of the attacks around the country. She was shocked to learn the Washington transportation outage wasn't the lead story. It was far from it.

Monocacy Farm, South of Frederick, Maryland

The story ended as it began. The people who had initiated these attacks came together for a toast at the Civil War–era farmhouse overlooking the river. They weren't politicians or elected officials. They were spooks, spies, and soldiers. Government officials and bureaucrats—accountable to no one but themselves.

They shared a glass of champagne and cheered on their successes of the evening, hurtful as they were to their fellow Americans. They acknowledged their task had just begun. Standing before them, the host of the gathering closed the meeting with the following words:

"One man's luck is often generated by another man's misfortunes. I, for one, believe that we can make our own luck. It will be necessary to achieve our goals as laid out in our carefully crafted plans.

"With this New Year's toast, I urge all of you to trust the plan.

Know that a storm is coming. It will be a storm upon which the blood of patriots and tyrants will spill."

He raised his champagne glass into the air, and everyone in the room followed suit.

"Godspeed, Patriots!"

And so it began …

Book Two: *Doomsday: Haven*

The story continues with the introduction of Ryan and Blair Smart, and their four-legged kids, Chubby and The Roo.

My mother taught me a German proverb that goes like this — *Wer im Spiel Pech hat, hat Glück in der Liebe.* Or something like that (My German is a little rusty). This translates to mean *he who is unlucky in game or gambling, is lucky at love.*

Well, Ryan and Blair Smart were lucky in both. The married couple from Florida spent each day of their lives together and loved every minute of it. They were not gamblers, but on one fateful night before Halloween, they decided to take a stab at winning the largest Megaball lottery in history.

They won. Now, they faced the daunting task of what to do with their money.

The Smarts were genuinely concerned about the direction their country was taking and vowed to never let outside influences disrupt their happiness. They wanted to find peace and serenity in their daily lives while preparing for the eventual collapse of American society.

Over the next two years, their lottery winnings were transformed into the Haven, a community developed on the site of the Hunger Games movie set located at Henry River Mill Village in North Carolina, an hour or so west of Charlotte.

The community was designed to use the existing structures on the land, plus modern ones specifically purposed for creating a preparedness community. The Smarts set about to assemble a team, all of whom had an important skill to contribute to the Haven. Through direct contact and the recruitment of like-minded thinkers they met on social media, the Haven became a reality.

And it was just in time. In the midst of a quiet New Year's Eve celebration, the proverbial crap hit the fan.

OUR OTHER CHARACTERS

As a new day dawned on a new year, our characters found themselves in various states of disarray. As the reader found out in book two, they all had a common goal—get to the Haven. The journey was not easy for any of them.

HAYDEN BLOUNT was in a state of limbo. She was scheduled to appear before the United States Supreme Court on behalf of the President as he fought the 25th Amendment action taken against him. She was self-reliant and confident in her capabilities, but by the same token, she wasn't going to risk her life unnecessarily by staying in the metropolitan Washington, DC area as society collapsed around her.

Hayden prepares for either eventuality and travels to a nearby Walmart to purchase additional ammunition and supplies. After stopping by the gun range to retrieve her firearms, she sees a group of people spray-painting graffiti on a bridge support. The drawing of a fist raising a black rose high into the air was unknown to her, but left an indelible mark nonetheless.

TOM and DONNA SHELTON had survived the chaos of New Year's Eve with the only injury coming to Donna's ankle. As they rested in their hotel room, they are startled by loud knocking at their door. The police were evacuating the area around Time Square due to a dirty bomb scare.

With the assistance of a wheelchair, Tom and Donna made their way through Midtown Manhattan to a staging area where buses were provided for refugees to flee the city. One of the destinations to choose from was East Haven, Connecticut, a place that Tom knew well.

While Donna slept by his side, Tom decided to call upon a resident of East Haven whom he'd met in the past — George Trowbridge. During this meeting in which Tom asked for assistance to get closer to home, it was revealed that the two had been connected for many years.

Trowbridge was rich and powerful, and he'd purchased the loyalty of Tom Shelton with a handsome stipend in exchange for seemingly mundane tasks related to his command at Joint Base Charleston. The relationship had been hidden from Donna but she accepted her husband's explanation as their benefactor assisted them to Norfolk.

During the meeting at the Trowbridge residence, the sickly man provided Tom a letter to deliver to Meredith Cortland. Tom did not know anything about her, but Trowbridge assured him that their paths might cross.

MICHAEL "CORT" CORTLAND, wife MEREDITH, and daughter, HANNAH

The Cortland family had to make a decision. Cort had recovered and was released to go home. After seeing the news reports and speaking with his boss, a powerful Washington Senator, Cort knew that he had to take his family to the Haven.

There was just one problem. They knew nothing about it. Following an emotional scene in which Cort revealed some, but not all, of what he knew about the state of affairs and his reason for becoming involved in the Haven to begin with, Meredith acquiesced to their leaving Mobile.

Her bigger concern was now for her husband who wanted to fly. Gasoline shortages had struck the nation and societal unrest was rampant on the first day following the terrorist attacks.

DR. ANGELA RANKIN, TYLER RANKIN, and their children, **KAYCEE** and **J.C.**

The Rankins were caught in the midst of a region decimated by an EMP attack. Electronics were destroyed, the rural parts of New Jersey where they were located had no power. But the Rankins were fortunate that Tyler had an old Ford Bronco that was not susceptible to the electromagnetic pulse.

This would become both a blessing and a curse for the family. Having the only operating vehicle for miles, they immediately became a target for their desperate fellow man. Their first challenge was to get away from the Six Flags parking lot that was packed with dazed and confused New Year's revelers.

Then, they had to traverse the back roads through New Jersey toward their home in Richmond, Virginia. Except for a few skirmishes along the way, the family was almost in Virginia when they came upon the Chesapeake Bay Bridge-Tunnel. They entered the dark tunnel not realizing that trouble lay ahead.

Tyler gets ambushed by thugs who were robbing travelers in the darkness of the tunnel, but Angela came to the rescue. The family persevered and eventually made it home to Richmond where they came to the realization that they needed to wind up their affairs and head for the Haven.

THE HAVEN

Delta blended in with the team and he tried to reassure his kids, Skylar and Ethan that they would be safe. Skylar took to the community immediately, but Ethan had his doubts. He was more focused on reaching out to his mother and possibly bringing her to the Haven than assimilating with the other residents.

Around the Haven, preparations were being made. Security was established, duties were assigned, and the Smarts tried to implement the detailed plans they'd created over the prior two years. They hoped for the best but prepared for the worst.

It turns out, as the conspiracy surrounding George Trowbridge, his associates and the Schwartz family deepened. Trowbridge began to have his doubts about what happened to Cort on the ill-fated Delta 322 flight. Meanwhile, György Schwartz and his son, Jonathan, plot the further demise of the United States by inserting themselves into the chaos.

Jonathan was the henchman of the family while his father played global financier. One of the Schwartz family's favorite tools to manipulate financial markets was to fabricate societal unrest. To further their goals of collapsing the U.S. dollar, and destabilize American society, Jonathan calls upon the anarchist group known as the Black Rose, or Rosa Negra.

Well-financed by the Schwartz family organizations, the grassroots movement around the country was known for wreaking havoc on cities during political events. Now, they'd be called upon to take the fight to Main Street USA, America's heartland, where we all live in our neighborhoods, with two-car garages, and parks for our children to play in.

Book Three: *Doomsday: Anarchy*

THE SCHWARTZ FAMILY

On New Year's Eve, the fuse had been lit and now others were interested in joining the fray. One politician infamously said that you never let a good crisis go to waste. For the Schwartz family, this was their opportunity to bring down the house of cards known as the United States monetary system.

Markets like stability and financial profiteers like György Schwartz had the ability to disrupt that stability when a financial opportunity arises. However, the events of New Year's Eve were different. Making money was one thing. Collapsing a mighty nation like the United States was another.

It had been a dream of Schwartz's for many years to bring America to its knees, and now somebody had started the process for him. While the terrorist attacks were disruptive, they didn't accomplish his goal of collapsing the economy and the U.S. dominance over world financial markets. He didn't care if Russia, China or the hapless Europeans stepped into America's shoes, as long as the U.S was cut off at the knees.

Jonathan calls upon his minions in the Black Rose, also known as Rosa Negra. He believes that one man's anarchist is another man's patriot. As a result, it was easy for Jonathan to justify the violent methods employed by the Black Rose federation of anarchists.

He frequently likened their actions to those of the Sons of Liberty who opposed British rule in the pre-Revolutionary War days. Others saw them as a band of rabble-rousing thugs, loosely made up of groups from Occupy Wall Street, Antifa, and Black Lives Matter who were willing to use the disruption of society as a means to a political end.

Regardless, the Schwartz's devised a plan that would not only disrupt the psyche of Americans who chose not to engage in the fight brewing on the streets, but also enable them to profit from the societal collapse as well.

Using their vast financial resources, and the passions of the Black Rose movement, in the midst of the chaos that was initiated on New Year's Eve, the father and son threw gasoline on the fire. And, like the North Viet Cong soldier who would toss a grenade inside a village hut, only to run away and not observe the aftermath, the Schwartzes rushed to their jet for a planned escape to their safe place in New Zealand.

Their nemesis, George Trowbridge, had other plans for the father and son team. Using his contacts within the Federal Government, Trowbridge orchestrated a hastily obtained warrant for the arrest of the Schwartz's with the intent to have them detained indefinitely following the martial law declaration. In Trowbridge's mind, this would put an end to the feud between the power political opposites.

As the FBI closed in on the Schwartz jet sitting on an obscure tarmac, ready for departure, Jonathan saw the handwriting on the wall and narrowly escaped arrest. As he lay in the cold, wet grass, he vowed revenge.

Meanwhile, Trowbridge had another score to settle. He had become skeptical of his long-time associate, Hanson Briscoe, who was spearheading the events of New Year's Eve. The fact that Trowbridge's son-in-law, Michael Cortland, was nearly killed troubled the old man. He'd been around too long to get one-upped by Briscoe.

After a meeting in the Trowbridge home, Briscoe was allowed to leave but Trowbridge had made his assessment—the man who orchestrated the New Year's Eve attacks had to die. Trowbridge had big plans for Cort, and the attempt on his life could not be tolerated.

THE HAVEN

Meanwhile, back at the ranch, as they say, the Haven was busy implementing its survival game plan that had been a couple of years in the making. Ryan and Blair Smart had spent many months picking the right property for their prepper community and then planning to provide its residents with safety, sustenance, and medical treatment, all while trying to maintain some sense of normalcy.

WILL HIGHTOWER had been the first to arrive and was immediately rotated into a security shift. This left his children, Ethan and Skylar, alone during the day. Alpha, the head of the Haven's security team, had incorporated drone technology into their perimeter monitoring. His plan included using older kids to operate the drone's that continuously fed surveillance footage back to a series of monitors in the Smart residence, known as Haven House.

During Alpha's orientation of Ethan, the teen learned that his father had made no effort to locate a battery charger for his son's cell phone. This angered Ethan and he immediately devised a plan to leave the Haven and return to his mother and boyfriend in Philadelphia.

Using one of the drones as an aid, Ethan discovered a nearby home that was occupied by an elderly couple. He put the drone away, snuck over the wall, and stole the couple's car without saying goodbye or *arrivederci*.

The fifteen-year-old was sailing along, singing and allowing the wind to blow through his hair without a care in the world, until he reached Richmond. Then the old Oldsmobile ran low on fuel, and patience with the high-speed it had endured for hours, and the engine seized.

Ethan was naïve to the ways of the world. He thought he would be welcomed anywhere, anytime. He was wrong. At the end of his journey to Philly, he was badly beaten, stripped of his shoes, jacket, and cell phone, and left for dead next to a dumpster at a gas station.

Ethan's sudden, unannounced departure from the Haven caused more drama than Ryan and Blair wanted to put up with. The other important members of their team, the Cortlands, the Sheltons, and toward the end, the Rankins and Hayden Blount, arrived safely at the Haven by the end of the day.

Michael Cortland was tapped to be Ryan's right-hand man from an administrative standpoint.

As America descended into societal collapse, Ryan needed to focus on the safety and operations of the Haven. Cort, who was well organized and had fought trench warfare in DC, was the perfect man for the job.

In addition, Ryan called upon Tom Shelton to act as his advisor from a security standpoint. While Alpha was the warrior that the Haven needed under the circumstances, Tom was a seasoned commander whom Ryan could trust.

And, as it turns out, so could George Trowbridge. The Sheltons and Cortlands were astonished to find one another and when Tom presented Trowbridge's letter to his estranged daughter, Meredith, some tears were shed. The letter also contained a suggestion to his daughter—you can trust Tom Shelton, and no one else. Time will tell if the advice from her father was sound.

The Sheltons had something in common with another important member of the Haven, although they didn't know it yet. As they traveled through Richmond, the Black Rose anarchists were up to their dastardly deeds and blocked the southbound lanes of the interstate. While the thugs were attacking motorists, a young woman fought back and cleared the path for the Sheltons to escape too. During the melee, they even noticed how some creature mauled the face of one of the attackers.

Unbeknownst to them, the young woman was Hayden Blount who arrived later that evening and the creature that mauled the face of the anarchist was her Maine Coon cat, Prowler.

The mauled marauder crossed the path of another of our characters—Dr. Angela Rankin. She and her husband, Tyler, made the decision to leave their jobs and home in Richmond to go to the Haven. While Tyler was purchasing a truck and trailer, Angela went to the VCU hospital where she worked to negotiate a leave of absence. While she was there, she worked on the patient whose face had been mauled by Prowler.

Also, while she and Tyler were making their arrangements to leave, their kids, Kaycee and J.C. were left home alone to do some chores and gather the family's things for a road trip. However, the Black Rose federation had different plans for the neighborhood. After gathering at a Schwartz owned-property to the west of the Rankin home, the thugs began to march toward downtown Richmond and the State Capitol with the intent to destroy everything in its path.

They broke into homes, terrorized residents, and generally wreaked havoc along the Rankin's street. When they approached the house to break in, Kaycee and J.C. devised a plan. J.C. found a space in the old house to hide and Kaycee locked herself down the hall in her parent's bedroom.

Armed with a shotgun, she waited. Two of the marauders found her locked away and threatened her. They started pounding on the bedroom door in an attempt to break it down. Kaycee didn't hesitate.

She racked a round into the shotgun and sent a blast of buckshot through the door and into the bodies of her assailants. The two bad guys scrambled to leave the house, begging for their lives as they went.

Tyler and Angela eventually arrived to comfort their kids and the family made their way to the Haven where they were late to arrive. Now, everyone who had purchased property or had been invited into the community was within the safe confines of the Haven.

But there was one among them who had a dark secret. He'd been unknowingly recruited into a conspiracy that might lead to the demise of everyone at the Haven, including himself. He too had been the recipient of mysterious texts.

X-Ray was an introverted, techno-geek who could have been a valuable asset to Ryan and Blair Smart. As it turns out, he was someone else's asset as well. He'd done as instructed by the anonymous benefactor who paid him well enough to buy the electronics gear he so desperately craved.

When the shock wore off from meeting the man he was instructed to watch out for, Michael Cortland, he found the burner cell phone that he'd procured before arriving at the Haven. He issued the required text message, careful to get the words just right.

The eagle's mark is in sight.

Then X-Ray waited, unsure of what this meant and how he was supposed to proceed. Then he received a response.

Tell no one.
Will advise.
Godspeed, Patriot.
MM

X-Ray was beginning to lose his nerve. He considered running away from the Haven as fast as he could. He wished he had a drink. He stared at the cheap flip phone, wishing it would malfunction. But then, it buzzed to life with another text message.

From Doomsday Anarchy …

X-Ray quickly pulled the phone out of his pocket and flipped it open. He pushed the select key to change the display to the text function. He read the message and then collapsed back into his swivel office chair.

Beware of those around you.
All is not as it might seem.
Godspeed, Patriot.
MM

"What?" he shouted again. "Beware of who? You? Jesus!"

In a rare show of anger and raw emotion, X-Ray flung the phone across the room, where it careened off a lampshade and landed safely on the leather couch in front of the fireplace, its light-blue screen continuing to illuminate despite the attempt to kill it.

Doomsday: Minutemen begins now …

EPIGRAPH

"Cruelty has a human heart, and jealousy a human face; Terror the human form divine, and secrecy the human dress."
~ William Blake, English Poet, 1795
*****

"The Patriot's blood is the seed of Freedom's tree."
~ Thomas Campbell, Scottish Poet, 1795
*****

"The best medicine against the grapes of wrath
is a whiff of grapeshot."
~ Napoleon Bonaparte, the newly installed commander of
the Army of Italy, 1795
*****

"Our task is not to bring order out of chaos, but to
get work done in the midst of chaos."
~ George Peabody, 1795–1869
*****

"Scores will be settled …"
~ Early American idiom, circa 1795
*****

"It's never too early to start over, but it can be too late."
~ Unknown

PROLOGUE

One Summer day at Yale, 1984
Late Afternoon
New Haven, Connecticut

Secret societies have existed since the dawn of man—rituals, partnerships, alliances, clubs, and organizations whose activities were generally concealed from nonmembers. It should come as no surprise that Americans have created hundreds of secretive organizations since the days of the early settlers.

Early on, these clandestine groups were largely political in nature as the early colonists sought a means to break free from the grasp of British rule. The American Revolution had been centuries in the making. Successful revolutions never start overnight. Beginning with the early settling of the New World and the attempts to colonize Roanoke Island in 1585, the *Seeds of Liberty*, the important stones that were laid into the foundation of American freedom and independence, had been sewn.

Another secretive society was formed in 1832 at Yale University. A disagreement among collegiate debating teams resulted in a gathering of the school's class valedictorian, along with fourteen others, to become the founding members of the Order of the Scull and Bones, later modernized to Skull and Bones.

The exclusive Order of Skull and Bones existed only at Yale. For nearly two centuries, new *Bonesmen*, as they were called, were initiated into the secretive society. The seniors in the group *tapped* fifteen juniors at the university, literally, in a ritual evidenced by a tapping on the shoulder and a nod of the head. These select few became Bonesmen.

The family names of former Bonesmen were historically notable—Vanderbilt, Bush, Rockefeller, Goodyear, Taft, Weyerhaeuser, Kellogg, and Trowbridge. The Order of Skull and Bones helped one another to greatness in America, rising to become influential leaders in business, Supreme Court justices, and presidents.

From the beginning of its formation, the Order was under attack from professors who objected to its secrecy and from fellow students who claimed the Bonesmen enjoyed financial perks and educational favoritism.

One such group of students started a new school newspaper at Yale called *The Iconoclast*. In its first volume, the editorial board of the paper dared to take the Bonesmen head-on. They tried to expose members of the Order and the alleged control over the university's financial dealings the Bonesmen exerted.

Year by year, the deadly evil is growing, they wrote in their inaugural issue. *Out of every class, Skull and Bones takes its men.*

The article closed with this statement: *It is Yale College against Skull and Bones!! We ask all men, as a question of right, which should be allowed to live?*

One thing was certain, *The Iconoclast*, a publication named for a person who attacked cherished institutions, was not allowed to live. The paper was immediately shut down, and many of its student-editors were expelled from Yale.

The legend of the Skull and Bones grew further when, in 1856, the Tomb, a windowless, brownstone meeting hall, was constructed. To this day, outsiders claim strange, occult initiation rites are held twice a week. This was all speculation, of course, because Bonesmen never speak of what happens within the structure's walls.

Within the Tomb was lodge room 322, the supposed *sanctum sanctorum*, the holy of holies, that contained pictures of the founding Bonesmen, together with the emblem of the file and claw.

The old engraving had become a symbol for the Skull and Bones with a meaning known only to them. Even the number, 322, had a special significance. Speculation had always run rampant, with no definitive answers emerging.

One summer day at Yale, in 1984, the Bonesmen gathered at their private island retreat, known as Deer Island, on the St. Lawrence River. The forty-acre retreat was intended to give Bonesmen, students and alumnae alike, the opportunity to rekindle friendships, negotiate business deals, and discuss the politics of the day.

On that particular summer weekend, a divisiveness grew within the ranks of the Bonesmen. President Ronald Reagan had pleased the conservative members of the Order while enraging the liberal constituency. In a rare showing of the breaking of the ranks of the Skull and Bones, the two disagreeing groups congregated in separate parts of Deer Island.

The purpose of the agreed-upon separation was to allow cooler heads to prevail so the political acrimony could subside. The alcohol was locked up, and the most influential Bonesmen of the time hoped the arguments could be stopped.

What actually happened during the cooling-down period would go down in history. The conservative contingent, led by George Trowbridge and Hanson Briscoe, used the rift as an opportunity to plan for the future. The two men could see the direction the country was taking, and in their opinion, it was a path reminiscent of Rome as the empire began to collapse.

Trowbridge was a student of history. He recognized that collapse had happened to every empire in human history. It was, as he deemed it, a natural law that an empire achieves a certain level of success, its height of power and economic security, and then it implodes.

In his mind, debauchery and decadence began to rule the day during the time of the Roman Empire, and its decline came soon thereafter. It became a society that was mired in political unrest. Trowbridge, Briscoe, and the other Bonesmen on the right side of the political spectrum agreed and made a solemn vow—this will not happen to America.

Beginning that summer weekend, through the next three and a half decades, those Bonesmen, and others who agreed with their underlying premise, prepared for the day when they thought America would reach the breaking point.

They were opportunists who wielded great power over the military-industrial complex and the politicians who controlled the purse strings. For decades, secretive alliances were formed. Politicians were bought. Rank-and-file employees of the government, the media, and strategic businesses were brought into the fold. An army, of sorts, was built, awaiting the moment when they were given the signal. A signal that would come from a single source—*MM*.

The collective minds of these Bonesmen had come together that evening in October at Briscoe's Monocacy Farm to celebrate their attempt to rescue America from a certain decline into anarchy. They set their plan into motion. It was a plan that had been developed, revised, and finalized, waiting for the right moment. It was a plan that was to be trusted.

To these Bonesmen, the only way to save America was to bring it to the brink of destruction in order to build it back in the vision of the Founding Fathers. Their efforts created a framework, a plan, to give the nation a second chance.

Trust the plan.

PART ONE

CHAPTER 1

Haven Barn
The Haven

Blair Smart never looked back upon her life and thought—*what might've been*. As a high school freshman, she was pretty, popular, and full of potential. Then, one fateful day, while riding in the pickup truck of a classmate with her friends, the sixteen-year-old driver sped up a hill toward a railway crossing, hitting the tracks too fast, and lost control. Blair, who was sitting in the lap of a friend, was thrown forward into the windshield, causing significant injuries to her back and spine.

The surgeries and recovery associated with the accident forced her to withdraw from high school and abandon the extracurricular activities she enjoyed. For months, as she fought through the pain—both physical, from the accident, and emotional, due to her withdrawal from her normal activities—Blair tried to focus on her future.

Years later, when she first met Ryan, he told her that his father always suggested that he go to college. "*You trade four years for forty*," Ryan had relayed to her his father's sentiment. Four years of college would set him on a career path toward retirement.

Blair would never forget the conversation the two of them had over beers at a beach bar on Longboat Key, Florida. They talked about the board game *The Game of Life*. After you start the game, you quickly have to make an important choice that sets the tone for your life. One path, college, enabled you to make more money in salary, but it took longer to get into the real world, so to speak. The other path, career, threw you right into life and the school of hard knocks.

At age fifteen, due to the accident, Blair's choices in the Game of Life were taken away. Her dreams of college and becoming an attorney were over. She was facing physical therapy, home-schooling, and a goal of attaining a GED rather than walking in the graduation processional with her friends.

Yet she still had options. She was pretty and most certainly could find a husband, have kids, and follow the path of motherhood that so many of her girlfriends had in mind. Or she could enter the business world and find her own way.

Which she did. With the bulk of her physical therapy behind her, Blair got a job in a beauty salon. Not as a stylist, but as the receptionist. Within just a few months, her organizational skills impressed the owner and she was elevated to the position of office manager. By seventeen, she'd abandoned hope of being an attorney but still pursued her paralegal training. This also led her to training to become a private investigator.

The consummate overachiever, Blair had barely blown out the candles on her eighteenth birthday cake when she applied for, and received, her licenses in Florida as a paralegal and a private investigator.

After meeting Ryan, the two worked together and developed various businesses together. Some were successful and others, not so much. But they didn't care as long as they had a roof over their heads and they could be at each other's side.

When the Smarts won the lottery, they could've followed in the footsteps of other mega-millions winners by throwing lavish parties, spending money on toys, or impressing friends with expensive trips. Instead, they stuck to their plan, which focused on the safety and future of their family.

Now, as she stood in Haven Barn watching introductions being made and small talk exchanged between the strangers who knew nothing of one another, her chest swelled with pride. None of the people gathered for the morning meeting realized that they were all brought together for a purpose, one that was conceived many years ago in the minds of Ryan and Blair Smart long before those lucky numbers had appeared on those ping-pong balls of the Florida lottery.

Fate determines who enters your life, but actions determine who remains.

"You! You're the young lady that helped us in Richmond!" shouted Donna Shelton as she rushed to Hayden Blount's side. "I'll never forget your face, even in the middle of the chaos."

"You're the gold Yukon?"

"Yes, dear," replied Donna. "Tom! Tom! Come here, quick!"

Tom Shelton was speaking privately with Ryan when Donna got his attention. He excused himself and rushed over to her side with a concerned look on his face, until the recognition overcame him.

"Impossible," he began. "It's you! My God, this is an amazing coincidence! My name is Tom Shelton."

Donna exuded exuberance. "I'm his wife, Donna. I can't believe we've crossed paths again."

Hayden was also in shock at the unexpected turn of events. Her eyes darted around the room as she noticed the others pausing their conversations to listen in. "My name's Hayden Blount, and I work in DC. I was on my way here, of course, when the whole thing happened at that bridge overpass."

"This is like the *Twilight Zone*," said Donna as she spontaneously hugged Hayden. "Young lady, I don't know how we can thank you enough."

"Let me echo my wife's sentiments," added Tom. "We'd been traveling in New York City and had been given a ride to nearby Norfolk from a, well, a friend." Tom glanced at Meredith Cortland, who gave him a knowing smile.

Donna picked up on his sudden pause and continued for him. "And here we are. What a small world this is, right?"

"It sure is," said Hayden.

Tom recovered and his curiosity got the best of him. "Hayden, I have to ask you something."

"Okay," she replied with a hesitant look on her face. Hayden lived in a world full of opportunists and vultures in Washington. Her legal training always kept her on guard.

"During the melee, one of the men was trying to get into your vehicle," Tom began. "Suddenly, he fell backwards onto the pavement, and his face was …" He grimaced as his voice trailed off.

Hayden nodded and allowed herself a slight smile. "Prowler didn't take too kindly to the guy invading his space."

"Prowler?" asked Donna.

"He's my Maine coon cat, and let's just say he's bigger than the average cat."

"More like a lion," quipped Alpha from the other side of the room. Hayden glanced in his direction and then realized everyone had stopped talking as they became intrigued by the chance encounter between Hayden and the Sheltons.

"He's a big one," added Ryan. "What happened?"

"This guy, one of a dozen or more who attacked us, was trying to grab me through the passenger window," Hayden replied. "Prowler was pissed. He did some real damage to the guy's face."

"I can attest to that."

Hayden and the Sheltons turned their attention to the woman's voice.

"I'm Dr. Angela Rankin, a doctor at VCU. I was working in the ER when this patient came in, handcuffed to a gurney and escorted by police. We'd never seen anything like it. The consensus was he was attacked by a bobcat or something larger."

"No, just Prowler, although he's as large as many dogs. He's, well, very territorial."

The room erupted in laughter, except for Cort, who said, "There are a lot of coincidences here, including one that I haven't mentioned yet. By the way, I'm Michael Cortland, but you can call me Cort. This is my wife, Meredith, and our daughter, Hannah, is with us too."

"Are you gonna tell them?" asked Meredith.

"Yes, I think so," he replied. "A couple of things. First, and I haven't mentioned this to Delta over there." Cort pointed in Delta's direction, who waved.

"My real name is Will Hightower, but around here, I'm Delta."

Hayden smiled at Will and introduced herself with her moniker while at the Haven. "They call me Foxtrot."

"Foxy!" shouted Alpha.

"In your dreams, buddy," Hayden threw it back at him before turning back to Cort. "Go ahead, please continue."

He glanced at Delta and explained, "When I met your daughter last night, I remembered something that I needed to ask you about. Were your kids traveling alone, possibly from Philadelphia to Atlanta? She might've been wearing a light blue sweat suit?"

"Yes, exactly," replied Delta. "How would you—?"

"They walked right in front of me along the concourse when I was waiting for my flight to Mobile."

Delta perked up. "Wait. Hold on. The kids were on Delta 322 from Philly. I was at baggage claim to greet them."

"Delta 322 was the flight that continued to Mobile, and I was on it. Well, at least until it landed in the Gulf of Mexico."

"Huh?" asked Tyler Rankin. Angela squeezed her husband's hand and he allowed them to continue.

Meredith picked up the conversation, as she noticed Cort suddenly became withdrawn as he recalled the memory of New Year's Eve. "There's more, everyone. Cort was within reaching distance of Delta's kids in the Atlanta airport. Also, the Sheltons met with my father, who lives in New Haven, Connecticut. They knew one another when Tom was in the military."

"That's right, and then Hayden helped us in Richmond, and the guy who attacked her landed in Dr. Rankin's ER."

"Angela, please. Doctor is so formal."

"Is this crazy or what?" asked Alpha.

Blair smiled to herself. She understood how these things work. The universe finds ways to put souls together. That was how she and Ryan found one another. Some occurrences were just too inexplicable to be explained away as mere coincidence.

Fate. Destiny. Call it what you will. Blair knew it was meant to be.

CHAPTER 2

Haven Barn
The Haven

To some, it might seem like an episode of the television show *LOST*, but not to Blair. She knew all of these people intimately, more so than any of them realized. The School of Hard Knocks had taught her well as she entered adulthood in her teenage years. Everything she and Ryan had experienced in their lives, both before they met and after they were married, led up to this moment. Their successes gave them the opportunity to create the Haven and bring everyone together. But their failures and practical knowledge enabled them to create a group that would mesh under pressure. The fact, however, that they had interacted with one another in so many different, unexpected ways was more than just fate. It was almost supernatural.

"Guys," began Ryan, interrupting the conversation, "we're gonna have more opportunities to get to know one another and trade stories about your journeys, but we've got some important business to discuss first. Would everyone please gather around the whiteboards with me?"

The group wound up their conversations with one another, and Blair heard promises of several people to talk later. She studied the faces of the residents she and Ryan had handpicked to be the core members of their team.

To be sure, everyone within the Haven had a role to play or they wouldn't have been selected. Those within the community had been screened, vetted, and assessed as to how they would advance the Smarts' goal of creating a safe haven during a time of societal collapse.

She stood at the back of the room, watching Ryan begin the morning meeting, and she considered the strengths of the five diverse groups of people who had now coalesced together as an extended family.

Blair expected that the connection between the Sheltons and the Cortlands would reveal itself. Naturally, Tom Shelton could never know she had the ability to peek into his financial affairs and had seen the regular monthly deposits into his account from an obscure limited liability company in Providenciales. Blair knew how their banking system worked, and a few phone calls to Barclay's Bank in the Turks and Caicos enabled her to gain access. Then she'd traced the origins of the LLC back to George Trowbridge's company.

At first, she wasn't sure whether the relationship would be a problem. She noticed that social events attended by Trowbridge never mentioned a daughter. Likewise, none of the images posted on Meredith's Facebook or Instagram accounts referenced her father.

She filed it away as information that was good to know, but not necessarily a reason to exclude either of the families from the Haven. As it turned out, it drew them closer together, and Ryan's intuition from a year ago that Tom and Cort would make excellent advisors in the event of a collapse was spot-on.

"All of you have found your way to the Haven from different directions and under exceptional circumstances," said Ryan in a loud tone of voice to get everyone's attention. "Every bit of knowledge you gathered along the way, all of your experiences, will help us formulate a plan to protect everyone in the community."

Alpha stepped forward. "Ryan and Blair have created an excellent security plan, and we've got a great team in place to implement it. But as Sun-tzu wrote in *The Art of War*, know thy enemy as you know thyself. We have to anticipate what happens next in the event the crazies bring their happy asses to our doorstep."

Hayden laughed. "Trust me. Crazy never takes a vacation in DC. From what I've seen, it's consumed everyone outside the Haven too."

Ryan stepped forward. "One of the things that will help us is to develop a working theory of what's happening. It should come as no surprise to any of you that I detest the media. All of them. They all lie, exaggerate, tell half-truths, and manipulate Americans to advance their own narratives. Their actions disgust me, but it is what it is. We need to determine if this situation is going to get worse, and whether we need to be prepared for the proverbial golden hordes descending upon us from nearby towns and cities."

Alpha stepped forward. "We all recognize the fact that the Haven isn't exactly a secret in the community. Ryan and Blair built this place like a fortress for a reason. However, that most likely garnered the attention of the locals, and in a panicked crisis, word can spread quickly. Having a working theory of what's happening and who's behind it will help us explain, predict, and understand the causes of the collapse, and how we should adjust our security plan."

"Because security is all important," added Ryan. "If you can't defend it, it isn't yours."

Members of the group began to talk to one another, and Cort moved closer to the whiteboard. He gestured toward the markers, and Ryan stepped aside to let him lead the conversation.

Cort began to create a freehand drawing of the United States. He wrote in the names of the cities that were directly attacked—Seattle, Chicago, Detroit, Los Angeles, Washington, New York, and Philadelphia. Then, using a green marker, he wrote the words *Atlanta concert* and *Delta 322* in smaller print over their approximate locations on the map. Finally, using a red marker, he wrote EMP next to Philadelphia; cyber next to DC; drone next to New York, followed by the various means of attack next to the other cities in the Midwest and Los Angeles. Next to Atlanta, he wrote the word *terrorist*. Next to *Delta 322*, he wrote the letters *RFW*.

"Okay, thanks for bearing with me and I hope you can read my chicken scratch. My mom always said I wrote like a doctor but thought like a lawyer."

The group laughed along with Cort.

Ryan spoke first. "I'm seeing a pattern."

Cort nodded. "Good, Ryan. Me too. You go first."

"Let's talk locations," continued Ryan. "Except for your flight, all of the attacks took place in major cities, although the attack at the Mercedes-Benz Stadium appeared isolated and unconnected."

"But the timing," interjected Delta before Cort raised his hand to stop him.

"We'll get to that in just a moment," said Cort. "Ryan's correct, but let me take it one step further. What else do these larger cities have in common?"

"Dense population," replied Tyler.

"True, but there's more," said Cort. "We touched on this briefly last night before everyone arrived. Consider the demographics of these six metropolitan areas."

Angela reeled off several characteristics. "Inner city. Minority. Poor."

"Exactly, Dr. Rank—um, Angela," said Cort as he pointed the marker at her. "I'm a student of politics and, like Hayden, deeply in tune to the thinking of DC. Everything nowadays is looked at through the spectrum of a political lens."

Hayden nodded in agreement. "I'm not a politician, but it's apparent that these cities weren't just chosen because of their population size. They were picked because of their political proclivities."

"Yes!" exclaimed Cort. He turned to the map and ran his fingers around the interior of the U.S. border. "Where are the large-scale attacks on San Diego? Dallas? Houston? Kansas City? Or any of the major Southeastern cities. In my opinion, the traditional liberal voting enclaves were targeted."

"Ethnic cleansing?" asked Ryan.

"Sort of," replied Cort.

"Richmond was falling apart at the seams," added Tyler. "It wasn't attacked, but it was feeling the heat."

"Charlotte, too," added Meredith. "We saw gangs attacking one another in the street with clubs and rocks."

"Same thing in Richmond," said Angela. "These people dressed in black broke into our house and tried to attack our kids. Then they moved down the street and ended up in a brawl with these guys wearing red caps."

"The people in Charlotte were dressed in black too," added Meredith.

"I saw them in DC before I left," added Hayden. "They were spray-painting graffiti that looked like a fist holding a black rose in the air on a bridge abutment."

"We saw it in Richmond as well," added Meredith. "It was next to our truck just as the fighting began. You know what? They were all dressed in black too."

"Rosa Negra," mumbled Ryan.

"What?" asked Hayden.

"Rosa Negra. They're an anarchist federation made up of the worst of the worst from Antifa, Black Lives Matter, and the Occupy Wall Street groups. Rosa Negra means the Black Rose. That's their symbol."

"Are they on the East Coast?" asked Cort.

Ryan nodded. "Yeah, believe it or not, not all anarchist activity occurs in Seattle or Portland. The Black Rose is well-funded, organized, and at the beck and call of György Schwartz, the international money guy."

"The scourge of the right," said Cort. "Schwartz and his organizations fund a lot of left-leaning political activity around the world. My father-in-law hates him."

Meredith furrowed her brow and gave Cort a puzzled look.

"It sounds to me that what y'all witnessed in Charlotte and Richmond is the resistance fighting back," said Ryan.

Blair had teased Ryan about spending so much time on conspiracy theories concerning Schwartz and the so-called resistance. The point he continuously made to her was that the people who dressed up in their black garb and hid their faces didn't have the kind of money necessary to fund their activities. He bought into the theories that the resistance was a tool of the Schwartz family to destabilize American society and draw attention to their political beliefs. *Maybe he was right?*

"To me, this is only a small part of the overall picture we're looking at," said Delta. "You guys who know politics are probably correct. Here's what I want to know. Who pulled the trigger to begin with?"

"Big triggers," added Alpha. "The advanced weaponry you guys have described did not come from your local gun shop. This is heavy artillery in today's age of modern warfare."

"Especially the EMPs," said Ryan.

"I can shed some light on part of it," interjected Tom. "From what I'm hearing of the power outages in Eastern Pennsylvania and New Jersey, the EMP had to be targeted, low trajectory, and fired from a fairly short distance. My guess is that it was delivered from an underwater location."

Cort stepped closer to Tom. "Russians? They have the capability and their sub warfare program is on par with ours."

"They certainly have the cyber capabilities that were used in DC and other parts of the country," added Ryan.

"All true," replied Tom. "But toward what end? The Russians use cyber and electromagnetic pulse technology as a precursor to an invasion. They haven't been beating the drums of war, nor are they amassed at our borders. In fact, they've reached out to the president to offer aid, according to the news reports."

"Subterfuge and propaganda," interjected Alpha.

"Maybe, but not likely," said Cort. "Consider all of the scenarios. Why would the Russians risk getting their operatives caught in Atlanta and New York during the terrorist-like attacks on those locations? And why take down my flight? If they were going to deploy their radio frequency weapon to cause maximum damage, they would've tried it out on Air Force One or the chopper taking the president out of Mar-a-Lago. If they stuck with EMP weaponry and cyber, at least they'd have plausible deniability going for them."

The room became quiet as everyone absorbed the theories being bantered about. Hayden pushed her way to the front and took the red marker from Cort. On a board next to the one Cort had been using, she wrote Rosa Negra on the left side and then drew two arrows in the center, one pointing left and the other pointing to the right. She paused for a moment and turned to the group.

"How many of you have received strange text messages since New Year's Eve?" she asked as she raised her hand, indicating she was a recipient.

Tom Shelton raised his hand. "I did on New Year's Eve, and then another one after that. I must admit, the tone and tenor of the message was similar to the ones that I received when I was at Joint Base Charleston."

Hayden turned to the whiteboard. "I received them as well. Very mysterious and cryptic, but they had one common element. They were signed …" Her voice trailed off as she wrote the letters *MM* on the whiteboard. She turned and made eye contact with Tom, who nodded.

"Same here," he said.

Hayden replaced the cap on the marker and tapped the board with the end. "MM. Who is this mystery person or group, and what does MM stand for?"

The group looked at one another. Some shrugged and others shook their head side to side, as they were unable to give an opinion. Then the voice of a young boy provided an answer from the back of the room.

"Minutemen."

CHAPTER 3

Monocacy Farm
South of Frederick, Maryland

Hanson Briscoe's uneasy feeling followed him from his meeting with George Trowbridge and was firmly ensconced in his psyche by the time he returned to Monocacy Farm. The damp, cold Maryland winter was unforgiving on his aging body, and the spacious rooms of the antebellum mansion did little to take the chill out of his bones. Despite the roaring fire in the large ballroom, Briscoe's sense of foreboding prevented him from relaxing.

He allowed himself a touch of brandy in his morning coffee as he prepared for the second wave of disruptive attacks within the United States. The next target would be popular with many, and a source of consternation for others. Despite the symbolism behind the next step, the real purpose was to create uncertainty by cutting off the ability for information to be disseminated to everyday Americans.

He'd pulled open the ceiling-to-floor velvet drapes that covered half a dozen television monitors on the wall adjacent to the foyer. He rarely powered on the screens, opting instead to watch important news matters inside the privacy of his study. Typically, the ballroom was used to host political events such as fund-raisers and election night parties, when his candidates were expected to win, of course.

One by one, Briscoe powered on the monitors to reveal nonstop coverage from both the cable news networks and the Big Three—CBS, NBC, and ABC. Each of the networks either interviewed pundits who did their best to prognosticate, or the screens displayed images of chaos transmitted from around the country, depicting an America on the brink of collapse.

Briscoe pulled out his phone and initiated a series of texts to his cyber operatives around the world. It was important for the cyber sleuths to be misdirected to potential locations outside North America. He was keenly aware of the problem of attribution when cyber attacks were initiated, especially when it came to an attack on the nation's critical infrastructure. Thus far, anyone with an opinion was able to point a finger of blame at the perpetrator of the New Year's Eve attack. His next move would add to the confusion and provide even more arguments as to who the guilty party was.

He sent the final text message instructing the well-paid and highly talented cyber warriors to initiate the next step in his intricate plan. He settled into an overstuffed settee in front of the screens and watched the images come in from Richmond and Charlotte. The news reports interspersed graphics with the live feeds showing the spray-painted graffiti of the Black Rose Federation, who'd suddenly become a prominent source of coverage.

He sipped his coffee and winced, not at the temperature but rather at the strength of the brandy that he'd added to the cup. A second sip took away the sting of the alcohol, and he allowed himself a smile as he considered that he might just partake of several more cups of the concoction before the day was over.

"La Rosa Negra," he muttered aloud to no one. Briscoe was alone in the spacious home, as the staff had been told to stay away while he conducted this next phase of the plan. They were all good people and he trusted them, to an extent, but he also wanted to be alone with his thoughts.

Briscoe was wrestling with the failed attempt on Michael Cortland's life. He knew that it was a power play that could've reaped big rewards for him, considering the ill-health of Cortland's father-in-law, George Trowbridge. Everyone within their circle of trust, a close-knit group formed years ago during a Skull and Bones retreat at Yale, knew that Cortland was the heir apparent to the Trowbridge legacy and power base.

Briscoe, like his ancestors before him, had grown weary of living in the shadow of others. He believed he'd earned the right to carry the torch of power once Trowbridge passed away. Not Cortland, who'd never been involved in the *company business*, as his fellow Bonesmen referred to their geopolitical machinations.

The fortuitous turn of events that landed Cortland a seat on Delta 322, the aircraft carrying the original target, Congressman Pratt, was too good for Briscoe to pass up. To be sure, he hadn't received the flight manifest before the chopper took off from the remote area in the Florida Panhandle en route to the oil platform off the coast of Alabama. However, he still had the ability to call off the assassination and downing of the aircraft. He'd chosen to look the other way and allow things to play out.

He never imagined Cortland would survive. At first, he scrambled to prepare his excuses for the mistake. Then, time passed and Trowbridge didn't contact him. When he was summoned to the Trowbridge residence, he thought his days on earth were over, but the conversation was businesslike and even cordial. He left there feeling he'd been watched over by a guardian angel.

All of which had resulted in this melancholy mood that had overtaken him since his trip to East Haven. The guilt of allowing Cortland to be put at risk of dying was beginning to weigh on him, and he was now seriously considering a mea culpa, an acknowledgement of guilt and a plea for forgiveness from the man whose wealth and contacts made this entire operation possible—Trowbridge.

Suddenly, one of the screens turned to gray snow, an indication that the CNN news network had been unplugged. MSNBC suffered a worse fate. Smoke suddenly appeared to come out of the computer monitors embedded in the news hosts' desk in front of them. They were startled at first, but when sparks shot out of electrical outlets near their feet, the newscasters shrieked and pushed away from the desk out of fear.

The news sets from Fox News, C-Span and NBC News also experienced sudden bursts of smoke and sparks from their computer equipment. These network studios were housed in the same building in the four-hundred block of North Capitol Street in Washington.

Within sixty seconds, all of the monitors either produced a blank screen or snowy static. Briscoe smiled once again as he poured the rest of the coffee and brandy down his throat with a wince. The harshness on his throat didn't prevent him from standing up to pour another half cup of coffee, with half a cup of brandy. Sure, it was early, but unplugging the American news networks was a moment worth celebrating in Briscoe's mind.

He stood by the butler's cart, taking another sip and enjoying the monitors that were devoid of any feed whatsoever, when a shadow crossed his vision just outside the ballroom's massive doors leading to the back veranda.

Then he heard a muted thud. It was metallic sounding, but somehow coupled with the sound of his marble floor. Briscoe could sense the intruders. He tried to appear nonchalant as he slowly set his coffee cup on the cart.

He pulled his cardigan tight around his chest and nonchalantly walked toward the fireplace. The roaring blaze warmed his body, and just as he reached the hearth, that point at which the view of the ballroom was obscured by the curtains, he dropped to his knees, pulled back the area rug, and grabbed a stainless-steel ring that was inset into the wood floor.

Briscoe quickly opened the hatch and dropped to the top rungs of an old wooden ladder. As he'd practiced many times before during his lifetime, he deftly slid the rug over the top of the hatch and slowly closed the door, leaving no indication that he'd escaped.

He'd barely reached the dark, dusty basement floor when he heard the glass break in the rear doors and heavy footsteps pounding the floor above him, causing centuries-old dust and dirt to rain down upon his gray hair.

From the early days of the settlers, who feared attacks by Indians, through the days of the Civil War, antebellum mansions had safe places and tunnels built in to their foundations to protect the owners from attack. Briscoe didn't hesitate to use the labyrinth of tunnels to hide until dark, allowing him to escape into the cold morning air at Monocacy Farm that day.

When he crawled out of a root cellar nearly a quarter mile away from the mansion, he was shoeless and shivering. But he was alive.

CHAPTER 4

Haven Barn
The Haven

Blair swung her body around in search of the voice that had snuck up on her. She was so enthralled with the recollection of the events by the group that she hadn't noticed J.C. and Kaycee Rankin, who'd entered the conference room behind her.

"Kids, why aren't you back at the cabin?" asked Tyler with a stern admonishment. He began walking toward them when Cort interrupted him.

"Wait. What did you say, young man?"

J.C. stood a little taller so he could be heard. "Minutemen. MM is used for Minutemen in some of the books I read about the American Revolution."

Blair looked down at the youngster in disbelief. "You read books about the Revolutionary War?"

"Yes, ma'am. My dad says they won't teach about it in school, so me and Peanut have to learn it on our own."

"Peanut?" asked a confused Blair.

"That's me, ma'am. My name is Kaycee, but they all call me Peanut."

"O-kay," said Blair, drawing out the word as the sudden appearance of the kids and their interaction with the adults threw her off guard. Blair wasn't around kids very much so they were somewhat alien to her, although her first impression of the Rankin children changed her point of view.

Tyler and Angela had rushed to the kids' sides and were about to escort them out of the conference room at Haven Barn when Cort asked young J.C. a question.

"J.C., do you recall in the books any examples of the colonists using the initials MM on letters or marked on buildings?"

"Yes, sir, and carved on trees too. It was a way to let the other people in town know who the good guys were."

Cort waved to J.C. and encouraged the boy to join him by the whiteboard. J.C. pushed his way through the crowd, and when he arrived at the front, rather than taking on a shy demeanor, he took charge of the room.

"I always liked the stories about the Minutemen because they reminded me of my dad. He's a firefighter and he's always gotta be ready *at a minute's warning*, just like the first Minutemen who fought for the revolution."

"You learned this on your own?" asked Blair, surprised that the child would be interested in such matters.

"Yes, ma'am," replied J.C., and then he went on to explain. "Two years before we declared independence, local towns tried to eliminate soldiers who might have been loyal to England from their local police and army forces. They wanted the patriots' names to be kept a secret, so they told the men to be ready on a minute's notice to fight the Indians or the British, or whatever was necessary to protect the town. That's how they became Minutemen."

J.C. caught his breath and continued. "The first Minutemen were used in Massachusetts, and when the war started at the Battles of Lexington and Concord, the Minutemen led the charge."

Blair made eye contact with Ryan and smiled. He knew she was impressed with the kid. J.C. elaborated somewhat more and then yielded the floor back to Cort.

"This makes sense, especially from a symbolism standpoint," Cort began to explain his theory. "Someone, or a group, most likely, has decided to take things upon themselves to escalate the war of words between the left and right to a whole new level. I'm sorry to say this, but I'm beginning to see a pattern here that may have well-intended purposes based on the principles of our nation's founding, but the execution of which will result in the deaths of millions of Americans."

"Wait, hold up," interrupted Delta. "Are you saying our side started this mess? I mean, conservatives used their resources to attack typically liberal parts of the country, the consequences be damned?"

Tom was quick to respond, "Delta, this is all speculation, but I, for one, am prepared to rule out a foreign country. They've never had an incentive to broadside us like this without a larger plan. The events of New Year's Eve were intended to stir an already boiling over pot, in my opinion."

"I agree with Tom," said Cort. "Nobody's laid claim to the attacks. The weaponry was too advanced to be in the hands of terrorists. All of the attacks, including the downing of my plane and the incident in Atlanta at the stadium, were perfectly timed to coincide with the larger operations. This could very well be an inside job, in a manner of speaking."

"We attacked ourselves? I can't believe that," said Delta.

Ryan moved in to calm everyone down. "I can. Given time, I can give you a couple of hundred examples of governments using false-flag activity to manipulate their citizens." A false-flag event was a covert operation undertaken by a group, or a government, with the intent to misdirect the source of the action, but was ultimately used to manipulate the citizens of the nation under attack.

"It's not that surprising," added Cort. "Adolf Hitler once said if you tell a big enough lie, and tell it frequently enough, it will be believed."

Delta continued to argue against the notion. "You've already said that nobody has claimed responsibility. Now you wanna blame our own government and, in the process, point the finger of blame at conservatives?"

Ryan shot a glance at Alpha and then over at Blair. He welcomed dissenting opinion, but Delta seemed to be a little over-the-top in his counter-arguments. Blair suspected the weight of his decision to fetch his son, Ethan, or not, was causing him to be emotional.

"Delta, we're still in the early stages of this attack on America, and for all we know, it's not over yet," said Cort. "That said, the facts as we know them are beginning to point to a coordinated effort from within our own government because the tools were possessed by us. And, without stirring up too much controversy or upsetting the president's legal counsel, who is with us, war and turmoil favor the commander-in-chief from a political standpoint. When a president is under siege politically, like ours is, it helps him to divert attention away from scandals and to focus the public's ire upon America's enemies."

Delta was still stinging from Cort's rebuke the night before at Haven House after the disappearance of Ethan. He let his attitude show in his response. "Our president is tougher than any namby-pamby politician in office. He can fight his own battles without attacking our own. I refuse to believe he had anything to do with this."

Cort shot back, "Who else would have the authority to order these types of strikes?"

Tom kicked at a dust bunny that lay at his feet and hesitated before speaking. Finally, he mumbled loud enough for those at the front of the room to hear him, "You'd be surprised."

Ryan intervened because he saw the meeting getting off track. "Okay, okay. Let's not argue amongst ourselves over speculation. It's a bunch of bickering that may have led us to this debacle to begin with, if what we know is true."

J.C. continued to stand in the midst of the adults, who were arguing over who to blame, when he raised his hand. "Um, his name is Alpha, right? And you're Delta?"

"That's right," replied Alpha in his baritone voice.

"My name's J.C. What kind of cool name can I have?"

The ladies in the room laughed at the youngster's confidence as he inserted himself into the adult conversation.

"He's quite a charmer, isn't he?" asked Donna.

"Just like his daddy," said Angela, who gave Tyler a playful shove.

Alpha walked up to J.C. and put his hand on his shoulder. "Well, J.C., the code word in the military alphabet for J is Juliett."

"No way, not a girl's name!" protested J.C.

"Hey, I have an idea," said Hayden. "Since the young man is so charming, as all of us ladies will attest, let's designate him R for Romeo."

"Yeah, Romeo!" exclaimed J.C. "I'll take it!"

"Romeo it is," said Ryan. "And how about Kaycee?"

"She's Peanut," J.C. quickly answered.

"No, I'm grown up now and I want a code name, too. What's the name for K?"

"Kilo," replied Alpha.

"K for Kilo and Kaycee. Works for me!"

The adults got a good chuckle, and the exchange with the kids worked to ease tensions in the room. Angela gathered up the newly designated Kilo and Romeo. The two kids protested briefly but then agreed to find their way back to the cabin.

While the group continued conversations between themselves, Blair looked around the conference room. That was when she noticed that X-Ray, who'd stood off to the side the entire time and never once contributed to the conversation, had disappeared.

CHAPTER 5

Haven Barn
The Haven

Delta had tossed and turned all night, regaining his former self as Will Hightower, estranged father to two kids, one of whom had run away and likely committed a felony in the process. After he and Skylar had returned to their cabin, the two talked it through. His daughter had been remarkably calm under the circumstances and, frankly, much more rational than he was.

Skylar reassured her father that Ethan could take care of himself. She broke sister-code and revealed to Delta all of the misdeeds Ethan had committed since the divorce and Delta's subsequent move to Atlanta. This caused Delta even more angst as he continued to pile heaps of guilt upon his shoulders, but Skylar, wise beyond her eleven years, continuously reminded her father that Ethan had experienced a lot as a teen, and if anyone could make it on his own, it was her brother. He might not be able to survive in the woods, but he could survive on the streets.

Nonetheless, after their heartfelt conversation—during which Skylar promised to be by his side the whole way, or stay at the cabin and fend for herself, which she had grown accustomed to doing anyway back home—Delta was finally alone with his thoughts.

He was torn between doing what he thought was the right thing for his child and the logical conclusions that invaded his thought processes. Naturally, Delta assumed his son was headed home, to Philadelphia, where hopefully Karen and even that louse Frankie, her boyfriend, would be waiting.

He would be searching for a needle in a haystack. Ethan was not responding to his phone calls. If Ethan had run into trouble, either by running out of gas or running into the kinds of thugs roaming the streets like the Sheltons and Hayden had, then it most likely would've happened by the next morning. Likewise, if he was able to travel home without difficulty, he'd be there already. In either event, nobody had attempted to call him.

Delta had to make a decision because people at the Haven were relying upon him, especially his young daughter, who'd be left in the care of complete strangers if he struck out without her. After what he'd heard that morning from those who'd had bad experiences in Richmond, he began to fear for Ethan's safety even more. As the morning meeting broke up and everyone went about their daily chores, he felt obligated to pull Ryan and Blair aside to discuss his options. The Smarts were heading toward their Ranger four-wheeler when Delta caught up with them.

"Hey, guys, can I talk to you a minute?"

Blair grabbed Ryan by the sleeve, who was anxious to get back to Haven House for a follow-up meeting with Tom and Cort. They both stopped and waited for Delta.

"You need a ride back to your cabin?" asked Ryan.

"Well, um, sure, but that's not the reason I need to talk with you alone. Can you give me a lift and I'll go over it on the way?"

"Hop in," replied Blair, who volunteered the front seat to the longer-legged Delta.

Ryan fired up the Ranger and got the heat going as they slowly made their way out of the sawdust and pine needle parking area that surrounded Haven Barn and onto the gravel road that ran through the heart of the former *Hunger Games* movie set.

Delta jumped right in. "I barely slept last night, trying to decide what to do. You know, I have an amazing kid waiting for me up ahead. Sky gave me great advice and reassurances that she'd be fine whatever I decide."

"Including taking her along?" asked Blair with a hint of disapproval.

"Nah. I told her that was not an option under any circumstances. Naturally, I believe in the old African proverb 'If you wanna go quickly, go alone. If you wanna go far, go together.' If Ethan got in trouble while on the road, he'd need my help right away, and I can't necessarily protect one child while trying to rescue another. I could lose them both."

"Do you think Ethan is in trouble?" asked Ryan, who periodically glanced in the rearview mirror at Blair to gauge her reaction to the conversation.

"I've heard nothing from Ethan or his mother. It's impossible to tell, although I could argue no news is good news."

"You're assuming he went back home, right?" asked Ryan.

"I talked to Sky about that, too. He doesn't have any close friends, and we didn't have any other family except Karen's sister in upstate New York. He wouldn't pass Philly to go there."

"What are you gonna do?" asked Blair, who wanted to cut to the chase. She'd been annoyed by the drama from the beginning.

"It's a tough decision. I feel like a crappy parent by not chasing after him. However, I have no way of contacting him. He could be anywhere or stuck somewhere in Richmond facing the same issues the others came up against."

"Exactly," said Ryan. "Richmond is too dangerous. I'd advise you to drive around the city if you're going back to Philly to look for him."

Delta paused and responded, "Yeah, except Ethan doesn't know what we know. He would've taken the direct route through the city, right into the heat of the frying pan. Besides, I'm not worried about any of that. I can handle myself."

"Sooo?" Blair was growing impatient.

"Okay, Meredith and Donna both promised to watch over Sky for me and, without saying it, they are fully aware that something might happen that would prevent me from coming back. You know?"

"Yeah," said Blair. "You're chasing after a runaway teen and leaving a loving, vulnerable daughter behind."

"I know, Blair. That's not lost on me. But am I a piece-of-crap father for not trying?"

"Delta, who cares what others think about you?" Blair was blunt in her response. "I know you've talked to a lot of the others to get opinions and advice. Here's mine. Stay put. Take care of that beautiful little girl. Ethan's fifteen going on thirty, from what I can see. He seems street smart. Just because he's not eighteen, or technically not an adult, doesn't mean he can't fend for himself."

Ryan glanced over at Delta. "Man, I've got to agree. Either trust that Ethan makes it home or he comes to his senses and returns to the Haven. You should be here, either way."

Ryan wheeled the Ranger into the parking area in front of Delta's cabin. Skylar came out the front door, waving to them with a big smile on her face. She was holding up the painting that Blair had commissioned her to create.

Blair was the first to exit the Ranger and approach Skylar, who proudly presented the painting of their cabin to Blair.

"Miss Blair, it's perfect timing. I just finished it for you. Whadya think?"

Blair accepted the watercolor painting from the young artist and a slight tear came to her eye. She studied it for a moment, dropped to one knee and gave Skylar a big hug.

She whispered into the child's ear, "I absolutely love it, Sky. Thank you so much for making it. Would you like to come up to the house and help me pick out the perfect frame, and then we can find a place to hang it?"

"That would be awesome," responded Skylar. "And while we're there, we can talk about any other paintings that you'd like commissioned. I'm getting better at this. Practice makes perfect, right?"

"It sure does. Now, go get your coat on and we'll ride up together, okay?"

"Deal!" shouted Skylar as she bolted back into the cabin.

Blair turned around to Ryan and Delta, who were standing in front of the idling Ranger. Her demeanor immediately changed as she walked straight up to Delta and looked into his eyes.

"If you abandon that sweet girl to chase after a kid who's nothing but trouble," she snarled, "you'd better not come back, or I'll shoot you myself. C'mon, Ryan. Delta has work to do."

CHAPTER 6

Haven House
The Haven

Tom and Cort were pacing on the front porch of Haven House when the Smarts, with Skylar in tow, arrived. Blair hustled Skylar inside for a mug of hot chocolate while Ryan escorted the guys into his study. The guys worked together to build a fire and then got settled into the distressed leather chairs to talk.

"Okay, guys, there's a whole lot more to this Minutemen, patriotic rigmarole than meets the eye. I need some straight shootin' here. Did we attack ourselves?"

Both Tom and Cort began speaking at the same time.

"Here's the thing—" started Cort.

"It may take some—" began Tom.

They both stopped and gestured to one another to go first. Ryan made the decision for them.

"Listen, it's just us now. If either one of you are gonna equivocate and blow smoke, then I don't wanna hear it. I can do plenty of that on my own."

Cort laughed. "You sound like Senator McNeill. He was never interested in long stories with no ending."

"Neither am I, 'cause we don't have time. From what I've seen on the news, unrest is spreading outside the big cities into midsized towns as well. Richmond and Charlotte are just examples based upon our personal experiences. Before the meeting, there was a report out of Florida that there was a shoot-out between militia types and a bunch of college kids in Gainesville, for Pete's sake. Nearby Durham had a similar incident near Duke."

"I think we saw that developing," added Tom.

"Here's my point, y'all," continued Ryan. "I love our location and the security we have in place. But if half a million people race out of Charlotte and head for the hills, as they say, although in this case, it would be the Smokies, we're gonna have our hands full."

"We can all speak frankly, right?" asked Tom.

"Absolutely," replied Ryan. "What's on your mind, Tom?"

"If, and this is a huge if, our government, or those who pull the strings of government, orchestrated this attack, it's possible that—" Tom caught himself and abruptly stopped as if he didn't want to say the words aloud.

Cort, however, didn't hesitate. "What Tom's trying to say is that if we were behind it, based upon the targets and methods, it's quite possible that the president will order our National Guard to stand down and let the fire burn itself out."

"Chicago, Detroit, LA, Seattle," Tom began before he took a deep breath. "They'd be on their own without government intervention."

"They'll kill one another in the streets," added Ryan.

"Exactly," said Cort under his breath. "It's tantamount to ethnic cleansing."

"Or a reset," said Tom. "Listen, I've worked around these people for a long time. Patriotism is just another way of saying we want things the way they used to be. You know, when America worshiped the flag and was proud of its leaders. A time when the nation was not self-absorbed or hung up on political correctness and social justice."

"They want us to tear each other apart, but not just on social media," added Cort. "They want us to fight it out and let the best side win. And, I suspect, if the other side begins to gain the advantage, you can rest assured another attack of some kind will occur to even the playing field."

"Are you guys both saying that we can expect lawlessness? Intentionally?" asked Ryan.

Cort and Tom looked at one another and nodded their heads in unison. The room remained silent for a moment before Cort spoke up.

"Here's what I envision happening, and most likely the media will scream bloody murder."

"What?" asked Ryan.

"I understand Washington and I also know this president. He's very streetwise and he knows how to play the game now. I see him marshaling his assets by using traditional methods of helping those in need through the Red Cross and FEMA."

"But it's too dangerous in the streets," interrupted Ryan.

Tom smiled and looked over at Cort. "I see where you're headed. Ryan is correct. It's too dangerous to send FEMA and the Red Cross out there alone. They'll need protection. The president will say something to the effect that if we focus on keeping the peace, we won't have the resources to help the needy."

"They, whoever *they* are, want a second civil war," surmised Ryan with a sigh. "Listen, don't get me wrong, there's no love lost between me and the radical leftists who've tried to take over this country. But don't you think wiping out innocent Americans in an effort to create some kind of *reset*, as Tom called it, is a little much?"

Cort smiled. "A revolution is a struggle to the death between the future and the past. Conservatives, by their nature, try to hold on to America as it was envisioned by the Founding Fathers. Liberals, or Progressives, as they like to call themselves now, see our nation as evolving from the eighteenth century, and our political institutions need to keep up with this natural evolution of society."

"Peaceful revolution doesn't work," added Tom. "Most times, to create drastic change within a society or government structure, you necessarily require armed conflict. Consider the Civil War. Slavery was entrenched in the South and many other states across the Sunbelt. Those in Washington tried, through legislation, to halt the practice, and they were met with strong resistance."

"If you oppose peaceful change, then you're necessarily making violent revolution inevitable," interjected Ryan.

"Yessir," said Tom as he leaned back in his chair. "Somebody way above our pay grades decided that the time was right for both sides to duke it out for the heart and soul of our country. The question becomes whether we can sit it out on the sidelines."

Ryan stood and walked toward the windows of his study that looked out onto the front lawn. Blair and Skylar were walking through the yard together. Every few feet, Blair would stop and point something out to Skylar, who'd make notes on a pad she toted under her arm. Ryan sighed and turned to his top lieutenants.

"Call me selfish, but we have a duty and obligation to the ones we love right here at the Haven. I'm not interested in relitigating the past or doing the dirty work of others by getting involved in a second civil war. Make no mistake, however, if their war comes to our doorstep, then they'll get their fight."

CHAPTER 7

Haven House
The Haven

"All right, boys, what did I miss?" Blair announced her late arrival to the meeting with a question. She had given Skylar another project to work on, and the child immediately got to work. Blair saw it as a way to keep Skylar focused on something other than the drama surrounding her brother.

"Well, the country's going to hell in a handbasket," replied Ryan.

"I knew that before New Year's Eve," said Blair with a chuckle as she backed up to the fire to warm her body. "Anybody have an opinion as to why? I mean, all of a sudden, somebody fired the first shot, am I right?"

Ryan laughed and looked at the guys. "She's wise beyond her years. No amount of college degrees or residing in the Washington swamp can substitute for good old-fashioned intuition. Right?"

"I agree," said Tom, who then turned his attention to Blair. "Our consensus is that a second civil war is coming, and the people who pulled the trigger, as you say, are powerful and have access to all the toys in our military's arsenal. The guys on the other side, the usual suspects, are more adept at a ground war, speaking, of course, in military parlance."

"Gentlemen, the second civil war is already upon us and it's been raging for some time," said Blair. "Ask the families of fallen police officers or those who've lost loved ones to MS-13 gang members. Or the wife of Steve Scalise, the congressman who was nearly assassinated while playing softball. The way I see it, the second civil war has already begun, only the guns are now bigger and badder."

Ryan joined his wife's side and put his arm around her shoulder to help her warm up. "The question we were about to address is how this affects us."

"Well, I can tell you this from news reports this morning that cities are burning and neighborhoods are being destroyed. Innocent bystanders are getting caught up in the fight between the thugs who are coming from all around and the armed militia that have always vowed to take up arms in the event of societal breakdown. I'm hearing the media use words like *lawlessness, collapse,* and yes, *civil war.* The pundits are no longer looking for a bogeyman from abroad. They're starting to point fingers of blame within our borders."

"At who?" asked Tom.

Blair chuckled. "My goodness, Tom, who else? The Commander-in-Chief. The wild accusations are everywhere. Not only has he committed these heinous acts in order to save his hide in front of the Supreme Court, but he's delaying sending in the military to save the cities. They're calling it a form of ethnic cleansing."

"Told ya," said Cort, looking at Tom. "You have to wonder whether the people who instigated these attacks knew the suspicion would naturally be cast upon the president. Hayden said as much when she and I talked briefly this morning. Her firm acknowledged that the president stands to gain politically by what happened New Year's Eve."

"Now he has a crisis to deal with, and the media is hammering him over it," interjected Blair.

"True, but as president, he can come to the rescue," said Tom.

"Or let it play out," Cort quickly added. "Think of it this way. If he was aware, or even if he has conducted the same analysis as we have, delay in restoring order benefits him. He can walk the fine line between helping those in need and bringing order to the streets until the balance is tipped in his favor."

"Listen to what you're saying, Cort," began Ryan. "Innocent people are getting slaughtered in order to gain a political advantage, am I right?"

"Yes," replied Cort dryly. "It's no different than the first Civil War. Consider this. When General Sherman began his march through the South from Atlanta to Savannah in late 1864, the Civil War was over for all practical purposes. Lincoln didn't stop his advance or try to rein him in. He allowed Sherman to deliver a message to the Southerners who still wanted to hold onto the old ways. Don't doubt me on this, Sherman wanted to wipe out the Southern way of life and kill as many Confederate sympathizers as he could in the process."

"And you think that's what might be happening here?" asked Blair.

"I do," replied Cort.

"Bottom line it for me," said Blair. "How does it affect the way we protect ourselves?"

Ryan took that question on. "It's all about security. We have enough supplies to weather the storm. We just need to stay abreast of the news and especially what's happening outside our walls. If we're about to be overrun by scared citizens, or mobs laying waste to the farms around us, we need to be forewarned that they're coming our way."

Blair sat in Ryan's chair and brought up X-Ray. "Well, our newest member of the team was supposed to keep tabs on all of this type of stuff. Have you guys received any reports from X-Ray as to whether we're threatened by a mass exodus or refugees out of Charlotte, for example?"

"No, not yet, but I haven't asked for that either," replied Ryan. "We're still trying to get a handle on all of this as we speak."

"Has he provided you any intel, using Tom-speak, about what's going on around the country?"

"No, not yet," replied Ryan. "I know you're wary of X-Ray, and I'm keeping an eye on him as well. He has the ability to monitor military and governmental communications that will give us a heads-up on anything that directly impacts the Haven."

"That's great, and I'm anxious to see his work product," began Blair. She was operating the Haven like a business. "There's another thing I want to address about him. Did anyone else notice how he was acting during the morning meeting?"

"What do you mean?" asked Ryan.

"He was fidgety and unsocial," she replied. "I didn't see him make an effort to interact with anybody."

"Well, I can say this from my brief encounters with him around the Haven so far," started Cort. "It may just be his way. He's kind of an introverted geek."

"So, does that explain why he disappeared in the middle of the meeting this morning, just as you began your discussion about the text messages, the attacks and who was behind them?"

None of the guys had an answer for that, so they remained silent.

After a moment, Blair said what was on her mind. She swiveled in Ryan's chair so she could look directly at Cort. "It's time for some brutal honesty here, Cort." Blair's piercing eyes lowered as she studied him. She casually pointed as she spoke. "You have a close relationship with Meredith's father, George Trowbridge. As do you, Tom. Now, I'm assuming, correctly I believe, that you two have never met before coming to the Haven, yet there's this connection. A connection to a very powerful mover and shaker in Washington. One who most likely has the ear of the president, as well as his political opponents."

"Where are you headed with this, Blair?" asked Cort, who was uneasy with her challenging tone.

"All of the attacks of New Year's Eve have a certain common thread, as you pointed out earlier—political demographics. But what does the attack on your flight have to do with the rest of it? Coincidence? No way."

Cort answered quickly. "Based upon our theory that the folks who pulled off these attacks is a friend of the president, I believe the target was the man who was charged with taking him down through the impeachment process—Congressman Pratt."

"I have another theory and, Cort, you're a smart guy, so I'm sure this has crossed your mind," continued Blair. "Who else on that plane might be a possible target for a complex, highly unusual assassination attempt?"

Everyone's focus was on Cort when Ryan's phone rang, interrupting the tense moment.

CHAPTER 8

Near Cofer Road
South Richmond, Virginia

Ethan Hightower's head was pounding. He couldn't breathe and was having difficulty opening his eyes. But despite the beatdown he'd received outside the gas station in South Richmond, he was alive, and somehow, he was not lying in the cold against the green dumpster where he'd landed when the thugs were done with him.

As he became more conscious, he struggled to catch his breath, causing him to begin a fit of coughing and choking on his own saliva. He reached for his throat only to moan in pain as his badly bruised arm betrayed him.

"Momma! Na-na Jean! He's awake!" A young girl's voice pounded in his concussed brain, but he didn't mind. It was a sign that he was alive and being cared for.

"Stand aside, Celeste," an elderly woman said. "Let me have a look."

Another voice addressed Ethan. "Young man, don't try to talk or move. You're in pretty rough shape, and we don't rightly know how bad it is for you on the inside."

"Celeste, get the child's sippy cup with water and also a cold wet cloth. He's got a powerful fever and we need to cool him down."

Ethan managed to open his right eye to see his caregivers. A heavyset black woman in her forties hovered over the top of him, studying his facial movements. He glanced toward his feet, and a much older woman, possibly the child's grandmother, peered at him over her wire-rimmed glasses with a concerned look on her face.

The young girl, Celeste, Ethan presumed, arrived holding a child's sippy cup with a picture of Bambi on the side. He tried to reach for it, but his arm was too sore to move. He suddenly became aware of the bruises and painful cuts he'd received from the beating.

"Hold still, young man," said the elderly woman. "We're gonna get some water in your mouth and a wet cloth on your forehead. There ain't no reason for you to talk, so just lie still for a minute."

The ladies doted over Ethan for several minutes in an effort to make him comfortable and to hydrate his body. After five minutes of cold compresses on his sweating forehead and neck, Ethan was feeling better and was able to take some of the woman's pain medications.

"Thank you," he barely mouthed the words, but they clearly understood what he was trying to say.

"You're welcome, young man," the elderly woman said. "I'm sorry that we couldn't take you to a hospital, but we didn't have enough gas to go into the city, and the ambulances ain't runnin' in South Richmond."

He looked around the room with his eye that was open and noticed he was in a bedroom. "How?" Ethan attempted to ask how he'd arrived in their home.

The mother spoke up. "My son found you when he was out looking for food last night. He thought you were dead at first, but then felt your pulse. We didn't know what else to do because the police don't even bother to come down here, so we all worked together to carry you to our house down the street."

Ethan closed his eyes and began to visualize the blows descending upon him by the men at the gas station. He seemed to be reliving the beating because he winced and his body shook as he recalled the attack.

"Hey, hey, take it easy," said the mother. "It's over, okay. You're safe."

The elderly woman spoke up next. "Young man, you need to see a doctor or something. Do you live around here? Can we call your parents for you?"

Ethan took a deep breath and then exhaled, gathering the strength to reply. The small sips of water were working wonders on his throat and mouth. He opted to try his other arm that hadn't been injured. Anticipating the pain, but grateful it wasn't there, he motioned for the mother to come closer to his mouth.

"Okay," she said as she placed her ear near his mouth. "Celeste, grab Na-na a pencil and paper. Hurry."

Ethan began to whisper to her, ignoring the pain as he mouthed the words. The mother repeated what he said.

"Mom. Philly. Two-six-seven. Three-two-two. Twelve-fifty."

The older woman repeated the number and then looked down to Ethan. "Young man, do we have it right? This is your momma's phone number?"

Ethan shook his head side to side. "No," he whispered.

"Who is it?"

The mother put her ear to Ethan's mouth and then repeated his words again.

"Frankie. Mom's boyfriend." She pulled away and looked down to Ethan. "You want us to call your mom's boyfriend and not your father?"

Ethan nodded and closed his eyes before falling asleep.

CHAPTER 9

West of Danbury Airport
Near the New York-Connecticut State Line

Jonathan Schwartz ached all over. He was never one for exercise, choosing instead to control his weight by instructing the staff at the Schwartz Estate in Katonah, New York, to monitor his calorie intake. He rarely took his meals in public, in part because he feared assassination by poisoning or being rendered incapacitated, which might make him susceptible to being kidnapped. His father grew up in a world of post-World War II Nazi sympathizers and Russian mob activity that often resulted in the rich being kidnapped for ransom. He'd warned Jonathan to watch his back, and soon it had become ingrained as part of his lifestyle.

As he began the midnight trek from the airfield at Danbury, Connecticut, back towards the estate, he cursed himself for letting his guard down. He should've known that his family's enemies would use the occasion of the martial law declaration to their advantage. After all, he had rallied the Black Rose Federation to move into the suburbs of traditionally conservative cities to wreak havoc. It was a game of chess and he'd been blindsided.

He continued walking along the deserted stretch of country road, wondering how his father was faring in a cold, dark holding cell in the basement of a federal courthouse somewhere. He was certain the Department of Justice would keep his location well hidden, and any information concerning his arraignment out of the press, if he was even entitled to one under martial law.

His father might have been the big prize for the people behind the feds swooping down upon them the night before, but they certainly intended to have him arrested as well. Whoever gave the order must know that the son of the powerful financier wouldn't sit idly by as his father was persecuted under what could amount to dictatorial rule for many months.

But first things first. He'd been walking along Ridgebury Road toward the New York state line, dashing into the woods as the occasional vehicle passed. At one point, he stopped and retrieved his dismantled cell phone and the SIM card that he'd removed while on the tarmac next to the awaiting jet. He contemplated putting the phone back together for a moment to call a member of his staff or one of the family's many operatives for assistance, but he resisted the urge. He knew the moment he placed the SIM card back into the device to activate it, he'd be on the feds' radar and the manhunt would intensify.

He eventually turned west when he came upon a farm located northwest of Ridgefield, Connecticut, and just a mile from New York. Earth Root Farm was a locally owned micro-farm specializing in organic crops produced with non-GMO seeds.

Like any farming operation, including a small local operation like Earth Root Farm, the lights were on well before dawn as the employees prepared for their day.

Jonathan was growing weary of the long walk and realized that he'd only traveled a third of the way to the estate. He was also keenly aware that their home was probably being watched. He crouched behind a granite boulder that was perilously close to the narrow tree-lined road that swept by the farmhouse and barns.

In the driveway sat an old, slightly banged-up white Ford pickup that looked like thousands of others that traveled the roads of rural New York and Connecticut. It was idling, most likely to warm up its old bones for another day on the farm.

Jonathan inched around the large rock and climbed up a slight incline until he could get a better view of the front of the two-story farmhouse and the pickup. The truck was unattended. He considered his options and the likelihood that the vehicle would be immediately reported as stolen. Then he thought about the fact that local law enforcement would be slow to react due to the circumstances surrounding the New Year's Eve attacks, and most certainly the Connecticut police would need to get approval to enter New York State to pursue the stolen vehicle. That would take days with New York City still in the throes of mayhem.

He decided to go for it. He raced across the lawn, his leather shoes crunching in the partially melted snow that had refrozen overnight. Without hesitation, he eased open the driver's side door and slid into the warm cab of the truck. The vehicle was parked on a hill that sloped back toward the road. He placed it in neutral to avoid the reverse lights illuminating on the truck's rear end. He released the parking brake and it slowly rolled backwards.

Jonathan's sweaty palms gripped the wheel. His eyes darted between the side-view mirrors, to ensure he wasn't headed for a ditch or a tree, and the house, to make sure his theft hadn't been discovered.

Relief swept over him as the four wheels reached the pavement of Mopus Bridge Road, and he was able to easily turn the steering wheel to point the pickup toward the west. With one final glance toward the house, he eased into drive and slowly drove away, using only the moonlight to illuminate the one-lane road.

After he narrowly avoided striking a concrete barrier designed to prevent vehicles from driving into Mopus Creek, he felt more comfortable turning on the headlights, enabling him to pick up speed, but not so fast as to draw attention.

A minute later, he saw a single green sign that read *New York – State Line* sitting cockeyed on the shoulder of the road. Crossing that border just bought him time to escape into obscurity while he devised a plan to help his father and exact his revenge on George Trowbridge.

During the twenty-five-minute drive toward the estate, the only place he could think to go at the moment, he considered the obstacles he faced by not being able to communicate with members of the Schwartz security team and his most trusted operators. Undoubtedly, the most obvious bank accounts used by the family were frozen by the Department of Justice, and his credit cards were locked.

There was still money, precious metals, and weapons hidden at the estate, but he couldn't risk going onto the property. To satisfy his curiosity, he drove near the estate, being wary of roadblocks or traps. Unsurprisingly, the roads leading to the Schwartz Estate were patrolled by New York state troopers and the occasional black Chevy SUV, whose appearance screamed federal law enforcement.

Traveling into Pennsylvania was Jonathan's next logical move. The family had a remote hunting lodge off U.S. Route 222 near Reading. It was rarely used and had been held by a charitable trust since the seventies. The FBI ranks were thinned as they investigated the attacks of New Year's Eve. He seriously doubted they'd have the manpower to stake out a property owned by an obscure charity that the Schwartz family hadn't funded since the early eighties.

With a newfound resolve, and the confidence that he'd formed some semblance of a plan, Jonathan Schwartz picked up speed and headed across the Hudson River into New Jersey just as the sun rose on a new day.

CHAPTER 10

George Trowbridge's Residence
Near Pine Orchard, Connecticut

George Trowbridge winced as his medical team helped him to sit upright in bed. The mental strain surrounding the events of the last few days were beginning to take a physical toll on his body as well. Despite his doctor's admonishments to avoid the news reports and to turn over his business dealings to someone else, Trowbridge ignored the well-intentioned instructions and carried on business as usual.

His longtime aide, Harris, stood at the foot of the bed and powered up the monitors for him to view the latest news. "Sir, do you want the volume on any network in particular?" he asked as the monitors came to life.

"Not yet, closed-captioning will suffice," replied Trowbridge, who patiently waited for the nurses to finish taking care of his bodily waste. He'd grown accustomed to the embarrassment and humiliation of allowing others to clean him up each day. It was part of the medical routine to keep him alive, but disconcerting, nonetheless. When they were finished, he waved his arm toward a member of the house staff. "Please close that as you leave. We're not to be disturbed until lunch."

After the door closed, Harris turned to his boss and asked, "Where would you like to start?"

Trowbridge furrowed his brow and ignored the question. He studied the monitors that displayed a variety of news feeds with visuals from across the country.

"We are witnessing the collapse of a great empire," he began as he adjusted himself in the bed. "Throughout history, military, political, and financial leaders have sought to create great empires modeled after ancient Rome. Over time, nations were formed that spread their wings across continents and oceans. Take Spain, for example. With its mighty armada, it was able to conquer the New World, and the gold harvested allowed them to gain greater influence throughout Europe."

"Much to the detriment of Great Britain," added Harris. "The cost of the colonies and the many wars that they fought in the eighteenth century took a heavy financial toll on their coffers."

"That opened the door for the great American experiment, the United States, to take over in the nineteenth century and beyond," continued Trowbridge. "However, Harris, like all great empires, America was destined to collapse, and we were well on our way to yielding the title of greatest nation-state to the Chinese. Like Rome, we rose as a republic, with minimal central control, but we began to crumble under the weight of an expanding federal bureaucracy."

"We're not even taking into account the rapid change in societal values that our country has experienced in the last five decades," said Harris, who, unlike Trowbridge, was a devout Christian. "Rome was fraught with debauchery, declining morals and values, together with a general attitude of self-absorption."

"I can't disagree, Harris, but frankly, I believe those types of societal issues are secondary to the bigger factor associated with the size and intrusion of government in people's lives. The Founding Fathers never intended to create an out-of-control, centralized bureaucracy to exert authority over its citizens. They envisioned the state government, those legislators closest to the people they govern, determining what was best for their citizenry."

Harris pointed toward a monitor that showed President Xi Jinping commenting on the situation in America. "Depending on how this plays out in the States, is he the heir apparent to the world's next great empire?"

"Most likely," replied Trowbridge. "I'm not so sure it will come to that. Invariably, the last people to understand that their empire is collapsing are those who live within it. Americans, who are self-absorbed, as you put it, would be the last to truly understand that their days are numbered. Most look at the gradual decline of the last fifty years to be a temporary setback, one in which a rebound is sure to follow."

"And you disagree," interjected Harris.

"I do. Historically, once an empire has been knocked off its pedestal, it's replaced by a rising power that is typically more productive and forward thinking."

Harris wandered toward the monitors and tapped the ones that depicted the chaotic scenes from cities like Charlotte and Richmond. "How does instigating this help?"

Trowbridge allowed a slight smile and responded, "We were sinking deeper into the abyss, Harris. It required a drastic change, a catalyst, to set the nation back to where it was."

"But not so far back that we couldn't compete on the world stage, am I right?" asked Harris.

"That is the plan. The United States, its political leaders, and its populace needed a wake-up call. Those who sat on the sidelines and watched the decline of our society and the nation's standing in the world must now become engaged."

Harris walked over to the bed and set the remotes on the medical table next to it. "A civil war may be the natural result of this plan. Warfare is often the death knell of a declining empire. Great Britain is an example of that."

"True, but that's an example of a nation that spread itself too thin by fighting outside its borders and meddling in the affairs of others. I believe the president will see this as an opportunity to close ranks, bring our military closer to home. If not to quell the unrest, then as a protective shield against any military power, whether from Beijing or Moscow, taking advantage of our moment of weakness."

"This will set the foreign policy of our nation back to the start of the twentieth century," Harris opined.

"Certainly, and one would hope that our new leaders, the ones who emerge out of this difficult time, will learn to pay attention to our own before we interfere in the affairs of others."

Harris was not convinced. "But, sir, what about the argument that we can maintain peace throughout the world while keeping the Russians and the Communist Chinese in check from expanding their power?"

"Harris, we're too powerful to be challenged at this point militarily, unless, of course, like the Brits of centuries past, we become spread too thin. Make no mistake, I will have an opportunity to get a message to the president. He thinks like I do, and I'm sure he'll agree that pulling our military forces closer to home is the right course of action."

"And in the meantime, do we continue to stand down while the nation tears itself apart?"

Trowbridge grimaced. "For the time being, yes. Today, Briscoe will initiate another important step in the plan. Redefining the role of the media."

Harris smirked. "After that, Briscoe will be eliminated."

"As planned," added Trowbridge.

CHAPTER 11

The Armageddon Hospital
The Haven

Angela stood in the center of the building that was once part of the *Hunger Games* movie set, and prior to that, it was a storage facility for bales of cotton used in the textile mill operated nearly a century ago. The transformation from storage to dystopian cabin to Armageddon Hospital was remarkable.

She was impressed with the Smarts' commitment to providing the makeshift hospital with as many modern tools as possible to care for wounds, including serious trauma injuries like those she was accustomed to treating. She and Tyler had often discussed what would happen if America was ever attacked or subjected to widespread societal collapse.

The medical care system was overloaded under normal conditions, but if the nation was subjected to a significant collapse event, health care providers would be immediately overwhelmed.

The Smarts attempted to address the same concerns by creating the functional equivalent of a walk-in clinic, adding advanced medical equipment under the assumption that hospitals and trauma centers would be unavailable to residents of the Haven.

Tyler brusquely opened the door, startling Angela. "Okay, I've got our little monsters in their designated places and threatened them within an inch of their lives if they wander off."

Angela laughed. "Good luck with that. Listen, I've only begun to check out what's available to us, but I'm impressed. Look."

Angela walked Tyler through the facility, showing him the fully stocked cabinets. "They've got a great mix of OTC medications and even some prescription basics."

"I'll have to ask how they pulled that off," added Angela as she stood to the side, allowing Tyler a closer look.

"Online sources," he mumbled. "Probably out of Canada. You know how that works, babe. You call into an eight-hundred number from a website. They ask you a handful of questions just like a physician's assistant does at your general practitioner's office, and maybe you have to take a pic of your arm in a blood pressure cuff. They'll prescribe just about anything except scheduled narcotics."

Angela shook her head and smiled as she examined a bottle of a commonly prescribed medication for Type II diabetics. "And all for the low, low price of thirty-nine ninety-five."

"Yep, that's about right," said Tyler. He closed the cabinets and moved on to a larger enclosure. Inside were several military-style rucksacks packed full of emergency medical supplies. He lifted one up and felt the weight. Then he opened a couple of them and confirmed they were packed with the same supplies.

"Whadya think?" asked Angela.

"I hope we never have to use this stuff," replied Tyler glumly. He took a deep breath and exhaled, clearly overwhelmed by the possibility. "Ryan has assigned a vehicle to me."

"A truck? I didn't hear it when you pulled up."

"No, something more mobile. Come take a look."

Tyler grabbed his wife by the hand and led her through the front entrance. An olive-drab green Cushman electric golf cart sat in front of the hospital. It had a black roof with a solar panel affixed to it. Angela noticed the panel first.

"Battery operated? With a solar panel?" she asked as she left Tyler's side and bounded out into the parking area. She immediately began to inspect the vehicle.

"Yeah, these guys have thought of everything," replied Tyler. "Apparently, the local high school upgraded their own portable gurney cart, and Blair happened to be over there when it was delivered from Cushman. It's just like the one you see on football games when a player gets hurt."

"Impressive. It's got room for your medical gear, and look, it's even got hooks for you to set up an IV drip while you care for the patient. They must've consulted with doctors on this recently. The hospital wasn't this far advanced the last time we came here."

Tyler pointed back toward the door and led his wife by the arm inside. "Believe it or not, Ryan said he put things together based upon internet research and made a lot of the purchases on Amazon. He'd planned on calling us this month anyway and, well, um, here we are."

A small office was located at the back of the building and Angela entered it for the first time. There were several bookcases filled with medical books dealing with all manner of ailments and injuries. A metallic box sat on the edge of the desk and she opened it. Two iPads with chargers were contained within the egg-crate-style foam cushioning. There was a laminated page containing instructions and Angela read some of them aloud.

"These iPads contain PDF files as reference materials for the Armageddon Hospital. There are downloads of trauma medicine techniques, a *Physicians' Desk Reference* to help with identifying and dispensing medications, and specialty manuals on treating patients such as infants and the elderly."

"These guys have done their research," said Tyler. "They even stored all of this in a small Faraday cage."

Angela continued reading. "The two iPads are identical and loaded with the same materials. Please keep them charged by only removing one at a time during the charging process."

Tyler listened to Angela describe more of the contents of the iPad and looked behind the partially closed door.

"Check this out, babe," he said cheerily. "I guess it's official. Congrats on your new job."

Tyler removed a white lab coat from the back of the door. It was embroidered with the words *Dr. Angela Rankin, Armageddon Hospital.*

"Let me see," she said as she rounded the desk. Angela pulled the jacket on and was pleased with the fit. She reached into one of the pockets and retrieved a stethoscope. "I like it."

A voice interrupted them. "Well, it certainly suits you." The sudden entrance of Donna Shelton startled the Rankins. "May I be your first patient?"

"Hi, Donna," greeted Tyler as he stood to the side so she could enter. "I was just leaving anyway. Ryan wants me to begin driving the roads and trails of the Haven so I become more familiar with everything. I guess I'm gonna double as an EMT and ambulance driver."

Angela exchanged a fist bump with her husband and then rewarded him with a kiss on the cheek. "Enjoy your first day on the streets," she said with a chuckle.

Tyler smiled at Donna, grabbed a trauma kit, and bolted out the door, leaving the two women alone.

"Come on in, Donna, and take a seat," began Angela. "I'm just now getting acquainted with the hospital, so I hope what you wanna talk about isn't too serious."

Donna sat down and her shoulders immediately slumped. She subconsciously rubbed her chest just below her neck and then pulled her cardigan a little closer together.

"Unfortunately, I'm afraid it might be."

CHAPTER 12

Monocacy Farm
South of Frederick Maryland

Briscoe managed a laugh, born out of exhaustion and fear, as he thought about how a person's sixth sense worked. Leaning against a two-hundred-year-old oak tree, he surveilled the grounds between the house and where he'd emerged out of the tunnel. His eyes searched the woods, looking for any signs of movement indicating that his pursuers were aware of his location.

"Left for love, right for spite," he mumbled to himself as he thought of an old saying. An oft-repeated myth was that if your ears were ringing, it was a sign that someone was talking about you. If someone was speaking about you in a fond way, your left ear would ring. If it was your right ear, it meant they were speaking poorly about you. Then, as the superstition goes, if you begin saying names of people who might either love you—or hate you, if the right ear is ringing—you could then determine who triggered the sensation. Once the person's name was said, the ringing would stop, and the culprit would be revealed.

Of course, Briscoe knew that the changes in blood flow, such as after a fit of anxiety followed by unusual physical activity like he'd just subjected his body to, was the likely culprit. But in his state of semi-delirium, he couldn't resist the urge to repeat the names of those who might wish him harm. Only one name caused the ringing to stop—George Trowbridge.

Briscoe gathered himself up and began to dart through the woods toward the caretaker's house located about a mile away. He was old and out of shape, but he'd managed to muster the adrenaline and drive to escape from his attackers. As he jogged through the sparse underbrush, using the trees as cover, he considered his plight.

Trowbridge likely knew all along that Briscoe was extremely negligent in not overseeing the downing of Delta 322, or worse, the old man knew of his intention to kill Cortland. Either way, he was now a marked man, and he was sure his friends were few and far between.

He stopped short of the clearing overlooking his caretaker's home. The elderly man had managed the grounds and the housekeeping staff for nearly thirty years. Clarence Johnson had approached Briscoe one day and said his family was destitute. He'd been incarcerated for stealing from a convenience store and was released after four years in the Maryland state prison.

Briscoe needed help around Monocacy Farm and gave Johnson a job as a groundskeeper. Over time, the man proved himself to be a loyal, hard worker and was elevated to being in charge of the sizable staff that maintained the property and served its guests.

Briscoe waited over an hour to ensure that the caretaker's home wasn't raided by his attackers. During that time, he became increasingly paranoid about whom he could reach out to for help. His network of hackers might have been tipped off by Trowbridge's people. His phone could've been monitored. Or they were simply waiting for an opportune moment.

Either way, no one had appeared after the botched mission to take his life, so Briscoe forced his stiff and shivering body toward the kitchen door at the rear of the house. When he saw Johnson making coffee, he gently tapped on the door and spoke in a hushed voice.

"Clarence, open up. It's Hanson. Please hurry."

"Mr. Briscoe, is that you?"

"Yes, please open up."

Johnson came to the door and he was quickly joined by his wife, who wrapped herself up in a housecoat to ward off the cold air. Briscoe moved into the warm kitchen, and Johnson took a glance outside before closing the door.

"Listen to me. Close all the curtains and blinds."

"But, Mr. Briscoe, why do——?"

Briscoe, cold and frightened, became agitated with his caretaker. "Because I said so, Clarence. Somebody broke into the main house and they tried to kill me."

"What?" asked Mrs. Johnson as she poured a cup of coffee, almost spilling it as she heard Briscoe's statement.

"Now, who's gonna kill you, Mr. Briscoe? You're a very powerful man."

"People more powerful than me," he replied. "Please do as I say."

Briscoe wandered around the room for a moment as his body started to warm. Mrs. Johnson brought him some towels and offered one of her husband's flannel shirts to change into. The shirt was massive on Briscoe's wiry frame, but it was welcome and warming.

Briscoe had to make a decision. Could he trust his longtime employee? Or would they fold under pressure, the type of painful coercion that his operatives would be capable of administering?

The Johnsons had left him alone with his thoughts as he sat in the living room, which faced the driveway. He was beginning to feel more confident that he'd evaded his assassins, for now, but his next step was more uncertain.

Despite the fact that Briscoe felt like he was in charge, at the end of the day, everyone's loyalty was to Trowbridge. The man's failing health did nothing to sway power from the others who'd come together after that night on Deer Island in 1984. Briscoe furrowed his brow and snarled as he thought about his place in life. He was no different than his ancestor and namesake, John Hanson, the first president of the Continental Congress, who never garnered the respect he deserved.

"Well, I'm nobody's stooge," grumbled Briscoe aloud. He stood from the sofa overlooking the front yard and turned to find Johnson standing in the kitchen observing him.

"Mr. Briscoe, what can I do to help you?" he asked.

Briscoe closed his eyes and slowly shook his head. He'd made his decision. "Clarence, do you still have that handgun I gave you years ago?"

"Yessir. I've never shot it, but I kept it tucked away in the nightstand like you said. All the bullets are still in the box, too."

"Good, I need it back."

Johnson made his way to the bedroom, and Briscoe adjusted his pants, which were now fully dry. He removed the caretaker's flannel shirt and adjusted his sweater to look more presentable. He subconsciously felt for his cell phone to ensure it was still tucked away in the sweater's pocket.

Johnson returned with the weapon, the bullets, and his wife by his side, who spoke first. "Mr. Briscoe, maybe we should call the police. I mean, if there are people trying to kill you, the police can help, right?"

"Not this time," he replied unemotionally. He reached his hands out and took the weapon and ammunition from Johnson. It was a .38 revolver, something easy for Johnson to load and fire in the event of an intruder. Briscoe accessed the cylinder and checked to see if it was already loaded. He saw that it was empty, so he quickly inserted six bullets.

As he shoved the remaining bullets into his sweater, his palms became sweaty as the realization of his next step hit him. *Loose lips sink ships*, and Briscoe couldn't leave a witness as to his whereabouts.

To be sure, Hanson Briscoe had killed before, but not like this. He gave orders and others fulfilled their duties. He watched the aftermath from afar, usually in the safety and comfort of Monocacy Farm. He took a deep breath and steadied his nerves.

Without hesitation, he quickly grabbed a pillow off the sofa next to him, shoved the barrel of the pistol into it, and fired a round into the chest of the man who'd been his loyal employee for decades.

His quick actions and the muffled sound of the revolver stunned the couple. Mrs. Johnson gasped and covered her mouth in astonishment as blood poured out of her husband's chest, the wound causing him to drop to his knees beside her.

Briscoe grimaced, but didn't hesitate as he turned the gun on her, also shooting her in the chest. The couple, barely alive, were now lying together on the hardwood floor next to the kitchen where they gathered together for morning coffee before attending to the affairs of Monocacy Farm.

Briscoe tried not to look at their faces as he covered them with the pillow and fired another round into their skulls, finishing the job. He stood and stared at the ceiling before hurling the blood-soaked pillow across the room.

"Damn you, George Trowbridge! This is on you! You will pay for what I've been forced to do!"

CHAPTER 13

The Varnadore Building
Uptown Charlotte, North Carolina

Uptown Charlotte was anything but *uptown* in many respects. Charlotte was a city of distinct neighborhoods, growing together over time as the Queen City became a regional financial hub and the second most influential metropolitan area along the southern Atlantic seaboard other than Atlanta.

Uptown Charlotte, the central business district of the city, had been split into wards over time that were divided geographically by the interstate system. As was true in many American cities, new growth, spurred by the arrival of major corporations like Bank of America, Duke Energy, and Wells Fargo, dominated the landscape. The rapid population surge associated with the influx of corporate America brought noticeable change to the city's landscape.

New construction left behind pockets of abandoned buildings, low-income housing, and dilapidated retail structures. Just on the eastern outskirts of Uptown Charlotte was an area along East Independence highway where skeletons of once-proud structures barely stood, rotting away from the elements and vandalism.

These were the parts of the United States that became the target of Schwartz-owned organizations. Using the massive war chest of cash at their disposal, the Schwartz Foundation acquired buildings that remained largely vacant as a city modernized all around them. Jonathan Schwartz and his father took advantage of U.S. tax laws to reduce their liabilities to the government while also using the buildings to funnel monies from foreign income sources back into the States.

In the meantime, the crumbling structures could serve a secondary purpose—a staging ground for anarchist activity.

The Varnadore building east of uptown was a seven-story, brick and glass office building built sixty years ago. Once the offices of Charlotte's major real estate firm and builder, The Ervin Company, it was now abandoned and surrounded by others structures in similar condition. But the empty storefronts that once sold pool tables, hot tubs, and grandfather clocks all had one thing in common. They were owned indirectly by the Schwartz family. Now they were being utilized by Joseph Jose Acuff, who'd adopted the street name Chepe, to lead a ragtag group of assorted malcontents who had been brought together to ravage Charlotte.

Chepe had arrived in Charlotte late the night before, but the midnight hour didn't necessarily mean that the people of the city were tucked away safely in bed awaiting another day of work, school, or play. The city was already under siege by those who would become Chepe's army, and the Ghost Face Gangsters, who'd migrated from Georgia in search of a new locale for their criminal activities.

These two groups, coupled with the usual opportunists who sought the opportunity to break into storefronts and steal televisions as a display of their social angst, instilled fear in local residents. The police force was completely overwhelmed. The governor of North Carolina was hesitant to deploy the National Guard, and those who attempted to resist the anarchy taking place in the city were met with brutal, deadly force.

After Chepe met with his new lieutenants to get a clear picture of the state of affairs in Charlotte, he joked that he could've stayed back in Richmond and simply let his minions burn Charlotte to the ground without his involvement. However, he had been given an order from Jonathan Schwartz himself. He'd learned that the Schwartz family was successful in creating chaos when chaos was called for, and he intended to follow their instructions.

The ground-floor lobby of the Varnadore had been beautifully appointed in mid-century modern décor at one point in time, but as the building was abandoned and later purchased for a dime on the dollar by Schwartz interests, the vagrants moved in and tore out the old wood-stud walls to build fires during the wintertime. Now the lobby was a large open space, its broken tile floor, concrete walls and ceiling creating a cold, dungeon-like feel.

Two men had pulled several wooden crates toward the center of the room so that Chepe could stand tall above his new charges. He began to deliver a speech that he'd used many times to rally his fellow anarchists.

People of all walks of life needed motivation to act outside of their comfort zones. A shy child needed special encouragement to stand in front of a room to speak. A new resident needed to be prodded to join a gathering of their neighbors. Would-be rabble-rousers, those who spent their time flapping their jaws on social media, had never contemplated taking their anger to the streets to effectuate change. They did their part from the comfort of their sofas and through their weapon of choice—a computer.

Chepe needed to elevate their involvement. They needed to do more than wear a funny pink hat in the form of a vagina. They needed to do more than lie down in the middle of the street and block traffic or carry signs in support of people who were from another country. They needed to do more than throw eggs at a politician's home or pour paint on a socialite's fur coat.

Chepe took a moment to introduce himself and then he further quietened the crowd. Over a hundred men and women had crowded into the ground floor of the Varnadore building, with several dozen more standing above him on the balconies of the second and third levels. The group was somewhat raucous, filled with anticipation of their new leader, who they knew was sent by the family who'd helped fund their activist gatherings in the past.

"First, I want all of you to pull down your masks," Chepe ordered. He pointed to the variety of face masks worn to obscure the identities of the anarchists. Many had donned the Guy Fawkes masks worn by members of the Anonymous group. He picked them out of the crowd and explained why.

"There are many in this country who drape themselves in the flag and declare their patriotism to be greater than all others'. Let me tell you something, the patriots, the Founding Fathers whom they revere so much were no different than we are. Think about it. The new land was ruled and colonized by Great Britain. Those colonists who rose up against the crown to take America from the England were looking for change. They formed a resistance. And they were rewarded for their efforts with a new nation.

"The Loyal Nine, the men known by many as part of the Sons of Liberty, were the leaders of this movement as it began in Boston. Their resistance required soldiers, but not in the sense of an all-out war. Instead, they needed people loyal to their cause who'd do whatever was necessary to unnerve the British soldiers and harass the politicians who'd kept their foot stomped on the chest of the people.

"Hiding in secret and gathering in buildings just like this one, these men rallied their operatives with fiery speeches. They also recruited people like yourselves who'd been shunned by the upper crust of society. They didn't live in neighborhoods like Eastover, Wessex Square, and Myers Park. They weren't welcomed into social clubs like Carmel or Providence.

"They sought to shake things up just like we are. We know that the only way to get attention is to bring it upon ourselves. Like Guy Fawkes, who attempted to kill King James in 1605, and those like him, insurgents like ourselves learned to take the battle directly to those who want nothing to do with our cause. Followers of Fawkes adopted the masks like yours, with the oversized smile and red cheeks, upturned mustache and the pointed beard, as a show of support.

"Together, the American Revolution movement, using the muscle and enthusiasm of the downtrodden, created a new nation. And once they did, they could take off their masks, come out of hiding, and be proud of their accomplishments.

"So my question to you is this. How are we any different from the Sons of Liberty and the men they recruited to stir things up?"

"We're the same!" shouted a man in the rear of the room.

"We need a new nation!" yelled another.

"That's exactly right!" Chepe responded. "This nation has lost its way. It no longer respects the common man. It's all about corporate interests and lining the pockets of the rich. It's time that we show them what the power of the people can do."

"Freedom!" a woman yelled.

Chepe smiled and pointed in her direction. "Yes! Freedom. A free society of free individuals. No more capitalist economy, and do away with a nation-state that is governed by the wealthy. We deserve a society based upon equality of the human spirit, not one based upon a hierarchy established by wealth."

"We need to reclaim the streets!" a man near Chepe shouted.

"Take our country back!" added another.

"Exactly, and we'll start with one neighborhood and one city at a time," said Chepe. "Listen to me. We are not alone. All around the country, others like us are gathering and making their plans. While in the past we've tried to organize a nationwide movement, now we're focusing on our task of showing Charlotte that we're serious about real change.

"We will no longer fight behind masks and under the shadow of darkness. That's what they expect. The police, the politicians, the media expect us to sneak around like rats after the sun goes down. Not today. Today, we march into the homes of the wealthiest bourgeoisie of Charlotte, proud of our cause and determined to make our points.

"Nobody will expect this bold action. They will be unprepared. They will learn what happens when workers are exploited, when people are told to shut up, and when they use their wealth and power to hold us down."

"Yeah!"

"We're ready!"

Chepe allowed the demonstration to simmer and then he finally shouted over the crowd, "The fuse has been lit and it's time for war!"

The group roared its approval, and each of them symbolically removed their face coverings, from masks to bandannas, and slung them into the air as they congratulated each other on their newfound freedom.

Chepe stepped off the crates and began to wander through the crowd, receiving pats on the back and words of thanks. He knew what he was doing. With his gift of rhetoric, he was able to convince this mob from diverse backgrounds to move throughout Charlotte, destroying property and murdering if they chose to.

He gradually made his way to the front of the building and stepped out into the crisp, midmorning air. Chepe was contemplative as he stared out toward the glass towers of bank and insurance buildings in downtown Charlotte. He shoved his hands into his pockets and shuddered slightly as he warded off a chill.

Then his cell phone began to vibrate.

CHAPTER 14

The Armageddon Hospital
The Haven

Angela and Donna had spoken at length about the drone attacks on New York City and the probability that dirty-bomb materials might have been dropped onto Midtown Manhattan. Angela's first inclination was to conduct online research into whether Donna might have been exposed to the radiation and then determine what impact, if any, it might have had upon her. That was no longer possible, at least for the moment.

Between the power outages in the mid-Atlantic states and the unexpected cyber attacks on aspects of the nation's infrastructure, internet connectivity had been intermittent at best. Angela, whose field of expertise was in trauma care and who was not fully versed in cancer treatment, had to rely upon the volumes of materials downloaded by Blair onto the iPads kept in the EMP-protected box.

She and Donna studied the materials together, as Donna had a working knowledge of medical terms and procedures, especially as it related to her situation. As they reviewed the materials, they discussed the possibilities.

"I've always known that just because my breast cancer was in remission didn't mean the challenges were over," said Donna as she scrolled through the iPad, looking for relevant articles. She and Angela had both plugged their chargers into the outlets to bring them up to one hundred percent before stowing one of them away, as per Blair's explicit instructions.

"It must've had a profound impact on your life, as well as Tom's," added Angela.

Donna nodded. "When I found out that I had breast cancer, I was in shock. I was worried that I could die, which was terrifying. After spending hours at the infusion center, undergoing a lumpectomy and the chemo, I was struck by a range of emotions. My feelings were unpredictable. Some days I was sad and worried about my future and Tom's. Other days, I'd be mad at the world for what had happened to me. Unfortunately, I'd take out my anger on him."

Angela stopped glancing at an article in order to be fully engaged in the conversation. She sensed Donna needed to pour her heart out. "Tom seems like a strong man."

"Incredibly so," said Donna with a smile. "After my second chemo treatment, I was so sick that I couldn't stand to greet him. I became depressed and locked myself away in a guest bedroom to keep him away from me. It broke my heart because I could hear the sadness in his voice as he begged me to come out, but I didn't have the energy to lift my head up off the pillow."

"Yet you guys persevered and you beat it." Angela tried to change the tone of the conversation. Donna was, after all, a cancer survivor.

"Oh, yes. We're both survivors, in a way. My cancer was finally defeated after a year of chemo. I religiously followed up with my doctors, and my scans have continuously read clean for years. In fact, I just recently reached the five-year milestone."

"Which greatly increases your survival probabilities," interrupted Angela, who was aware of the importance of the clean screenings.

"You know, *survivor* isn't really the right term to use. It suggests something horrible like a car accident or the sudden death of someone you love, and you were lucky enough to get through it. Cancer, however, is not a onetime event. It continues forever, in a way. Remission isn't the same as being cured."

"I understand." Angela reached across the desk to take Donna's hand. "I imagine that you have to pay attention to every change your body goes through. A cold isn't just a cold anymore, right?"

Donna set the iPad aside and clasped Angela's young hand with both of hers. "Every ache and pain, each cough, or even a day of lethargy concerns me. It's never out of my mind. That's why I'm concerned about the effects of the radioactive substances released by those drones. You can't see it or taste it, but if it was there, it can invade my body quicker than someone else's."

Angela caught a glimpse through her window of Tyler's medical cart driving up the hill toward them, so she wanted to summarize her opinion for Donna before he arrived. "Donna, of course I'm not an expert, as you know, but I want to be honest. It is possible that the dirty bomb materials could exacerbate your cancer and hasten its return out of remission. I suggest you see me daily to monitor your vitals."

"Tom will grow suspicious if I'm constantly reporting to the hospital. I don't want to worry him unnecessarily."

Angela thought for a moment. "I have an idea. Why don't you work here as my assistant? It's my understanding that another potential resident with medical experience was turned away from the Haven. Meredith can handle the school duties with someone else. What do you think? Work here, and we'll monitor you without Tom becoming alarmed."

Donna smiled and stood to embrace Angela. The two women fought back tears as they bonded over Donna's illness. Finally, they broke their embrace just as Tyler was entering the building.

Angela whispered into the older woman's ear, "I almost lost both of my children to horrific deaths. They both live life with vigor and an amazing spirit. Always remember that saying you only live once is a myth."

Donna paused and became emotional. Angela reached down to touch the older woman's cheeks, comforting her as she regained her composure. Donna mustered the energy to add one more thought.

"The fact is that you only die once. You live every day."

PART TWO

CHAPTER 15

Eastover Neighborhood
Charlotte, North Carolina

Chepe had many weapons at his disposal, but the enthusiasm of his followers was his greatest. To be sure, the truckload of military-grade equipment ranging from fully automatic weapons to grenade launchers would allow him to launch a major assault on governmental targets. But those were wholly unnecessary for the first day of their attack on Charlotte.

His first goal was to instill fear in those who wanted nothing to do with the fight between haves and have-nots. By directing his teams into the affluent neighborhoods of Charlotte, he'd not only intimidate those who have influence over government, but he'd also provide his fellow anarchists the pleasure of knocking *the man* down to size.

Chepe had several lieutenants who'd worked in community organizing and shadowy anarchist activities throughout Charlotte in the past. He used them to create several teams that would descend upon locations throughout Mecklenburg County, starting around two o'clock that afternoon.

By spreading throughout the metroplex, Chepe followed the suggestion of his lieutenants who'd intentionally started fires in a way that the locals couldn't efficiently respond to. He hoped this would work as well. And, he confirmed, the Guardian Angels who'd confronted his people in Richmond were not active in Charlotte. He expected to have free rein as he moved from one wealthy neighborhood to another.

Chepe led the way from the Varnadore Building toward Queens Road, which was located in the heart of Eastover. What he found astonished him and almost forced him to move on to another location.

Shops and restaurants along the street had been looted, and some were smoldering from fires having been set inside them. Men wearing khaki pants and Izod sweaters were pushing shopping carts along the sidewalk, filled with all types of foods and clothing. The looters of Eastover were no different than those in the French Quarter of New Orleans after Hurricane Katrina. They were just better dressed.

There was a mob scene outside the Harris Teeter grocery store at the corner of Queens Road and Providence Road. The ornately designed building that lent the appearance of a colonial mansion was being emptied by local residents. Every window was broken out, including the one facing Providence that used to display an image of a fresh ear of corn. Only the lower part of the husk was visible, as the rest had been broken out to make room for both women and men to step into the store, only to later emerge with armfuls of groceries.

"Where are the cops?" asked Chepe as he looked in all directions from where the driver had paused next to a Methodist Church across from the store.

"Chasin' their tails," a man in the backseat responded. "Here's what you haven't seen yet. The difference in Eastover and the poorest neighborhoods in Charlotte is these folks are being polite to each other."

The three men in the car with Chepe burst out laughing and immediately began to mock the wealthy looters.

"Oh yes," one of them began in his best, proper English accent. "May I have a jar of that Grey Poop-on." The man intentionally misstated the word *Poupon* for effect.

The driver joined in the playful banter. "Naturally, sir. Would you please pass me a tube of Preparation H? Oh, no, not that one. I don't use generic. The other box with the big *H* on it, por favor."

This caused the men to break into uproarious laughter, but Chepe remained stoic as he studied the activity. His job was to generate chaos and create panic amongst the wealthiest residents of Charlotte. It appeared societal collapse had undertaken to do that for him. He began to rethink the use of his resources.

"What's the plan, boss?" the driver asked Chepe.

Chepe pondered for a moment. If the rich were out of food and resorting to looting, albeit in their country-club attire, what could he do to make their lives worse?

Cut off their sources of food to force them to turn on each other, he thought to himself.

"Contact the other teams." He began to give his instructions. "Tell them to locate the largest grocery stores or warehouse clubs like Sam's and Costco. Precisely at two o'clock, tell them to hit the stores hard and drive everybody out. Do whatever they feel is best to convince the shoppers that the store is closed indefinitely. Once they're afraid to venture out of their McMansions and gated communities, they'll begin looking closer to home for sources of food. Let's see if *love thy neighbor* applies then, right?"

The men laughed, and each of them picked up their two-way radios to reach out to the other teams. Chepe exited the vehicle and walked to the other six cars in their caravan to spread the word. Part of the team hustled off to the other end of Providence Road, where they'd stage an attack on the Laurel Market.

Chepe stood in the street for a moment, studying the determined faces of the people exiting the stores. Their eyes darted about, most likely concerned about law enforcement arresting them. Or they were afraid their neighbors might recognize them. These people didn't understand hardship, Chepe thought to himself. They only understood being judged.

The calls had been made and his team gathered around him. Both men and women stood in a semicircle behind Chepe as they marched toward Harris Teeter. Two visions immediately popped into his mind.

He thought of the video clips he'd watched when white people pounded clubs and baseball bats in their hands as the race riots in Selma, Jackson, and Memphis exploded in the sixties. The broken bodies and the blood streaming from them left a lasting impression on his young mind during his high school years.

The second vision was that of the Statue of Liberty, standing proud as a symbol of freedom and peace. He'd devoted his life to helping people out of oppression in a nation that prided itself on its freedoms. Yet, in the not too distant past, men in pressed-white shirts carrying clubs would beat another man down just because of the color of his skin.

Chepe, a white man who felt guilty for the privileges he'd been afforded as a result thereof, felt compelled to make up for the wrongs of the past. The brutal attacks on the residents of Eastover was only the beginning of what was to come in Charlotte and surrounding areas.

Emboldened by his memories, Chepe, without warning, began to run toward the grocery store, holding a fully extended telescopic police baton in one hand and a nine-millimeter handgun in the other.

The guttural cry emitted from his throat caused his comrades to pause in surprise, but then they joined the fray, running after Chepe as if they were Mongol hordes attacking unsuspecting villagers in a valley.

CHAPTER 16

Haven School
The Haven

"Well, you guys, it's our first day of school," said Meredith cheerily as her new young charges got settled into their seats. The schoolchildren of the Haven ranged from six to twelve. After a long discussion between Meredith, Blair and Ryan, they all agreed that teenagers would help the community better by working under the direct supervision of adults and being homeschooled in the evenings. The youngest children, those under six, were being cared for as part of a day care program in the Katniss Everdeen home as designated in the *Hunger Games* movie. The rest, representing grades one through seven, were to report to school.

Teaching a multigrade class presented some challenges for Meredith. The first challenge had to do with the maturity of the students. Developmentally, both from a social standpoint and an educational perspective, there was a vast difference between a six-year-old and a twelve-year-old.

Over the past several decades, children had grown up much faster than their counterparts in the middle part of the twentieth century. It wasn't just their exposure to things on television, or what they learned from other children. Technology enabled them to advance as well.

Meredith took the approach that the broad range of kids simply meant that some had greater learning capabilities than others. The older kids could remain more focused while the first or second graders might require more supervision.

She planned on adopting a balanced literacy format. She'd teach reading and writing lessons as a whole group, and then she'd divide the kids into smaller groups, which she could give individualized attention based upon their skill set.

The same would apply to math curriculums and the social sciences. History could be taught to them all in a way that was easy to understand and that encouraged interaction between Meredith and her students.

Meredith's daughter, Hannah, was her oldest student, followed closely by Kaycee Rankin and Skylar Hightower. The three girls bonded almost instantly although Kaycee was more mature and adultlike than the other two.

Young J.C. was not the oldest of the boys in the combined class, but he was the undisputed leader of the young men. He exuded confidence and commanded the room when he spoke. He was a born leader and would provide Meredith an excellent assistant, especially in history matters.

They were nearing the end of their day when Ryan and Alpha arrived at the school and pulled Meredith aside. She gave the kids orders to put their books away and straighten their desks while she stepped into the library to speak with the guys.

"Gentlemen, have you come to check up on me?" Meredith said jokingly.

"Well, we wanted to make sure they hadn't tied you up and stuffed you into a closet on day one," replied Alpha with a laugh. "I remember this time when I was in grade school. A bunch of us—"

Ryan raised his hand and shook his head from side to side. "No, Alpha. Meredith doesn't need to hear your childhood war stories."

"But she might need to know that—"

"Nope, not today. Tell her what you need."

"Okay," Alpha said, disappointed that he couldn't continue. "As you know, we have a perimeter-security program that involves drones. Some of the teenagers are involved in that, as well as a few adults volunteered. Truthfully, the adults can't seem to grasp the maneuverability of the quadcopters. You know, you can't teach an old dog new tricks."

"Hey, that probably applies to me," complained Ryan.

"Me too," said Meredith, who got suddenly serious. "Let's cut to the chase. Are you thinking of pulling some of these kids out of school?"

"No, no," Alpha quickly replied. "It'll be an afternoon and weekends thing. Um, they don't come to school seven days a week, do they?"

"Sunday school at church, but that's it on the weekends," replied Meredith.

"Then do you think any of the kids have both the skill set and the maturity to be worked into our rotation? We're talking about a few hours after school and free time on weekends."

Meredith fidgeted as she considered her new batch of students. The oldest kids made the most sense, but neither Skylar nor Hannah had the requisite maturity level. She immediately chastised herself for sheltering Hannah and not preparing her to be a young woman.

"Honestly, I can only recommend Kaycee at this point, although her brother is perfectly capable of handling himself. That kid could probably drive a truck if you asked him to."

"Of course. I remember him from the morning meeting, but how old is he?" asked Alpha.

Ryan and Meredith replied simultaneously, "Eight."

"Really? I don't know, guys," said Alpha skeptically.

"I tell you what," Ryan began, stepping in to make a decision. "From what I know of those two, they are very tight knit, and they've managed to survive a situation in their home where they worked together to avoid being attacked by a bunch of thugs. Alpha, can you assign them their own quadcopters, but have them work together?"

"Sure. I can designate them to the Henry River sector. The Rankins live down there anyway, and their cabin is centrally located along the entire stretch. They can practically work from home while staying completely familiar with one stretch of the Haven."

"I'll tell them, but I want to do it outside of the earshot of their classmates," said Meredith. "Let me speak to them after class lets out and I'll send them down to HB1. Is that okay?"

Alpha gave her a thumbs-up and headed toward the door. Ryan was about to leave when Cort arrived at the school.

"Hey, what did I miss?" asked Cort.

Ryan fist-bumped Cort and replied, "We're recruiting soldiers. Meredith said Hannah would make a fine gunner."

"Wait, what?" Cort had a look of concern on his face.

"They're just kiddin', dear," replied his wife, followed by a playful shove directed at Ryan. "Mr. Smart, why do you wanna scare my husband like that?"

They all shared a laugh. Alpha and Ryan left, leaving the Cortlands alone.

"Is everything okay?" Meredith asked.

"Yeah, um, I guess. I need to talk with you about your father. Is class almost over?"

Meredith studied him and then replied, "It is. The kids are cleaning up now. I need to pull the Rankin children aside to talk to them about being part of Alpha's drone squad. He'd like them to help monitor the riverbank during their off-school free time."

"J.C. is kinda young. Why not Hannah?" asked Cort.

"I'm sorry, but she's not ready, Cort."

He smiled and reached out to hug his wife. "I understand. Listen, take your time. I wanna take a look around the school."

Meredith kissed her husband on the cheek and dismissed the class. The Rankin kids were beyond enthusiastic when they were told of their new role within the Haven. They bolted out the front door and didn't notice Cort standing to the side observing their interaction with Meredith.

"Mom, are we going home now?" asked Hannah. "I need to start on my homework."

"Honey, I need to talk to your father for a moment. Can you wait for us, or do you want to get a head start and I'll meet you back at the house?"

Hannah hugged Cort. "Hi, Daddy. Bye, Daddy. I'm gotta get

started on learning algebra. You know, it's kinda like solving a puzzle, except you use numbers. I'll see you later." Hannah spun around and skipped through the door and down the stairs of the Little Red Schoolhouse.

Her parents watched for her a moment and then Cort said, "The world needs mathematicians, too, you know."

"I know. I'm not ashamed of how we've raised her, although I admit I've sheltered her too much. It was a mistake and now she's thrown into a cold, cruel world."

Cort hugged Meredith and consoled her. "You've sheltered her, and I've sheltered you. We do it because we want to protect the ones we love and hide the ugliness of the world from their view."

"Yeah, I guess you're right."

"Ironically, that's why I'm here," began Cort as he broke their embrace. He looked down to the wood floor of the schoolhouse like a young boy who'd been caught cheating on his math test. "There's more to your father than you know, and I have to tell you the truth about a few things. I want you to know that I love you and I didn't want to lie about anything, but I thought it best to keep certain things to myself."

Meredith touched her husband's cheek and smiled. "You're a good man and an excellent husband. There's nothing that you can say that will ever change how I feel about you. Now, you can start by cleaning the chalkboard and slapping the erasers while you spill the beans about dear old daddy."

CHAPTER 17

U.S. Route 222
Near Lancaster, Pennsylvania

Briscoe mustered all of his strength to control his speed and emotions. He'd left the Johnsons' bodies lying in a pool of blood in the home that he'd provided for them since he'd elevated Clarence to the position of caretaker. They'd become like family to him, and just hours ago, he'd summarily dismissed them from employment by execution.

Once he'd cleared Maryland and entered Pennsylvania by taking a number of country roads and detours, his paranoia subsided. He turned his attention to the man who'd ordered his death—George Trowbridge.

Briscoe understood that word would spread among those he used to consider trusted friends and allies. Their loyalty would turn directly to Trowbridge, especially if the old man explained his reasons for ordering the hit. Briscoe was fully aware that Trowbridge had the ability to call upon federal authorities to track him down, asking them to cast aside anything else on their desk, including dealing with the collapse of America.

Traffic was light on U.S. Route 222 as he approached the quaint town of Lancaster, Pennsylvania. He had more than a half tank of fuel and several hundred dollars in his pocket, money taken from the Johnsons.

Initially, his only thought was to make his way to Canada and call on a childhood friend who lived just over the Maine state line in Saint Stephen. There were numerous places to cross the Saint Croix River in that desolate part of northeastern Maine.

But then what? His life had been ruined by a miscalculation. He'd made a play, and it failed. Did he deserve to die? Should he be exiled? Not in his opinion. As he carefully drove through Lancaster, eyes darting in all directions to determine if local law enforcement was looking for the Johnsons' vehicle, Briscoe's attitude changed.

He went from a frightened fugitive, deservedly on the run for a wrong that he'd committed, to a man hell-bent on revenge and desperately in need of an ally.

A student of military history, Briscoe, like so many others, liked to quote Sun Tzu, the Chinese general and military strategist from the fifth century BC, who once wrote "The enemy of my enemy is my friend."

Briscoe smiled and laughed out loud as he said, "Trowbridge has no greater enemy than the Schwartz family."

Because it had been barely two hours since he'd left the caretaker's home and, most likely, the Johnsons' bodies had not yet been discovered, Briscoe chose to pull into a gas station that remarkably still had fuel. While the attendant pumped the tank full, *to the top of the throat*, as Briscoe had requested, he scrolled through his Notepad app on his phone.

He periodically received briefings on the Schwartz family, not only as it related to their financial dealings, but more importantly for Briscoe's purposes, he kept tabs on their political activism and the groups they used to promote their ideologies.

One of their go-to guys for instigating unrest was Chepe. Briscoe scrolled through his notes and found the dossier that had been created on the DC Antifa leader. He'd been arrested a couple of years prior for aggravated assault, ethnic intimidation and making terroristic threats in connection with an Antifa mob attack on two Hispanic-American Marines.

The Antifa members, calling the men Nazis and white supremacists, attacked them on the street despite the Marines' denials of association with any such groups. Calling the men racist terms, *spics* and *wetbacks*, Chepe led the charge as the men were brutally assaulted by the mob.

However, using the best criminal lawyers from Philadelphia that money could buy, courtesy of the Schwartz legal defense fund, Chepe's trial was continuously postponed until an underling within the Antifa ranks stepped forward and admitted guilt. The man, who had no family and no criminal record, received a minor sentence plus probation, and most likely a generous compensation package from Jonathan Schwartz.

Briscoe had notes on all of this as well as the most recent report on Chepe's activities. His last known whereabouts were in DC, but the news reports Briscoe had watched out of Richmond had all of the earmarks of a Chepe-led operation. If Chepe was making waves, he was funded by Schwartz. That meant he had access to Jonathan.

The attendant finished pumping the fuel and Briscoe paid him. Then he scrolled through the dossier and found Chepe's cell phone number provided to Briscoe's operatives courtesy of their NSA contacts.

Briscoe started the car and pulled into a parking lot so that he was out of plain view of any passing police cars. He took a deep breath and placed the call. After several rings, a single-word answer set the wheels into motion that would turn one family's life upside down and bring another's closer together.

One man's gain is another man's loss.

"Yeah." Chepe's voice was brusque but hesitant.

"Chepe, please do not hang up until you hear me out. My name is Harlan Briscoe, and I'm known to Jonathan Schwartz although we're not necessarily friends."

Briscoe waited for a reaction from Chepe. For several agonizing seconds, there was silence on the other end of the line. He pulled the phone away from his ear and looked at the display to see if the call was still connected. He nervously continued. "Hello?"

"I don't know either one of you," said Chepe in a monotone voice.

Briscoe was relieved that Chepe stayed on the line, so he treaded lightly as he continued. "Okay, I understand that and I'm not going to press you. All I'm asking is that if you were to speak with Mr.

Schwartz, you tell him that we have a common enemy and that I'm prepared to be his humble servant. Do you understand?"

"I do."

"Thank you," said Briscoe, his voice revealing his sense of relief at having jumped this initial hurdle. He took the next step, one that would either get him killed or guarantee his safety. "My phone number should show on your phone's display. Please provide the number to Mr. Schwartz and tell him that I will meet him anywhere, anyplace, under his terms. He can call me as soon as possible."

Briscoe heard a click and he glanced at the display once again. The call had lasted fifty-four seconds, too quick for a typical law enforcement trace. He surmised Chepe was aware of the surveillance parameters.

Now Briscoe waited. He hoped to have piqued Jonathan's curiosity. With his father arrested at the airport, a fact Briscoe had learned on his own the previous evening through a conversation with one member of the hacktivist team, it was probable that Jonathan was seeking allies as well. Briscoe hoped the two men could help one another.

He'd soon find out.

CHAPTER 18

Schwartz Lodge
Off U.S. Route 222
Near Kutztown, Pennsylvania

It had been many years since Jonathan had visited the hunting lodge off the Kutztown bypass northeast of Reading, Pennsylvania. One of thousands of real estate holdings his family had throughout the United States, the hunting lodge had been a place of refuge for his father during his early days of high-risk currency trading. He would come here with the family, hunt, smoke an occasional cigar, and teach Jonathan about geopolitics and financial market manipulation. It was an education his son could never receive in any business school.

The lodge was a two-story structure built in the seventies using cedar shake shingles and matching siding. The interior was built with post-and-beam construction, featuring soaring ceilings and a massive stone fireplace in the center that could be viewed from both the living and dining spaces.

Like most of the Schwartzes' residential properties, a property manager came around once a month to make sure the pantry was stocked with nonperishable foods that hadn't expired and that the utilities were in proper working order. The individuals were always instructed to be discreet and were well paid for their silence.

Schwartz surveilled the property for more than an hour before deciding to enter. He'd managed to evade the clutches of the FBI. While he didn't think they'd have the forethought to place agents at this obscure hideaway, he wasn't leaving anything to chance.

There was just one problem. The entry door's locking system

required that a code be entered. He had two options. One was to call the property manager and have him open up the lodge. The other was to access the code via his contacts in his cell phone. Either way, he'd have to activate the phone, which meant he could be discovered.

Schwartz wandered back and forth in front of the stolen pickup truck, yet another complication in his attempt to elude the authorities. He was anxious to ditch the vehicle so it couldn't lead to him.

Exasperated by the situation, he pounded his fist on the hood of the truck. "Dammit!" he yelled in frustration. The sudden outburst was stupid, and he immediately closed his mouth, looking around the dense woods to determine if he'd been heard.

The lodge was three miles from Kutztown and Route 222, a well-traveled north-south thoroughfare stretching from Allentown, Pennsylvania, into Northern Maryland. Jonathan was tired yet invigorated by the prospect of being able to ride out the storm at the lodge. If he was going to activate his phone, if only for a few minutes, he'd do it somewhere in Kutztown, where the FBI would presume he was just passing through.

He reentered the pickup and drove back toward the small town of five thousand people of primarily German descent. Within minutes, he was sitting in the parking lot of the Kutztown University of Pennsylvania. Apparently, classes had been cancelled, as there were only a few people walking around the campus.

During his escape, Jonathan had observed the change in the small towns as he drove away from Connecticut. Everything had come to a standstill. Businesses were shuttered, traffic was light, and he'd seen groups of people huddled around outdoor fires, carrying on animated conversations. The attacks of New Year's Eve had caused the nation to stop its normal routine, and after more than a week, there was no indication that the normal American way of life was anywhere close to resuming.

Jonathan took one last look around and began the process of reassembling his cell phone. He had half his battery life available, more than enough to locate the door-lock code for the lodge and then to power it down again.

He nervously fumbled with the device, his mind racing as he thought of the potential danger he was placing himself in. He finally powered on the phone and scrolled through the contacts in search of the code. Just as he found it, two-zero-two-nine, his phone rang, sending shock waves through his nervous system.

After his heart leapt out of his chest, he calmed his nerves when the display indicated that the caller was Chepe.

"Yes," he responded with trepidation.

Chepe, his most cerebral anarchist operative, was short and to the point. "I'll be brief. I know about your father. Someone has reached out to you. I believe he's sincere. Do you want his name and number?"

"What does he want?"

"To help. He claims you have a mutual enemy."

Jonathan's interest was piqued, but he wanted to remain cautious nonetheless. "Name and number."

Chepe responded and Jonathan closed his eyes momentarily as the ramifications of Briscoe reaching out to him sank in. Jonathan quickly switched his phone to speaker and pulled up his notepad.

"Repeat the number."

Chepe did, and then he awaited instructions.

"I'm here for you if you need me," Chepe said, drawing a smile from Jonathan. He had an ally, and maybe another one, in the form of Trowbridge's lead henchman, Briscoe.

CHAPTER 19

Near Cofer Road
South Richmond, Virginia

Ethan was still asleep when his mother, Karen Hightower, began to sob over his battered body. A combination of her tears and kisses on his swollen face stirred him awake. He was having difficulty opening his eyes at first, but then he recognized his mother's voice.

"Ethan, my baby boy. Ethan, can you hear me? It's your mom."

Ethan managed a slight smile, and then his eyes adjusted to the sunlight that was coming in through the windows. "Hey, Mom."

"My gosh, son. Who did this to you?"

"Some guys. I don't know. Doesn't matter. I'm alive."

Karen looked around the room and toward the faces of the family who had rescued her son. "Thank you, but, um. Ethan, where's Skylar? Was she—?" Karen broke down in tears and buried her face in her hands as she contemplated a similar beating being administered to Skylar, or worse.

Ethan was able to raise his arm now and touched his mother's shoulder. "She's fine, Mom. She's safe with Dad."

Ethan wasn't sure why, but his mother's demeanor immediately changed at the mention of Will.

"Where the hell is he?" she demanded. "Where was the dad-of-the-year while my child was being beaten half to death?"

Ethan shook his head side to side and tried to rise up in bed. He was too weak and immediately fell back onto the pillow. "It's not his fault, Mom. He kept us safe. I'm the one that left, you know, to come find you. This is all on me."

"Ethan, don't you even blame yourself for what happened here. Your father was supposed to take care of you. I knew I should've never let you go alone to—"

"No, Mom. It isn't like that. When things went bad, Dad had a plan. He took me and Skylar to this place. You know, it's kinda like one of those compounds."

"Like a cult?" Karen shot back. "Is he some kinda religious fanatic or something? I'm gonna call him right—" Karen fumbled through her pockets to find her cell phone. She tried to power it on, and then she remembered that the battery had died, and she didn't have a car charger.

Ethan cut her off before she finished her sentence. "No, Mom. It's a good place. Actually, a great place. I'm the one who chose to leave."

"Where is it, Ethan?" asked Frankie, who'd stood to the back and side of Karen while she reunited with her son. "Is it here in Richmond?"

"Hey, Frankie." Ethan managed a wave. "No, it's in North Carolina."

Frankie stepped forward and appeared puzzled. "Where? North Carolina? How did you get here?"

"Um, I borrowed a car from one of the farmers," replied Ethan, who was still short of breath. He was feeling better physically, and his emotional faculties had returned. He tried to downplay his theft. "I didn't want my dad to know that I was leaving on my own, so I took a car from a house outside the walls. I planned on taking it back when we went back there."

"Did you say walls?" asked Frankie.

"What kind of place is this, Ethan?" asked Karen, who was still distraught and somewhat angry. She fired off more questions. "Did your Dad not really have a job in Atlanta? Why would he be involved in some kind of cult compound in North Carolina? None of this makes any sense."

Ethan was growing frustrated. His mother had a tendency to overreact and become angry with anything related to his father.

Normally, around the house, he and his sister wouldn't bring anything up related to Will. Now he had no choice.

"Can you guys please prop me up? I really am feeling better. Just a little sore is all."

Frankie and one of the ladies who'd taken care of Ethan adjusted his pillows up against the headboard of the bed so he could sit up. He grimaced and groaned as he rose to a seated position, but he was glad to be upright. He was offered a glass of water with a straw, which he quickly drank down. With his parched throat quenched, and no longer being hovered over by his mother and Frankie, Ethan began to explain.

He relayed to them what had happened at Mercedes-Benz Stadium on New Year's Eve. The fact that he and Skylar were there unsupervised immediately raised the ire of Karen, who went on a rant before both Ethan and Frankie calmed her down.

Then Ethan explained that Will was also known as Delta and that he was an important part of the Haven as a member of the security team. He also told them about the important job he'd been assigned, operating their drone patrols.

"Mom, I was worried about you and got the feeling that Dad didn't want to reach you by phone. I don't know if that was true or if he really couldn't get through, but I decided to head home on my own to get you."

Karen calmed down as Ethan showed signs of improvement. He also was displaying a maturity that was unlike his general demeanor in the past several years. She turned the conversation toward his injuries and listened to the family members for their assessment of whether he needed to go to a hospital or not. The general belief was that Ethan, with bed rest, would recover more each day.

Frankie waited until the discussion of Ethan's condition was over before he pressed him for information on the Haven. "Ethan, they call the place Haven?"

"Yeah. It's really big. It stretches along a river on two sides, and the rest of the property is surrounded by walls and iron gates. They've got supplies and all kinds of people who have different jobs.

Some grow food. Others have special jobs like medical and teaching. They have a lot of security, like Dad."

"How did your dad find this place?" asked Frankie.

Ethan gulped and pointed toward his empty Bambi cup. One of the teenagers rushed to refill it for him. "I don't really know. All I know is that the security guys have nicknames. Dad's is Delta. The head security guy is named Alpha. He used to be in the military."

"Is this Alpha person the one who created the Haven?"

"No. Their names are Ryan and Blair Smart. I didn't see them much. She stays at their house, mostly, and he rides around the Haven on a four-wheeler. You know, everybody has a job. Even Skylar."

"What?" asked Karen with a huff. "What kind of job do they give to a child?"

"Mom, she's not a baby, and she was actually very proud of the job given her by Blair. She was told to draw a watercolor painting or sketch or something like that. You know, of our cabin."

"Will has a cabin there?" Karen asked. "How the hell did he pay for it when he's always behind on my support? He's the lowest of low." Her voice trailed off as she set her jaw.

"I don't know, Mom. I think he worked out some kind of deal or something."

Frankie stepped closer to Ethan's bed. "Hey, don't worry about all of that. Listen, Ethan. Um, do you think you could find your way back to this, this place called the Haven?"

"Yeah, I think so. It's not really that hard. It's west of Charlotte off I-40. From there, it's kinda tricky, but I think I can find my way."

"Frankie, what are you thinking?" asked Karen.

Frankie reached out for Karen's arm and pulled her to the side. "Let's give Ethan a little time to rest. There'll be plenty of time to talk. We've got a little road trip ahead of us."

CHAPTER 20

Haven House
The Haven

One of the outside patrols sped toward the front gate of the Haven, hunched over the steering wheel of his ATV, causing Alpha and Ryan to break up their conversation and draw their sidearms. The other two members of the gate security detail took up positions behind the solid block wall, prepared to shoot out the tires and possibly the driver if it was someone other than their own people. Fortunately, as the four-wheeler got closer to the gate, it slowed and the driver stood on the footrests to reveal his identity.

Alpha, still concerned about the sudden approach, kept his weapon ready and exited through the pedestrian gate to approach the car. His voice boomed, reflecting his annoyance with the driver's approach. "You wanna explain why you came barreling up here?"

"Yeah, sorry about that. There's a sizable group walking toward us."

Alpha was still annoyed. "You've got people watching I-40 all of this time and finally decide to tell us this?"

"No, it's not like that," the man quickly responded. "There's a lot of traffic heading out of Charlotte on the interstate, but they're not stopping at the Hildebran exit. Well, I mean maybe a few. But, mostly, they keep going west toward Asheville."

"Then where is this group you're talking about?" asked Ryan, who'd holstered his weapon and joined Alpha's side. He turned and motioned for the other sentries to open the gate.

"From the south," the driver replied. "You know, we've concentrated our efforts on the highway because of the thousands of people fleeing Charlotte. You know, there's really nothing to the south of us."

"Okay," said Ryan. "You said sizable. How many cars are there?"

"That's just it," the driver replied. "They're walking. They're coming toward the bridge up Henry River Road."

"How many?" asked Alpha.

"A few dozen. Interesting thing, though. We didn't see any kids. All men and women, both young and old. Also, we didn't see any weapons, or at least no long guns."

Ryan furrowed his brow and thought for a moment. "Okay, come on in and let me talk to Alpha."

The driver eased through the gate as Ryan ordered the gate secured. Alpha contacted two more members of the security team to relieve him and Ryan at the gate. When he was done, the two men stepped into the gatehouse and studied a topography/road map of the area surrounding the Haven.

Alpha traced his index finger around the map. "It seems odd that refugees wouldn't have any children."

"And if they were locals, why wouldn't they just stay home?" asked Ryan inquisitively. "Surely they know they're better off. I mean, where the heck do they think they're gonna go?"

"Not here," replied Alpha dryly.

"They're also unarm—" began Ryan before he caught himself as his fingers tapped an icon on the map. "Wait a second. I bet they're from Valley Haven, just south of Advent Crossroads. If I remember correctly, the campers come from all over the country for couples counseling, and just to get away."

"And get right with the Lord," added Alpha.

"Yeah, something like that. I don't know why they'd run them out of the retreat, but either way, it makes sense now. It's a place that kinda focuses on leaving your worldly possessions behind. You know, cars, cell phones, iPads, etcetera."

"Where do I sign up?" quipped Alpha, making a rare attempt at humor.

"You already did, buddy," replied Ryan before continuing. "Here's the thing. I didn't want to close the bridge crossing the Henry River along our southern perimeter because I felt like the locals needed the ability to come and go."

Alpha stepped away from the map and looked Ryan in the eye. "Yeah, but this is different. As we've discussed before, we gotta do what's best for us, right? We should've shut down the bridge from the beginning."

"I can't argue with that, Alpha. I really don't think we have a choice." Ryan glanced out the guardhouse window toward the driveway. "Do you still have the Department of Transportation barriers hidden down the embankment on the other side of the river?"

"Yeah, we have caution tape too. On the south side of the bridge, it'll look like the bridge is closed for construction. I'll position our people along the bridge to warn them off, with bullets if necessary."

Ryan nodded and wandered toward the gate. Henry River Road skirted the entire western perimeter of the Haven and was always an area of concern. His solutions for a scenario like this involved closing the bridge at the south and creating an armed roadblock at the northwestern corner of the Haven where the wall began. This prevented vehicular traffic from approaching their gates as well as large groups of pedestrians. He hadn't implemented these protections as of yet, so securing the bridge was the first step.

He didn't want to draw unnecessary attention from the local sheriff by closing off a county road to traffic, but it was time to hunker down. It was a matter of time before hungry, desperate refugees spilled out of Charlotte from their southeast to find their way to the Haven. Their security plan was sound, and now they'd have to take defensive measures to control the area just outside their perimeter walls. If the sheriff came around to complain, then Ryan would deal with him when the time came.

CHAPTER 21

Haven House
The Haven

"Looocy, I'm home!" shouted Ryan as he walked into Haven House, using his best Desi Arnaz imitation from the classic *I Love Lucy* program. Ryan laughed at himself as he realized that he was somewhat of a throwback to the sixties, when the show was popular. Although he was just a young boy at the time, the program was a favorite of his mother and they never missed an episode.

Ryan was barely through the front door when the sound of puppy paws came barreling through the house on the wood floor. Chubby and The Roo led the way, with the ten-pound-heavier Handsome Dan in hot pursuit. Ryan smiled as he recalled the GEICO commercial from years ago depicting a spoof of the Running of the Bulls held annually in Pamplona, Spain. In the commercial, rather than bulls chasing the brave young Spaniards, it was English bulldogs racing through the streets.

He dropped to his knees to greet the trio as they plowed into him, knocking him on his backside and rewarding him with wet sloppy kisses.

"Blair, help me!" said Ryan as Chubby climbed on his chest and shook her head side to side as if she was the conquering hero. Somehow, Handsome Dan learned from the girls that he could physically abuse Ryan as well. The large pup walked across Ryan's midsection, back and forth, until a misplaced paw caused Ryan to roll over in pain.

After a moment of enjoying the scrum, Blair came to the rescue. "Come on, guys, give the self-proclaimed king of the castle a break."

She knelt down to help her husband off the floor. "You're gettin' too old for this, Mr. Smart."

"Never," said Ryan as he sat up with a groan. "I let them think they're winning."

Blair covered her nose with her right hand and waved the air in front of her face with the left. "Dude, you need to take a shower. You're a little gamey."

"No, I'm not," protested Ryan. "I took a shower yesterday."

"Well, try using deodorant, then," Blair shot back as she stood over her husband. Ryan sat with his elbows rested on his knees as the three bulldogs circled around him like sharks.

"I do. I mean, I did. I use that Gillette clear gel. Remember, from those five-packs I bought on sale at Sam's Club?"

"It's not workin', 'cause you stink, sir."

"No, I don't," said Ryan and then he turned to the playful pups. "Guys, what do you think? You wanna sniff my pits?"

The Roo, whom the Smarts had labeled FOMO, an acronym representing the words *fear of missing out*, was the first in line to conduct a sniff test.

"Ryan! Stop that. Don't make my children sniff your pits. Use my deodorant if you have to or take a shower."

"I'm saving water, and deodorant," said Ryan with a chuckle as he stood up. The bulldogs heard something at the other end of the house, most likely the last remnants of the snow falling off a pine tree, and went tearing after it, roaring their disapproval at the disruption.

"We have a well," said Blair disapprovingly. "Several of them, as a matter of fact. Come sit down, but don't you dare flap those wings or I'll make you sleep outside with the other daddy hounds."

"Yeah, yeah," said Ryan as he slipped his L.L.Bean boots off and made his way to a chair at the dining table. "What's new in the news?"

"The good news is that there is literally no news," said Blair, who was always careful to use the word *literally* in its proper context rather than as a filler to a sentence, a practice adopted by vocabulary-starved millennials. "The cyber attacks were directed at all forms of media, print, television, and many websites. Somebody wanted to take away our ability to know what's going on."

Ryan chuckled. "It's a shame they didn't do that years ago. The country would've been better off."

"That's the truth," said Blair as she brought them both a bowl of potato cheese soup made with potatoes from the Haven's gardens and powdered cheddar cheese they stored in the Haven's prepper pantry.

"We have a possible situation headed our way, but Alpha's on top of it."

Blair crumbled some club crackers into her soup and took a bite. Her face contorted somewhat because it was too hot to eat. "So what's the sitch?"

"North of us, along the interstate, traffic is picking up with refugees streaming out of Charlotte, but for the most part, they pass our exit as they head toward the mountains. The problem is from the south."

"There's no population down there," interjected Blair. "How many people are we talking about?"

"About three dozen, and I think they're probably from the retreat."

"Valley Haven," muttered Blair as she tried another spoonful of soup. "They're harmless."

"I hope so, but you can never be too sure. Alpha has closed the bridge to any kind of traffic, and we intend to put the roadblock in place at the northern end of our perimeter wall soon."

"The sheriff will be pissed," said Blair.

"Yeah, but I think he has his hands full with all of the interstate traffic, some of which is on foot, I'm told."

Blair sat back in her chair and thought for a moment. "If you turn them away at the bridge, how are they gonna cross the river?"

"Old Shelby Road. It's only a mile or so downriver from here."

Blair didn't want to argue, but she was always good at playing devil's advocate. "As the crow flies, but they'll have to backtrack several miles to get to the bridge by road. Couldn't Alpha and some of the security guys escort them up Henry River Road until they move on?"

Ryan hadn't thought of that. "I suppose, but how many guys do we assign to the group to make sure they don't turn on us? A dozen? That pulls away from our other defenses just so these people aren't inconvenienced."

Blair wanted to add another thought when the ringing of Ryan's phone interrupted them.

"Hello?" he answered with a mouthful of soup.

Ryan listened for a moment and then interrupted the caller. "X-Ray, hold on. I'm gonna put you on speaker so Blair can hear this too."

Ryan changed the settings on his phone and set it on the table between them. "Okay, X-Ray, go ahead."

"Hi, Blair."

"Hey, X-Ray. What's new?" Blair exchanged a look with Ryan. She'd made it known that she didn't trust their newcomer and frequently asked whether it was worth keeping him around.

"Well, two things, actually. First, I've been monitoring some of the websites that are frequently used by white hat hackers. Supposedly, they're the good guys, but you can't always tell. Anyway, there's this Zero Day bunch, former Harvard students and their professor, who are frequently on the message boards of this one site. They claim to know about the virus that hit the *LA Times* first and then spread to Tribune Publishing."

"Okay, we're listening," said Blair, who shrugged and continued to eat. She usually liked people to get to the point and dispense with the preliminaries.

"Um, sure. Anyway, the virus was inserted through the *LA Times'* printing process and quickly found its way into their main servers. Once there, it became disseminated throughout the Associated Press network of media outlets. All of these media companies, whether print like the *Times* or the *Chicago Tribune*, or television, share information through the same networks. The virus attached itself to articles shared by the *LA Times* and then it spread like wildfire. It's traveling the globe now, and media companies worldwide are being shut down."

"Good, no more fake news," said Ryan as he finished off his soup. He let out a slight belch, drawing a disapproving look from his wife.

"Well, yeah, but it also impacts our ability to know what's going on," cautioned X-Ray. "I'm focusing on alt-web outlets, but they're not always reliable. I've stepped up my monitoring of local law enforcement and the frequencies used by known patriot groups operating in the area, like Camp Constitution, the Three Percenters, and of course, the Oath Keepers."

Ryan shrugged and smiled at Blair. She mouthed the word *whatever*, drawing a chuckle from Ryan. X-Ray was on top of the outage and keeping them informed at the same time. Blair had a hard time giving the young man accolades because of her wary feelings about him.

"Um, are you guys still there?" asked X-Ray after a long moment of silence.

Ryan replied, "Yes, of course. Anything else?"

"About Charlotte, something is going on there today," he replied. "There are reports of people being attacked and killed throughout the city. Now, I don't know Charlotte that well, but I jotted down the names of the neighborhoods as I heard them. These are the rich parts of town."

"Whadya make of that?" asked Ryan.

"Well, logic tells me that the poor are taking from the rich, by force, it appears."

"Yeah, that's logical, but not surprising," said Blair, who appeared unimpressed at X-Ray's conclusion.

"It's more than that, though," he continued. "This is kind of like the fires that were reported in those first few days after New Year's Eve. From what I've heard, the attacks were launched simultaneously at different wealthy neighborhoods around town. It's as if the unrest was orchestrated by someone who was attempting to take advantage of law enforcement being spread too thin."

"Okay," said Ryan. "You'll keep us posted, right?"

"Of course, but also be aware that the city is emptying out. I picked up on the scanner that road rage is happening all over the place as residents fight to get away from the carnage. Mostly they're headed south on 95 and northwest towards us."

A slight tap at the door caught Ryan and Blair's attention, as well as the sensitive ears of the bulldog brigade, who came racing from the back of the house toward the front entrance.

"Okay, X-Ray, thanks." Ryan signed off before disconnecting the call.

"Are you expecting anyone?" asked Blair.

"Nope, but it's starting to feel like Grand Central Station."

CHAPTER 22

Haven House
The Haven

Blair opened the front door while Ryan took their dishes and glasses to the kitchen. Tom and Cort nervously milled around on the porch with grim looks on their faces. Blair's first thought was, *Now what?*

"Hey, guys. Is everything all right?" she asked as she held the door open and waved them inside. Neither responded immediately, waiting until Blair shut the door behind them.

Ryan emerged from the kitchen. "Were we scheduled for something? Is there an issue at the front gate?"

Tom removed his jacket and hung it on a hook next to the Smarts'.

Cort was wearing his Yale sweatshirt with the *Y* logo on the front. He replied to their questions. "No, we, um, actually, this is about me. I think I need to tell you something, but I felt like I needed to run it by Tom first since he's more familiar with the situation."

Blair, who was standing behind the men, rolled her head on her shoulders and gave Ryan a look. She hated surprises. She and Ryan had planned the Haven down to every minute detail and went to great lengths to learn as much about their residents as possible before a collapse event brought them all together. However, as was always the case, the human dynamic could throw any organized universe into chaos.

"Grab a chair," said Ryan as he took a seat at the head of the table. Blair offered everyone something to drink, but they declined.

"Let me get right to the point," said Cort. "Earlier, I finished a long conversation with Meredith about this. Sometimes, a husband feels a need to withhold information from his wife in order to protect her. Or at least in his mind, he's protecting her." Cort paused, so Ryan tried to ease the tension.

"It's a fruitless exercise, my friend. Women have this uncanny BS meter that can see right into your head. You can't hide anything from them, trust me."

Blair added, "Yeah, Cort. Trust him. Ryan is a terrible liar, whether bold face or by omission. With him, what you see is what you get."

Cort managed a grin. "After talking with Meredith, she told me to come see you guys. Here's the thing. She and her father have been estranged for the last five or six years. Dear old dad, George Trowbridge, is probably one of the most influential people in Washington. His wealth and political power are rivaled by only a handful of Washington insiders."

"Did he ever hold office?" asked Ryan.

Tom laughed. "He didn't have to. He owned them already. Half of Congress and most presidents have been beholden to Cort's father-in-law."

"He's a *kingmaker*, as they say in political circles," added Cort. "In any event, when my wife and George had a falling-out, they both became stubborn and went a long time without speaking with one another."

"What happened?" asked Blair.

"Well, let's just say that George had a *daddy-knows-best* approach toward his relationship with her," Cort replied.

"Did he not approve of you as her husband or something?" asked Blair.

Cort chuckled. "Nah, just the opposite. After Meredith took me to her home for the first time, George practically recruited me to marry her. We had certain common interests at Yale."

"Like what?" asked Ryan.

Cort glanced at Tom for support. With an imperceptible nod that Blair picked up on, Tom gave Cort the green light to continue.

"I played basketball at Yale, but I was also determined to be a lawyer. During my junior year, I was tapped to join a group of students who'd carried on a tradition that dated back for centuries."

Ryan perked up. "Are you a Bonesman?"

Cort smiled. "So you're familiar with the Skull and Bones Society?"

"Sort of. I remember it was a big deal when George H. W. Bush ran for president. Then it came out that W. had been a part of it as well."

"Well, I'm a member, as is Meredith's father. During my time at Yale, a lot of alumni came to our gatherings, usually at a place called Deer Island. George wasn't one of them, although he was one of the more famous Bonesmen who'd never held political office."

"Why didn't he go?" asked Blair.

"When George was at Yale, there apparently was a falling-out among the Bonesmen at the time based on political differences. George, and many who were politically inclined toward the right, pulled away from the others. Since I've arrived here, I've had more free time to reflect on what I recall from the stories told by my fellow Bonesmen, and what George has relayed to me over the years. I think the rift was greater than any of them let on."

Blair was trying to make sense of all of this. "Okay, Meredith and her dad didn't speak for a while. I take it you stayed in contact with him?"

"That's correct, but it was more than a casual phone chat. He and I worked closely together on legislative matters. You know, exchanging information, discussing strategies. Things like that."

"That's it?" asked Blair. "I mean, that doesn't sound like some big national security secret. I guess I might've been pissed if Ryan had a secretive relationship with my dad and didn't back me up if there was some kind of disagreement. Is there more to this?"

"I think so," replied Cort. "He was grooming me, Blair. He never expressly admitted it, but I believe George was steering me from position to position in order to eventually take the reins of his empire. You see, Meredith is his only child, and she has no interest whatsoever in what he does. I check off all the boxes—family, politically astute, and most importantly, I'm a Bonesman."

Ryan leaned back in his chair and sighed. "I don't know, Cort. There could be worse things to become entangled with. From what you've described, your father-in-law is a wealthy, powerful, and respected man. He's kind of a middle ground to the Koch brothers on the right and the Schwartz family on the left."

"Yes, in the past he has played both sides of the aisle, oftentimes pitting one side against the other to get what he wants," said Cort, and then his voice lowered. "Until now."

"What do you mean?" asked Blair.

Cort took a deep breath and explained. He began to nervously rub his hands together and then wiped his sweaty palms on his pants. "I saw him on New Year's Eve before I flew home to Mobile. My visit was the reason I missed my earlier flight, and it was that hastily called meeting that placed me on Delta 322 from Atlanta to Mobile."

"What was the conversation about?" asked Ryan.

"It was almost, well, philosophical. George is in poor health. Meredith didn't know the extent of it until I filled her in this morning. Anyway, I believe he was preparing me for his death."

Blair could see that Cort was troubled and she leaned over to touch his arm. "Hey, the holidays do that to people, especially when they're old and alone. I wouldn't worry—"

Cort smiled, but he interrupted her. "We've never had a conversation like that before. Plus, it was what he said at the end that stuck in my head. His eyes looked into mine, like they were probing my soul. It was the eeriest feeling I'd ever experienced, other than almost dying in that airplane."

"What did he say?" asked Ryan.

"His last words to me were *either you control destiny, or destiny controls you*," replied Cort.

Cort's words hung in the air as Ryan and Blair considered their meaning. Finally, Blair asked Cort what they meant to him. His response shocked her.

"He knew."

CHAPTER 23

Haven House
The Haven

Ryan was beginning to get the picture. The group that lit the fuse on New Year's Eve had intended to inflict damage on certain groups for the purpose of fanning the flames of discontent. He wanted to probe Cort further so he could fill in the blanks of his own theories of what had happened.

"About what? The New Year's Eve attacks?" he asked.

"Yes, I think so," replied Cort. "I'm not totally sure as to why he would be involved in something like that, although I could speculate. Moreover, because of his poor health, I don't know how he'd have the ability to pull off coordinated terrorist attacks considering his circumstances."

"Yet his words were profound, and they did imply he knew what was about to happen," added Blair.

Cort hung his head and exhaled. "Yes."

Ryan looked at Tom. "You've been awfully quiet through all of this. What say you?"

"This was Cort's story to tell," replied Tom. "That said, take it from someone who's worked for George Trowbridge and his associates in the past, he, or one of his associates, was certainly capable of pulling off the type of coordination required to accomplish the attacks."

Blair stood up and wandered around the room. She rubbed her temples and then paused. "Why didn't he clue you in? Hell, why didn't he warn you? For Pete's sake, you were on an airplane that was shot down, possibly using some of his resources."

"Honey, sit down," said Ryan, who could tell his wife was getting agitated. "That was just a matter of being in the wrong place at the wrong time."

"If that's the case, it was pretty sloppy, in my opinion," said Blair, who continued to wander the floor. "If Cort is the heir apparent to some political machine or empire, you'd think the kingmaker, as you called him, would protect the prince a little better from being accidentally killed."

Tom spoke up. "We think Cort might have been the target, or at least by a stroke of luck, happened to be on the same plane as Congressman Pratt."

Now Blair was really confused. "His father-in-law tried to have him killed? That doesn't make—"

Cort stopped her. "No. No. He had no idea, I'm sure. It was probably somebody else."

"Someone went rogue, off the reservation, as they say," interjected Tom. "Cort and I believe that while Pratt was the initial and, I might add, obvious target, Cort's appearance on the flight's manifest as the last standby passenger to be boarded was either overlooked or considered to be a fortuitous turn of events for whoever spearheaded this operation."

The room fell silent as they contemplated Tom's words. Blair finally took a seat, but her body language spoke volumes. All of a sudden, this new wrinkle might put them all in danger. She was genuinely concerned.

Cort sensed the tension, so he addressed the elephant in the room. "I'm thinking what all of you are thinking. I may have been the target of the downing of Delta 322, and it's quite possible that the person or persons that orchestrated the attack may still be after me."

"I don't know, maybe," said Ryan. "How would they know that you were here?"

"Well, I knew it and apparently so did your daddy-in-law," replied Blair. "He gave the letter to Tom knowing that his path would cross with Meredith's. If we knew it, then these people who work for Trowbridge might know it, too."

Cort stood and adjusted his sweatshirt. "You're right, Blair, and I couldn't live with myself if I brought that kind of heat on the Haven. I think that Meredith, Hannah and I should leave."

"Come on, Cort, sit down," said Ryan, gesturing with both hands to have Cort return to the table. "Nobody's going anywhere."

Cort tried to argue. "I'm putting everyone here in danger. If there's a target on my back, they'll … Well, you've seen what they're capable of. They could drop a bomb here and leave a crater the size of Rhode Island."

Tom started laughing. "Cort, they're not gonna drop a bomb on the Haven. Ryan's right. Let's talk this through."

"I agree, Cort," said Blair. "Listen, you know me. I tell it like it is. If I thought you should go, I'd be escorting you to the gate myself."

"Me too," said Ryan. "Besides, where would you go? You can't go back home. You'd never make it to New England. Meredith and Hannah aren't made for hiding in the woods. You're staying and we'll figure it out."

"Let me add this, too," started Blair. "Even if you left, they, whoever they are, wouldn't necessarily know that you're gone. They'd come around looking for you and we'd have to fight them off anyway. At least you'd be here and add one more gun to the Haven's defense."

Cort was humbled and he slid back into his chair, slouching somewhat as his tall frame stretched well under the Smarts' dining table.

"Okay," said Ryan. "First, we have to keep this information within the four of us. I don't know how much you've told Meredith—"

"Everything," interrupted Cort.

Ryan looked to Tom. "How about Donna?"

"Nothing," he replied.

"Good grief," interjected Blair with an accompanying eye roll.

"Well, she's been feeling down lately, and I didn't want to add to her worries," Tom explained.

Blair, who was not a feminist, but certainly considered herself a strong woman, said, "Gentlemen, I'm gonna say this one time.

Women are not fragile. We bend, but we don't break. Consider this. We're capable of giving birth. Could any of you three do that? Hmm?"

Silence.

"Yeah, that's what I thought," Blair continued. "That said, in a stressful environment like this, and especially under the circumstances, the fewer people who know about this, the better."

"I agree," added Ryan. "We run this community like a business, doing our best to keep the emotions out of it. George Trowbridge obviously loves his family and must have some amount of confidence in the Haven. Otherwise, you would be somewhere under his wing, whether Meredith liked it or not."

Tom interrupted. "He's a man who keeps up with his assets. Sorry, Cort, not to insult your importance as a member of his family. Trowbridge invests a lot in people like you and me. He wouldn't put us in harm's way."

Cort reluctantly nodded.

"Good, it's settled, then," said Blair. "You're staying here. I want you to reassure Meredith that we'll do everything we can to protect you guys. Ryan might bring Alpha into it because special security arrangements may need to be put in place. I don't know. Whatever it takes, we'll do our best to make it happen."

Cort sat up in his chair, emboldened by the show of support from the Smarts. "Thank you. I will never forget what y'all have done for us."

CHAPTER 24

George Trowbridge's Residence
Near Pine Orchard, Connecticut

Trowbridge's health had taken a downturn as the aftermath of the attacks had begun to weigh heavily upon him. The desired results were being achieved. Certain parts of the country were in turmoil. Violence was widespread, and communities were in a lawless state. Local law enforcement was overwhelmed, and even when the governors dispatched the National Guard in some states like California, Illinois, and Michigan, they were instructed to perform crowd control only. Guardsmen were not asked to tamp down the riots with lethal force.

The president was safely tucked away at Raven Rock and, for the moment, he was content with bringing overseas troops back home for further deployment to the hottest zones of unrest. Harris, Trowbridge's aide, had spoken at length with the president's chief of staff on two occasions.

The administration was content with allowing the fires of collapse to burn on for another week or so until reservists were called up and overseas soldiers were recalled. Once the military assets were in place and ready for deployment under the martial law orders, the president would take the necessary steps by executive order to circumvent the Posse Comitatus Act.

Posse comitatus originated in ninth-century England and was later used as a means to incorporate the military in domestic law enforcement actions. Following the American Civil War, Congress passed a law prohibiting the president's use of military personnel in typically local law enforcement duties such as civil unrest.

The limitation did not apply, however, to the deployment of the National Guard. The Guard was activated by a state's governor but could not be activated by the president as a result of the Posse Comitatus Act.

The president's chief of staff told Harris that he would violate the act if he deemed it necessary to protect the American people, and deal with the consequences of it later. He suspected, however, that the leaders within the military would not act upon his orders. Therefore, he planned on ordering the Defense Department to reassign large numbers of military personnel to the National Guard to be deployed to select states.

He addressed the ramifications of the fuse lit on New Year's Eve. "A lot of Americans will die, Harris. I knew this in advance, and I believe the president is keenly aware of this."

Harris closed up his iPad and set it on a side table near the door. He joined Trowbridge by his bed.

"Sir, we were headed toward a second civil war anyway. I remember a poll taken a couple of years back that showed forty percent of those asked believed a second civil war would take place within the next five years, and sixty percent thought it would occur during their lifetimes."

"Harris, I will always wonder if I did the right thing by suggesting these attacks. The American electorate had shifted from being informed and placing their votes on distinctions between policy or procedure. Instead, they rallied behind their *team*, whether democrat or republican, for better or for worse."

"Sir, I personally believe this country needed to be shaken to its core. I thought 9/11 would do it. I felt like the patriotism on display in the years thereafter revealed a turning point away from the divide that began in the sixties."

Trowbridge laughed. "I remember. They all flew flags on their cars and wore lapel pins professing their love of country. And then the arguments about weapons of mass destruction and Saddam Hussein started in Congress, and our politicians were back to throwing stones and hurling accusations."

Trowbridge sighed and then continued. "The bottom line is this. There was no more time for nuance. There was only time for war. So, war it will be for the foreseeable future."

"How will it end?" asked Harris. "When the president takes control of the streets?"

"Maybe, maybe not. This conflict may be too large for our military to control. It may need to run its course." Trowbridge paused, managed a laugh, and then grimaced at the pain caused by enjoying the moment. "Harris, I'm like the weatherman. I'm not in control of the storm, but I can tell you where it's most likely to happen."

The two men fell silent for a moment as they stared at the blank television monitors. Ordinarily, several news networks would be displayed on the screens. After the cyber attacks of that morning, an actual news blackout had affected America.

Comfortable that the national approach to the collapse was being managed by the president in a satisfactory matter, Trowbridge was ready to focus his efforts on his adversaries. He bristled when Harris reported that Briscoe had eluded the hit team assigned to kill him at Monocacy Farm. Their careless mistake would send Briscoe into hiding and possibly out of the country.

Trowbridge was upset that he wasn't able to exact his revenge for Briscoe's betrayal. However, causing the man to scurry about like a cockroach when the lights were turned on was somewhat satisfying.

"Still no news on Jonathan Schwartz?" asked Trowbridge.

"No, sir. I have to tell you that the FBI's ranks are stretched thin at the moment. They have morphed from an investigative agency to one concerned with future attacks. I don't believe they're assigning the resources necessary to find Jonathan."

"And his father?"

"Tucked away in a holding cell at the federal prison in Petersburg, Virginia. It should suit him for many months until the dust settles around the country."

"Has the DOJ frozen their assets?" asked Trowbridge.

"Obvious accounts, plus those that we provided to them," replied Harris. "The Schwartz companies have real estate holdings all over the country. It's likely that precious metals and cash were tucked away, you know, just in case."

"Jonathan will stick his head up out of a hole, either to free his father or come at me. Are our people in place to fend off any direct assault on the property?"

"Yes, sir. We're at platoon strength on a full-time rotational basis with a second group of forty on standby."

"On the water, too?" asked Trowbridge.

"Absolutely. Yes, sir."

Trowbridge thought about Meredith and her family for a moment. He considered reaching out to Cort, but he was concerned that electronic surveillance might expose their whereabouts. He'd taken the steps to notify his closest friends to explain Briscoe's betrayal. He suspected that the word had spread throughout his fellow Bonesmen and the operatives they employed.

Trowbridge didn't lose sight of the fact that Briscoe had allies of his own and might look for a way to come at him. As he contemplated this, his lower back was struck with a sudden jolt of pain, followed by an onrush of chills that overtook him. His brow broke out in a cold sweat and he began to shiver uncontrollably.

Trowbridge was barely conscious as Harris summoned the medical staff into the bedroom suite to attend to the man whose health was deteriorating.

CHAPTER 25

Lancaster, Pennsylvania

Minutes seemed like hours as Briscoe anxiously awaited a phone call from Jonathan Schwartz. He'd told himself that after thirty minutes, he was going to continue driving north until he reached the Canadian border in Maine. If Schwartz called in the meantime, he'd take it from there. Otherwise, he needed to put some distance between himself and Monocacy Farm.

His vehicle was parked facing the midday sun, causing the interior to warm up. He hadn't slept all night and was exhausted. Despite his anxious state, drowsiness began to overtake him. Twice, Briscoe snapped his head upright as he drifted off to sleep. The third time, he was just about out when the phone vibrated on the seat next to him.

He immediately picked it up and looked at the display. He recognized the number, not because he'd spoken to the man on the other end of the line before, but because the briefings he'd received from his hacktivist team had included the number in a recent dossier update.

His mind raced as he thought of what he wanted to say. He set his jaw, straightened up in his seat, and prepared to enter a new alliance.

"Hello." He began the conversation full of trepidation.

"You've got less than sixty seconds," said the voice on the line. He recognized Jonathan's voice immediately. Over the years, he'd studied every public appearance of the heir to the Schwartz throne.

"George Trowbridge tried to have me killed, and I have no friends right now. I suspect you feel about him the same way I do. Perhaps we can help one another."

"I can handle things on my own."

"Maybe so, but I have an additional option that you might not have considered. One that would cut the old man's heart out, figuratively speaking."

"Tell me."

"Let's meet. I can assure you that I'm alone."

"Stay by the phone."

With that, Jonathan disconnected the call. Briscoe allowed himself a slight smile. He needed an ally, and while Jonathan Schwartz would not have been his first choice, he was an unlikely one, meaning that Trowbridge would never suspect it.

One thing that Briscoe knew that Trowbridge did not was the fact that each of the New Year's Eve attacks were compartmentalized. No one knew of the details for each of the operations except for Briscoe. Trowbridge might have his suspicions regarding the downing of Delta 322, but he wasn't certain. If Briscoe could finish the job by taking out Cortland, using Schwartz-hired operatives who'd shoulder the blame, then he might be able to sway his fellow Bonesmen to disregard Trowbridge's accusations as being irrational.

He could be *back in the saddle*, as they say.

The phone rang again. It was Jonathan.

"Hello."

"Meet me in the faculty parking lot at the University of Pennsylvania in Kutztown. How long will it take you to get here?"

"About two hours," replied Briscoe. He knew it would only take an hour, but he wanted to arrive early to check out the location.

"Come alone or I'll kill you myself," Schwartz snarled before disconnecting the call.

Briscoe pulled the phone away and dropped it on the seat next to him. He reached into his sweater pocket and felt for the revolver that he'd used to kill his caretaker.

"Oh, I'll be alone, just as you'd better be, my new friend. Both of us are capable of pulling triggers."

119

CHAPTER 26

Near Kutztown, Pennsylvania

Briscoe parked his vehicle two blocks from the university and chose to walk onto the campus to locate the faculty parking lot. Dressed in his cardigan, he looked somewhat professorial. Briscoe was not a public figure, and he seriously doubted that Jonathan would recognize him if they stood next to one another in a crowded subway.

He assumed that Jonathan was staying somewhere close; otherwise he wouldn't have suggested this location. Also, he'd probably been there before and knew it would be an easy location to surveil. As Briscoe traversed the sidewalks of the small campus, he checked his watch. He was early, by design.

Schwartz pulled into the parking lot alone and backed the stolen pickup truck so that the license plate was pushed against a retaining wall. He sat there staring ahead for a moment, and then he began to look around the parking lot. He checked his watch, all in plain view of Briscoe, who was standing to the side and rear of the pickup.

After ten minutes in which the two men assessed their surroundings, Briscoe decided to make the first move. To reassure Jonathan that he was alone, and to allow him the opportunity to run if necessary, Briscoe walked to the entrance of the parking lot and strolled in between the parked cars until he was out in the open. He casually walked past the front of Schwartz and then stopped to face him. The two men nodded to one another, and Jonathan casually waved him over as he rolled down the window.

"Good morning, Professor," said Jonathan with a hint of snark.

Briscoe studied his attire and smiled. "Yes, I suppose I do fit in." He paused and studied the pickup. "This appears to be a step down from your usual transportation."

Jonathan was remarkably loose and lighthearted. Briscoe studied his adversary. The son of the great György Schwartz appeared relieved to be talking with him.

"Hop in, it's stolen. You might as well join in the conspiracy."

Briscoe laughed. "Yeah, I have a stolen one as well. I really need to get it off the streets. Do you have a place where we can hide these for a couple of centuries?"

"Yes. We'll get your vehicle. I have a place about seven miles from here. There's a few barns on the property where they can be hidden away with years of dust."

Twenty minutes later, the two men had parked their stolen vehicles in a barn located at the back of the Schwartz property. They removed the license plates and slung them like frisbees into a nearby pond. Schwartz assured Briscoe that he'd have the vehicles destroyed as soon as he felt comfortable reaching out to his people.

Incredibly, the two men were nonchalant in their initial dealings with one another. It was as if they knew they couldn't turn to anyone else. The odd pairing resulted in a mutual respect that was necessary as they hatched a plan to fight back against the man who put them in this predicament.

It had been a long day full of a wide range of emotions. Incredibly, Briscoe felt safe in the presence of Schwartz, who was not known to be a violent man, although his employees were capable of it. Briscoe assessed his new ally's demeanor and wondered if Jonathan had personally killed anyone, like he had.

"Let's cut to the chase," began Jonathan after he poured Briscoe a glass of much-needed brandy. "We both find ourselves in similar circumstances. We're fugitives from law enforcement. We're also hiding from the tentacles of George Trowbridge. I'm speaking for myself, but I suspect you feel the same way. We don't know which way to turn and whom to trust."

"I agree. Honestly, I think that I could handle the legal matters easier than the personal vendetta Trowbridge has against me. Cops and judges can be bought. Trowbridge, however, cannot."

Jonathan took a sip of brandy and reached for a cigar humidor that sat on the coffee table between them. He offered one to Briscoe, who declined. After he clipped the end of a Davidoff cigar and lit it, he continued.

"While I would take great pleasure in ending Trowbridge's life, I've given this some thought. He will be protected and nearly untouchable. At present, I don't think I could find the professionals prepared to take on that task. I'm intrigued by the suggestion you made on the phone."

"George's weakness is his son-in-law, Michael Cortland," offered Briscoe. "I don't know the family dynamic, but I do know that George has never mentioned his daughter in my presence. I get the distinct impression that her husband is the apple of the father's eye."

"The son he never had," added Jonathan.

"Precisely. Cortland is our target."

"Rumor has it that Cortland was on the Delta flight to Mobile, am I correct?" asked Jonathan.

Briscoe peered over his glass as he nodded.

"And, may I assume that it was mere chance that he was on board that flight and, therefore, a level of plausible deniability was afforded the man responsible for the crashing of the aircraft."

Briscoe shrugged and toasted the air between the two men, indicating that Jonathan was on the right track.

"Because"—Jonathan stretched out the word—"why else would Trowbridge want to kill his number one guy?"

"Indeed, thus the reason we're here," replied Briscoe. "Two new friends sharing a brandy."

"All right, Mr. Briscoe. What's the play?"

Briscoe set his glass down and slid it closer to Jonathan, indicating he'd like a refill. While his host topped off his snifter, Briscoe laid out his proposal.

"Cortland and his family have arrived at a secluded compound a couple of hours northwest of Charlotte. This place, built in the last two years by a couple from Florida, was designed as a safe place in the event of a catastrophic event."

"Or events like the ones you triggered," interrupted Jonathan with a sly grin.

"Guilty as charged. I suspect that's a conversation to be had over another bottle of brandy. Be that as it may, I have eyes and ears everywhere. One of my people got word to me that Cortland and his family have arrived at this place they call the Haven. He likely considers himself safe there, and therefore, he's vulnerable to attack."

"Attack? Attack by whom?" asked Jonathan.

Briscoe took a deep breath and replied, "Time for me to make some presumptions. I know Chepe and how he operates. The Richmond unrest in the days following New Year's had his fingerprints all over it. Then, before the news blackout today, it appeared he'd moved on to a new target—Charlotte. Am I right?"

"Of course. Keep in mind, you started this fight, but we intend to finish it." Jonathan paused for a drink; then he asked another question. "May I presume that your people were responsible for the cyber attacks on the media?"

"Yes."

"Kudos. Fear of the unknown only serves to create paranoia in the masses. That plays to our benefit, you know."

"Don't care," shot back Briscoe. "This is not about who wins or loses initially, it's about the long game. We think the deck is stacked in our favor."

Jonathan stood and began to laugh as he cracked a window to allow the cigar smoke to billow outside. "Would history have been different if General Grant and General Lee sat down with a bottle of brandy in the early days of the Civil War to have a casual conversation like this one?"

"I don't think so," replied Briscoe. "Emotions ran high between the two sides then, as they do now. Sometimes, enemies need to fight it out for order to be restored."

"Well, as you said, that's a conversation for another evening. For now, tell me how Chepe and my army of anarchists in Charlotte can help."

PART THREE

CHAPTER 27

The Varnadore Building
Uptown Charlotte, North Carolina

"All right, people. We've got a slight change of plans," shouted Chepe to his group as they spoke amongst themselves. They'd had several successful attacks on affluent neighborhoods and upscale shopping districts around the Charlotte metroplex. None of their ranks were injured or arrested. All of them were energized by their successes.

After Chepe received the phone call from Jonathan Schwartz, he was somewhat dejected. After only a couple of days, his teams were hitting on all cylinders, working together to wreak havoc in the streets and frightening those who thought they could stay out of the fray.

What pleased him the most was the grassroots effort he'd generated. People who'd constantly been under the thumb of the rich, barely making a living wage, now saw an opportunity to better themselves and level the playing field. For years, these citizens of Charlotte had worked hard and sacrificed in order to make money for the people who lived in these oversized homes and drove fancy cars. Now the blue-collar stiffs of Charlotte got a taste of the good life by taking what they wanted.

Chepe likened it to rolling a boulder off a cliff. All the large rock needed was a little nudge and it did the rest of the work, tumbling down, gaining speed, and destroying everything in its path. Chepe wanted to nudge more boulders; however, Jonathan paid the bills, and Chepe would undertake the new mission.

"Everybody, please. Quiet!" Chepe finally had to shout to garner their attention. The group quieted to a low murmur, so Chepe began.

"You guys absolutely killed it yesterday! You should be proud that finally the fat cats and the one percenters got a taste of what life has been like for the rest of us. Way to go!"

The group burst out in applause and cheers, congratulating one another with vigor.

Chepe held his hands high in the air to calm the group down again. This time, they reacted much quicker. "We're going to continue to do more of the same, but I've got to do someone a favor. Is there anybody here from Hickory?"

"I am!" shouted a young man at the back of the room. "Well, not from there, but I went to school at Lenoir-Rhyne University."

Another man responded, "I was born and raised in Morganton, about twenty minutes west of there."

"Good, good," said Chepe. "Would you two come closer, please?"

The former college student in his early thirties and the local man, who was fortyish, made their way through the crowd, which parted as they approached the stack of crates Chepe used for addressing the group.

"I'm Earl." The older man introduced himself first.

"I'm Oliver, but they call me Ollie," the former student offered.

Chepe knelt down and spoke to them. "Have either of you watched the *Hunger Games* movie?"

"Yeah," replied Earl.

"Me too," said Ollie. "In fact, the film was shot just south of Hickory at a place called Henry River Mill Village. It's on the—"

Chepe finished his sentence. "River. I know. When was the last time you saw it?"

"Oh, it was back when I was in college. You know, right before the movie was shot."

Chepe looked to Earl. "How about you? Have you ever been there?"

"Oh, yeah. I used to fish those banks when I was a kid. It's been years, though."

Chepe waved one of his lieutenants over. He slid off the crates so the four of them could speak privately.

He gave his instructions to his lieutenant. "Get Ollie and Earl a car full of gas, binoculars, camping gear, food, and weapons. They'll be out front in just a few minutes. Go!"

The lieutenant scampered off, leaving Chepe with his two scouts.

"What do you want us to do?" asked Earl, who apparently was ready to assume the leadership role because he was older.

"Here's what I know," Chepe began in response. "In the last couple of years, the property was purchased by a group that converted it into some type of compound. You know, those whacky survivalist-prepper types that think the sky is always falling and the *guvment is out to get 'em*."

The trio laughed at the way Chepe mocked the preppers. He put his arms around the two men and led them toward the front entrance of the former office building.

"Yeah, I know the type," added Earl. "They lived all over Western North Carolina. Selfish, too. I remember talking to them when I used to hang out after high school. They hoarded all of this food and stuff with no intention of helping their fellow man if something went bad."

Ollie wanted to learn more about their mission. "Do you want us to check the place out? It's way off the beaten path, and there's literally nothing around it except for the river and a few farms."

Chepe glanced outside and saw that his lieutenant had pulled a car around. "Look and learn. That's all. I want you to make notes. Look at their security and write down any patterns that you notice. Try to make a map of the buildings. Heck, take pics with your cell phones."

"Um, the cell service isn't working," said Ollie.

Chepe explained, "I know that, but your phone still is. You can take pictures and we can analyze them when you get back."

"What are we gonna do then?" asked Earl.

"Maybe nothing," replied Chepe. "Just be as detailed as possible, but above all, don't get caught. If they see you scopin' the place out, we'll lose our element of surprise."

"Are we gonna attack the place?" asked Ollie.

"Not if I can find another way, and that depends on what you two come back with," replied Chepe.

The lieutenant opened the door and gave Chepe a thumbs-up. He pushed the two scouts toward the front door as Earl asked one final question.

"When do you want us to come back?"

"Be here at dusk tomorrow afternoon. That'll give you a full day and night of surveillance. Now go on and be careful. Do not get caught!"

The two men rushed out the door and Chepe watched as they sped off toward the Haven. He turned back to his fellow anarchists, who were anxious to learn about the evening's festivities. With a bounce in his step, he made his way back to his perch on top of the crates.

"Okay, sorry about the delay!" he shouted, drawing the group's attention back to him. "Yesterday, we opened up the eyes of the rich fat cats who get to complain about high taxes and government regulations during cocktail parties or at the country club while golfing. Today, we're gonna stick it to the government that these fat cats rely upon to protect them. We're gonna gather up some of our new friends who asked to join our cause, and we're gonna march on city hall."

The shouts of approval echoed off the walls of the lobby.

"Yeah!"

"Finally, we get to take our government back!"

"I'm tired of being under their thumb!"

Chepe smiled as he calmed the crowd down. "Yesterday was fun, but today has the potential to be dangerous. I plan on breaking out the heavy artillery and sending this city a clear message!"

More shouts of approval filled the air, and the group of anarchists worked themselves into a frenzy. All of them had a different cause they held dear to their hearts, but the one thing they had in common was they enjoyed destroying things.

On that night, Chepe wouldn't disappoint them as he prepared to try out the advanced weaponry delivered to him by Jonathan Schwartz. When he was done, Charlotte would be in shambles and its residents would be fleeing in all directions.

CHAPTER 28

Haven Barn
The Haven

Tyler and Angela joined the security team at the Haven Barn for the morning meeting. Ryan thought all of his top people, including the educators, should be there to start their day so they were aware of any potential risks, or special projects going on around the property. Because the Rankins were the last to arrive at the Haven and were still getting to know people, they stuck to themselves at the back of the conference room, taking it all in.

After a couple of days driving the roads and trails of the Haven, Tyler was thoroughly familiar with the layout and the various designations assigned to buildings and points of interest. He also dug into the medical supplies and other survival gear stored in the Haven's Prepper Pantry and in the Haven Barn. He supplemented the basic medical gear on his four-wheeler with other things that would benefit him in an emergency.

The meeting ended and he gave his wife a ride to the Armageddon Hospital, where she planned on perusing the medical files of all the residents at the Haven. Most everyone was healthy and only a few had prescription medication needs. Because they were likely to run out of their prescriptions soon, Angela wanted to review their files in order to find alternative health options.

She had not been a student of homeopathic and naturopathic medicines in the past, but Blair had provided her lots of reading material to learn more. Echo and his wife had been planting a number of dietary and herbal supplements to be used as prescription medications ran out. She was impressed with how the Smarts had planned for the eventuality of a long-term stay within the walls of the Haven.

"I love you, babe," said Tyler as he kissed his wife on the cheek. The two were enjoying their new life at the Haven and were comforted by how quickly J.C. and Kaycee took to the new way of life. Angela went inside the Armageddon Hospital to start her file reviews, and Tyler headed north toward the top of the Haven. He wanted to clear some fallen tree limbs that blocked a trail after the New Year's Day snowfall. He'd barely pulled out onto the gravel road when his two-way radio sprang to life.

"We've got two hostiles attempting to cross the river!"

"Location!"

"Just downriver from the bridge, near the cabins."

"Are they armed?"

"No, they're drowning. The current's carrying them downriver and—oh!"

Tyler tried to discern who was speaking. He assumed the security team knew each other's voices, because they didn't call out each other's call signs or names. All he could make out was that the voice reporting the hostiles in the river was a female and the other was a man, but not Alpha, whose voice was unmistakable.

He stopped the cart and got his bearings straight. The usually calm, meandering river had been overflowing the banks as melting snow in the mountains forced water toward the Atlantic Ocean. The Rankins' cabin was downstream from the bridge that had been closed off by the Haven's security team.

Tyler pressed the gas pedal down and spun around in the middle of the gravel road to head back toward the trail that led to his cabin. He hadn't been summoned by the security personnel yet, but in these cold temperatures, the people in the river were in great danger.

The radio chatter continued.

"I'm headed that way," barked Alpha into the radio. He began to use military parlance as he asked for a situation report. "Sitrep?"

"One of the guys got caught in a fallen tree," the female replied. Tyler recognized her voice now. It was Hayden. "His arm got tangled and the other guy crashed into him. Trust me, arms don't bend like that."

"Roger that. Call medical."

Tyler fumbled for his radio. He had only used it once to test it.

"This is Tyler. I'm en route with the cart. How far are they from the burned-out warehouse?"

Hayden responded, "Two hundred yards downstream and holding. One guy is still hung up in the branches. The other is holding onto the trunk of a tree to keep from being swept away."

"I'm here," said another member of the security team. "What do you want me to do?"

"I see you," replied Alpha.

Tyler swung through the clearing and slowed his pace so he didn't lose control of the cart. There was a small gathering along the bank just past the last cabin. X-Ray had stepped onto his front porch and waved at Tyler as he drove past. Less than a minute later, Tyler skidded to a stop next to Bravo and Alpha, who stood with their rifles pointed at the men.

He slid out of the seat and joined the others. "What are we gonna do with them? They can't hold on much longer."

"Good," replied Alpha. "When they let go, they'll float all the way to Conover—not our problem."

Before Tyler could suggest saving the two, Ryan pulled up in his Ranger. He had a pair of binoculars and took a closer look at the two men, one of whom was waving for help.

"Idiots," he mumbled as he passed the binoculars to Alpha. "What the heck did they think they were doing?"

Alpha responded as he studied the intruders' dilemma. "Hayden saw them first, upriver near the bridge. Who knows?"

Tyler offered a solution. "Ryan, I used to be a lifeguard when I lived in Hilton Head. I had to fish some people out of stormy seas before. I can get these two."

"Why?" asked Alpha. "They're not ours. Let them figure it out on their own."

Tyler grimaced. He couldn't disagree with Alpha, but he also was a medical professional whose job was to save people in danger, both good ones and bad ones.

He reached for the binoculars. "May I take a look?" Alpha tossed them to Tyler, who took a long look at the men who were tangled up in the fallen trees. "One guy has either a broken or dislocated shoulder. If he drops into the river, he'll likely drown."

"Okay, one down," mumbled Alpha. He cast a glance in Ryan's direction. "Do you want me to shoot the other one so we can go about our business?"

Ryan chuckled. "No, don't shoot him. Listen, this is something Blair and I've talked about at length. Here's our problem. Society has collapsed, but the cops haven't gone on vacation. We can't just go shootin' people. I've probably pissed off a lot of the locals by closing the bridge. If we shoot these two, the sheriff will be all over us."

"Fine, then let them get tired and float off to wherever the Henry River decides to take them," said Alpha.

"Or let me rescue them. Hypothermia will set in soon and they'll die if we don't help. Angela can treat them and then we'll escort them out of the Haven."

Ryan thought for a moment. "We do have a wet suit, just in case one of our people needed to get into the water."

"I know," said Tyler. "I've added it to my gear on the cart. I also have the two-hundred-foot nylon ropes and hooks. I can wrap the ropes around their waists and you guys could pull them back to shore."

Alpha stepped forward to get a closer look. "What about the guy with the busted-up shoulder? How's he gonna make it to shore with just us pulling him in?"

Tyler walked up next to Alpha. "He'll probably flail about, trying not to drown. The pain in his shoulder will be agonizing, so he'll scream until he passes out."

A slight grin came over Alpha's face. "Okay, I'd pay to see that. Let's reel them in, but if they give us any trouble, we're gonna throw them back. Deal?"

"No problem," said Tyler, who turned to get the wet suit on.

CHAPTER 29

Armageddon Hospital
The Haven

Angela raced out onto the deck of the Haven's medical facility and arrived at the parking area just as Alpha brought Tyler's medical cart to a stop. Tyler was wrapped in a sweatshirt and a camouflaged jacket, but he was still shivering uncontrollably.

"Ty, how bad is it?" she asked as she immediately grabbed his wrist to check his pulse. As she spoke to him, she studied his eyes to assess his level of mental acuity. "How long were you in the water?"

"Tah, tah, ten minutes," stuttered Tyler as a fit of shivers overtook his body.

Alpha raced around the cart to help Tyler stand. "Hey, Doc. It was more like twenty. He was having trouble freeing up this idiot, and then we couldn't get the rope out to him to tow him back to shore."

"Okay, okay." Angela was frantic, as she never imagined having to work on her husband. "I've got a fire in the cast-iron stove, and Donna's waiting with blankets. Get him inside first."

Angela went to the back of the cart and looked at the unconscious young man thrown in the back. They hadn't bothered to cover him with a blanket or jackets, opting instead to keep Tyler warm. She immediately saw that his shoulder had been dislocated. Just as she turned to get Alpha, Ryan pulled up in the Ranger with Charlie riding shotgun. She jumped out first.

"We've got another one," exclaimed Charlie. She threw open the rear passenger door of the Ranger and pulled out an older man, who was restrained with zip-tie cuffs. Like Tyler, he was shivering uncontrollably but didn't appear to be injured further.

"Okay, get him inside by the stove," she instructed Charlie before turning her attention to the injured man in the back of the medical cart. "Ryan, can you help me carry this one inside?"

Ryan nodded and then Alpha appeared from inside. "I'll get the other end, Doc. You take care of your husband before you deal with these ass clowns."

Angela's immediate concern was for Tyler and the risks to his body caused by being in the frigid water for so long. Hypothermia occurs when a person's core body temperature drops below ninety-five degrees Fahrenheit. To a layman, a three-and-a-half-degree drop below the normal ninety-eight-point-six degrees doesn't sound like much. However, a sudden drop coupled with the dampness of the water can be potentially fatal.

In a cold river, the body loses heat through the process of radiating through the skin, conduction with the cold surface water, and convection from the constant currents. Overall, hypothermia causes moisture within the body to evaporate.

Just a four-degree drop can induce mild hypothermia, or HT 1, evidenced by shivering and near normal consciousness. While she was concerned for Tyler's safety, he was a young man in great physical shape. His body would be able to withstand the loss of heat and potential dehydration associated with even a twenty-minute period of exposure to the icy water. His ability to answer questions, albeit off by ten minutes, relieved her concern. He'd warm up by the fire and be fine within the hour.

The other two men were in a much more serious condition. The older man, who was barely conscious, was no longer shivering. His demeanor and appearance indicated he was borderline incoherent, unaware of his surroundings. Angela's initial opinion was that he was suffering from moderate hypothermia, or HT II.

She'd examine him after she tended to the unconscious younger man. It was possible that his dislocated shoulder had resulted in more pain than the body could handle. The injured man was also relatively thin compared to the man who accompanied him.

Angela walked alongside the stretcher as Ryan and Alpha brought the younger man inside. She touched his neck and forehead. By her best guess, his body temperature was below eighty degrees, an extremely risky level. He was likely near death and clearly in severe hypothermia, or HT III.

"Get him off the stretcher and let's cut off his wet clothes," said Angela as she grabbed a gurney that was stored against the back wall of the Armageddon Hospital.

"What about this one?" asked Donna.

Angela was in her element. "Same thing. If he can't take his own clothes off, cut them off for him. Ryan, I need more blankets and another set of hands."

"I'm on it!" Ryan raced out the front door and called for Blair on the two-way radio.

Angela went to check on Tyler, who'd undressed himself and was wrapped in a white hospital blanket. His shivering had subsided.

"Whadya say, hero?" she asked as she popped a thermometer into his mouth.

"Hmm, ooh-kay," he mumbled, allowing the thermometer to bob up and down as if he were talking with a sucker in his mouth.

Angela checked her watch. "Three minutes, Ty. Don't move until I come back."

She turned back to the older man, who was now naked under another white cotton blanket. His front was open, exposing his genitals. "This isn't gonna be enough to keep him warm, or covered," she said, pointing down between his legs without staring. "Can we unhook his restraints until we get his body temperature up?"

"No," bellowed Alpha from the other side of the room. "We don't know anything about them."

Angela shook her head and wrapped another blanket around the front of the man. He began to shiver again and his eyes began to close.

"I'll get the other gurney," offered Donna, who quickly jumped into action.

"Guys, help me hoist him on the gurney. Cut loose these

restraints. You can cuff him to the rails if you want, but I've got to wrap him up better than this."

Alpha and Charlie lifted the man onto the gurney after his wrist cuffs were removed. All of the blankets fell to the ground, leaving him naked momentarily. After he was cuffed to the rails, Angela wrapped him up again and slid him against the wall next to the stove.

Blair suddenly burst through the door, carrying an armful of wool blankets. "These should help," she said as she stopped to survey the situation. She shook her head with a look of disgust on her face. "Tyler first."

"I'm fine, seriously," he said, rejecting the offer of the warmer blanket. Blair threw it in his lap anyway.

She handed one to Donna, who replaced the wet cotton blankets on the man cuffed to the gurney. The heavy wool had an immediate effect on him, and his eyes opened and darted around the room.

Alpha noticed that he'd become coherent and walked up to the gurney. He pulled his sidearm and cocked the hammer as he pointed the gun towards the man's forehead.

"Give me a reason, buddy," he hissed, causing the older man's eyes to grow wide.

Angela shook her head and turned to Donna. "Can you help me with this one? I've got to set his shoulder and then do some tests."

"What can I do?" Donna asked.

"Let's roll him over onto his back. Charlie, will you help Donna hold this kid down? I need you to provide resistance as I gently snap his shoulder back into place."

They got into position and nodded when they were ready. The young man's body was limp due to his lack of consciousness, making the procedure somewhat easier. Angela took a deep breath and pulled.

Crack!

"You broke it, good job," said Alpha, who was watching from the end of the gurney.

"No, I didn't," insisted Angela, who then ignored Alpha's laughing. "Okay, ladies, help me get him positioned so that I can wrap his entire body with blankets."

"I need to cuff him," said Alpha.

"No, not yet," Angela said with a hint of frustration at Alpha's interruptions. "He's not going anywhere."

"Now what?" asked Donna.

"The goal of treating hypothermia victims, regardless of stage, is essentially the same. First, you prevent further heat loss by using blankets and placing the patient in a warmer space than the outdoors."

"Okay, check," said Blair.

"Next, we have to be careful not to manhandle him too much. His body is very fragile right now and could deteriorate rapidly. He's susceptible to cardiac arrhythmia due to his heart muscle being irritated by the large drop in body temp. I really wish we had a heating pad or a couple of electric blankets to deal with this."

Ryan had reentered the hospital. "I'll get on the radio and ask around. I'm sorry, but I never thought of that when we were setting up."

"Thanks, Ryan," said Angela with a smile. She walked away from the unconscious man and approached Tyler. "The next few minutes will be critical. Let me check his body temp next."

She pulled the thermometer out of Tyler's mouth and looked at it. She patted him on the head.

"Now may I have a Dum-Dum?" he asked.

"No, but you'll live. Don't move."

Angela removed the protective shield from the thermometer and placed it on a rolling metal table near her office. She looked in a cabinet until she found a rectal thermometer.

"He's unconscious, so this will help us get a quicker, more accurate reading," explained Angela. After a minute, she checked the results. "Good, he's up above eighty. Eighty-four, to be exact. Let's keep him warm. In fact, Alpha, give me your socks."

"What? Why?"

"We need to warm his feet. It's important to get his extremities warm first."

"No, not gonna happen," Alpha objected.

"He needs his groin and armpits warmed, too," Angela shot back. "You wanna do that for me instead?"

"No," he said with a gruff as he began to unlace his boots.

Angela smiled and winked at Donna. She got a kick out of teasing Alpha. Warming the feet wasn't necessary to keep the young man alive, but it would help prevent frostbite and the possible loss of his toes.

After placing Alpha's warm socks on the man's feet, Angela stepped back and exhaled.

"Okay, now we observe and wait."

CHAPTER 30

Armageddon Hospital
The Haven

"All right, Angela, it's time for you to take your husband home," admonished Charlotte Echols as she shut the door to the Armageddon Hospital behind her. Donna and Angela had swapped two-hour shifts watching over their three hypothermia patients, and now Charlotte was going to take the graveyard shift until dawn. Tyler was fully recovered and was keeping Angela company while the two intruders were regaining their strength. After a brief visit with their parents, Kaycee and J.C. were taken to Haven House for a sleepover with Chubby and The Roo.

"Yeah, it's been a long day," she groaned, looking at her watch. It was just past midnight. "Charlotte, it's so late. Are you sure you and Echo are up for this? I can find someone else who is—"

"Younger?" Charlotte finished her sentence. "Don't you worry about me, Dr. Rankin. I've sat up many a night over the years caring for family members who were ill. On the farm, we took care of our own and didn't bother running to the hospital for every ailment. I can handle a six-hour shift until Tom and Donna arrive in the morning."

"I'm gonna speak with Echo," said Tyler as he made his way outside. He'd been acting as security, watching over the two men as they slept.

"So, Doc, do you have any special instructions for me?" asked Charlotte.

Angela walked over to the man whose shoulder had been

dislocated. "Well, as you know, this young man was in much more serious condition than his older friend. I've repaired his separated shoulder and I've immobilized it the best I can considering his restraints. I told Alpha he wasn't likely to go anywhere, especially in light of the fact that he's nude under these blankets, but you know how our head of security can be."

"Oh, yeah," said Charlotte with a snicker. "He can be brutish at times, but as my husband always says, he couldn't think of anyone he'd rather share a foxhole with."

"I suppose." Angela laughed as she felt the young man's face and forehead. His color was returning, and his vitals were near normal. She made her way to the other gurney.

"What about him?" asked Charlotte.

"This gentleman appears to have fully recovered. I have to say, Charlotte, Tyler fished them out of the water just in time. Just another five minutes and frostbite would've been the least of his problems."

"Does he understand what's happened to him? He's partially dressed, but still seems out of it," Charlotte observed.

"No, and it kinda concerns me. His condition wasn't near as bad as his young friend. He should've regained fully regained his faculties by now, or for sure when we dressed him. Ryan found a pair of fleece-lined Wrangler khakis and some wool boot socks to cover his lower half. I left his upper half undressed so I can check his vitals without fighting through clothing."

"He's still tied down with those plastic cuff things?" asked Charlotte.

"Yes, although not as tight as when they first brought him in. I was concerned about him losing circulation in his fingers and hands, complicating the healing process from his potential frostbite."

Charlotte walked to the IV-drip bag that was attached to the young man. "Do I need to change this? I've never done it before."

"Nope, he's good to go until Donna comes in at six. She's familiar with the process. Also, his catheter is in place and the bag has been emptied. No worries there."

"Good," said Charlotte with a laugh. "I don't want any part of that."

Angela smiled and headed for the door. "I get it. Listen, Echo has a radio, right?"

"Yes, always."

"Then please do not hesitate to wake me if there are any complications. I can be here in less than five minutes. Promise?"

Charlotte joined her and opened the door, allowing a rush of cold air to enter the room as they finished their conversation. The two women joined Echo and Tyler on the front porch of the Armageddon Hospital to talk about the day's events before the Rankins loaded up into the medical cart to head to their cabin for some much-needed rest.

"Good kids," said Echo as he and Charlotte watched them drive away. "They seem so young yet so mature. You don't see that much nowadays."

Charlotte nodded in agreement as she wrapped her arms through her husband's, enjoying the warmth of the hug. "We're lucky to have them both, and how about Tyler? I heard he had to argue with Alpha to go into the river after those two. That young man unselfishly risked his life for two strangers."

"Yeah, pretty amazing, really. I hope when these guys come to, they appreciate what everybody has done for them."

*****

Inside the hospital, the voices of the Echols were muffled and barely discernible. It wasn't their conversation that woke up one of their patients, but rather, the sudden rush of cold air that hit him, causing his body to shiver.

The older man had been in and out of consciousness throughout the entire ordeal. At times, he was oblivious to his surroundings, and other times he was completely lucid but chose to hide it from his captors. Because, after all, that was what they were. He and his young companion were prisoners, and the big man with the deep voice had made that abundantly clear.

That was why the prisoner didn't let on that he was conscious. He knew nothing about the people who had rescued him, only to treat him like a common criminal afterwards. His mind had raced as he listened to their conversations, wondering if they were some kind of cult. He'd made up his mind as soon as his ability to focus came back that he needed to escape.

So, after they loosened his restraints, enabling him to flex his hands and fingers, he got to work on the right wrist cuff that was closest to the cast-iron stove. The heat emanating from the stove caused the plastic to soften.

Through barely opened eyes, he studied his captors, who periodically left him alone or turned their attention to their other patient. Slowly at first, and then with increased vigor and strength, he twisted and turned his right wrist in the cuff until it grew larger. Eventually, it was large enough for him to slide his wrist out completely and then return it to the restraint when he was being attended to. When he was alone, he removed his right arm and worked diligently at stretching and twisting the left cuff until eventually it was loose enough to free his wrist.

Now, as the doctor and her husband, the fella who'd saved their lives, had left the hospital, the man had a decision to make. His buddy still appeared to be unconscious and incapable of escaping. He simply couldn't help that. He needed to go.

He considered overpowering the older lady who'd been assigned to watch them overnight. However, he was concerned the man on the porch was armed. He presumed that her husband was elderly as well, and his reflexes might be slow. But even a bad shot can find his target once in a while, and he didn't want to die. He'd cheated death once that day; getting shot at was pushing his luck.

He took a deep breath and steadied his nerves. All he had on were the khakis and a pair of socks. It would be cold, but his body now knew what extreme cold felt like. He decided a run through the woods in the cold, crisp Carolina air might actually feel good.

Decision made. He carefully slipped out of the restraints and quietly removed the covers, keeping one of the gray wool blankets to wrap around his upper body. He made his way past the other gurney, pausing to tell his unconscious friend that he'd send help, before approaching the rear windows of the building.

Moment of truth. Had these windows even been opened in the last century? They were made of heavy wood with lead glass panes. There were no locks on them, only carved handles at the top and bottom. With one final glance over his shoulder, he slowly pushed the window open, hoping that there were no loud squeaks or cracking noises.

Smooth as silk, he thought to himself as he hoisted himself through the window and into the dark environs at the back of the building. With a smooth, deliberate motion, he closed the window.

Seconds later, he disappeared into the darkness of the Haven.

CHAPTER 31

The Haven

"Okay, okay! Listen up!" Ryan tried to gain control over the frenzied mob that had descended upon the Armageddon Hospital. Echo and Charlotte had talked on the front porch of the hospital for a little over thirty minutes before they returned inside to warm up. At first, Charlotte thought her eyes betrayed her as she noticed the gurney was empty except for a pile of blankets. Echo immediately drew his weapon and moved through the building, thinking that the patient was hidden away in a closet or Angela's office. That was when Charlotte noticed one of the back windows was not quite closed.

Echo raised the alarm by contacting the main gate's security team, who then alerted Alpha, Ryan, and followed a contact list as part of their protocols. Within fifteen minutes thereafter, security at the main gate was increased, and Alpha had assembled his top lieutenants at the hospital, along with Ryan.

"Here's what we've got," Ryan began. "This man is in his late thirties or early forties. He's white, six feet tall, maybe two hundred pounds, with sandy-blond hair that's on the shaggy side. As far as we know, he's only got on a pair of khakis and gray boot socks. It's likely he's wrapped in a gray blanket to stay warm."

"How did this happen?" asked one of the male residents.

"It doesn't matter and we don't point fingers of blame here," Ryan quickly replied.

"What about our families?" asked another man.

Ryan raised his hands to calm down their concerns. "We have planned for this situation. As we speak, Blair is reaching out to all of you with kids, either directly via two-way radio or by sending someone to your homes. Our procedures require the children to be brought to Haven House, where we'll have beefed-up security. Blair and others will tend to their needs. While we search at night, only those of you who are experienced hunters will be used. If the manhunt extends into the daytime, then everyone with a set of eyes will be teamed up to hunt this guy down."

A female resident raised her hand. "What do we do if we find him? I vote that a bullet solves the problem."

"Yeah!"

"Me too!"

Ryan tried to gain control of the crowd once again. He reiterated their procedure in the event of an intruder. "We deal with problems as they are thrown at us, and the first order of business is to find this guy. Find him, hold him, and contact us by radio. Now, Alpha is going to organize us so that we can conduct our search in a grid pattern."

"Listen up." Alpha's voice boomed for all to hear. "Before I divide you into teams, let me give you some basics on hunting this guy down in the woods. First of all, it's gonna be dark for several more hours. We're hunting a frightened animal with nothing to lose. He doesn't know his way around the Haven, and he will likely follow established roads and trails to look for our perimeter."

"Is he armed?" asked one of the men.

"No, at least not yet," replied Alpha. "Our armory is locked up like Fort Knox, and all of you should've followed our instructions on securing your weapons. The only way he gets a gun is if he gets the jump on one of you. That's why we're going to travel in teams, using a buddy system.

"As you patrol the grounds, stay slightly separated but no farther apart than what your flashlight can illuminate. Use your lights, people. Don't play cowboy and think you're gonna sneak up on this guy. He's more likely to see you before you see him. Also, assume nothing. If you believe a briar patch is too sticky to hide in, think again. Animals use plant material as protection; this guy will too."

Ryan stepped forward. "As you guys know, I preach situational awareness all the time. If there ever was a time for focused awareness, it's now. Think of it as driving on ice and snow. Keep both hands on the wheel and have your attention totally focused on your surroundings. Do not take your eyes off the task at hand. Trust me, maintaining this level of concentration throughout the night will be tiring and stressful, but you cannot let your guard down. If you do, he will get one of your weapons, and that creates a whole nother set of dangers for us all."

"Ryan's right," added Alpha. "Eyes open and senses keenly aware of your surroundings. Also, do not shoot until you're one hundred percent certain that you need to. This leads me to the earlier question that was asked about what to do when you find him."

Alpha paused and glanced over at Ryan. "I want this sucker alive. I'm beginning to wonder what brought them to the Haven in the first place. Just a few minutes alone with the guy will give me all the answers I need. Now, let's split into groups and get started."

Blair had arrived for a moment to speak with Ryan. "I've got everyone secured, with help from the Sheltons, Cortlands, and Rankins to cover security."

Ryan pulled her to the side as Alpha issued his orders. "Do you want me to assign Delta to the house for extra protection?"

"Nah," replied Blair, who patted the AR-15 slung over her shoulder. "I've got everything I need right here."

Ryan was genuinely concerned for her safety. "I like Tom and Cort, and Tyler, too. But I'd feel better if I had an ex-LEO like Delta—"

"Ryan, stop it. I've got this. In fact, I'm sending Tyler and Angela back to the hospital to keep an eye on the other guy. Did you think of the fact that the escaped man will come back for his partner? Also, one of ours might get hurt while searching for him. You need your medical team ready, not holed up at the house with a bunch of kids."

Ryan exhaled. "You're right. It's just that I feel responsible for all of these people, and in a way, I wish I'd let these guys fall into the river or allowed Alpha to just shoot 'em like he wanted to."

"Yeah, on both counts. Now we've got a mess on our hands.

Listen, you've got a huge heart, and that's admirable in the real world. Things have changed now. The rules are being tossed aside, and our survival will be dictated by circumstances that may require killing people. Or, at the very least, not going out of our way to save them. That's neither here nor there. I've gotta get back."

Blair kissed her husband on the cheek and jumped onto her Kawasaki Prairie. Before she pulled away, she added one more thing. "Ryan, also, don't forget. These two may have friends who will come lookin' for them. What's happening outside our walls is just as important as finding the guy inside them."

*****

For hours, ten teams of two scoured the two hundred wooded acres of the Haven in search of the escaped prisoner. False alarms were common as frightened residents radioed in to Blair that they thought they heard or saw something near their cabin, only to find out it was members of the search teams.

As dawn approached, a lead brought them to the north end of the Haven in an area near the location where Ethan had scaled the wall when he stole the car from the adjacent farm. A shed containing farm, landscape, and logging equipment had been ransacked. Echo, who knew the contents well, said a machete was missing as well as a battery-operated Coleman lantern.

At first, Alpha ordered the search teams to remain in their designated sectors. He and Hayden, who'd been acting as rovers, raced to the equipment shed to meet with Echo.

"Well, now he's armed," said Hayden as she surveyed the wrecked contents of the shed. "You wanna change your order from capture to shoot to wound?"

"Not just yet, but we might have him cornered in the north sector. There are a lot of trees up here, some of which overhang the wall. After the kid ran off the other day, it was on my list of things to do, but the weather hasn't allowed us to put a crew together to cut them down."

The two paused their conversation as Ryan arrived in the Ranger. He jumped out of the cab and jogged up to the shed. "I've got our two infrared drones heading up this way. I told the operators to look for single heat signals rather than pairs. As day breaks, I'll increase the number of drone search teams."

"Makes sense," said Alpha. "Ryan, the guy probably has a machete. If he sneaks up on one of our people ..." Alpha's voice trailed off. He didn't need to say more.

"I know you wanted to interrogate the guy, but I'm pissed, and some of our frightened residents are turning angry."

"Can I issue a shoot order?" asked Alpha.

"Only if he resists," replied Ryan, who reached into his right pocket and retrieved a blue latex glove. He put it on his left hand and then pulled out a revolver from his left pocket, holding the weapon by two fingers. "Make sure he's dead and then I'll put this in his hand."

"Self-defense," muttered Hayden. "Nice touch."

"I saw it on a TV show," said Ryan with a smile. "Under most circumstances, it might not fly, but during the apocalypse, it makes for an open-and-shut case."

Hayden nodded. "Agreed."

"Good. You two go find this guy and raise me on the radio as soon as you can. I'll be back at Haven Barn, ready to react as needed."

CHAPTER 32

The Haven

Alpha and Hayden welcomed the sun's warmth as they worked their way along the wooded banks of the Henry River. This part of the Haven contained the most underbrush and uncertain terrain. Alpha, who knew every inch of the property, and Hayden, who was the security team's most experienced hunter, were a perfect pair to flush out the escapee.

"I've got a footprint," announced Hayden as she immediately crouched to the ground and readied her AR-10. Alpha slid in behind her and joined her on one knee. She pointed to it with her left hand and then immediately regripped the rifle.

Alpha had learned the art of tracking another human being in the military when he trained for jungle warfare. Whether he was searching for someone who was lost, backtracking himself after getting turned around, or chasing after a hostile, the art of tracking was part science, part survival instinct, and all about observing the details of your surroundings.

"He stepped into a track trap," whispered Alpha under his breath. "In the darkness, and in a panicked state, the guy didn't think to avoid these areas of damp surfaces. Look up ahead, there's another one sunk into the moss."

Hayden had adopted tracking techniques of her own when hunting deer. Wild pigs were easier to track in East Tennessee, where she spent most of her childhood hunting. Hogs tended to leave a big mess as they traveled. Between their heavy hooves and constant desire to forage for food, it was readily apparent which way a hog had moved through the woods.

Deer were more difficult. They were capable of long strides and were relatively light on their feet. She was able to discern a buck's intentions by following his tracks. They acted very much like an office worker driving home from work. They typically took a straight shot to their destination and then a sudden turn off the trail, like a motorist pulling into his driveway. The prints of the deer would become closer together and then suddenly veer off to one side or the other.

Hayden would also look for signs that the buck stopped to nibble a few buds or maybe pawed for beechnuts. That was when she'd study the terrain, looking for a spot to have a better view of the woods. This gave her an increased opportunity to shoot her prey.

"He's most likely discovered the wall and knows that he can't scale its ten-foot height," said Hayden. "I'm thinking he wants to follow the riverbank until he's cleared the end of the structure."

Alpha laughed and pointed ahead as he led the way. "He'll be in for a surprise, won't he?"

"Yeah, a lot worse than what he faced in the water yesterday."

"Come on," said Alpha as he led the way, setting a quicker pace now that they had tracks and daylight to assist them.

After several minutes, Alpha raised his fist and came to an abrupt stop. "He's been through here and it wasn't that long ago. Check out this spiderweb."

Alpha directed Hayden's attention to a broken spiderweb that hadn't been rebuilt. He'd been trained to check for aerial spoor, the clues or scent of the animal, or man, he was tracking. In this case, with the cooler weather, a spider would've begun to rebuild its web within an hour to an hour and a half. This web remained destroyed.

Snap!

Alpha turned and pointed to his right ear. Hayden nodded and pointed ahead, encouraging Alpha to lead the way.

With their rifles held at low ready, the barrels of the weapons pointed toward the ground in front of them, they followed the narrow path toward the point where the Haven's wall met the Henry River.

Arrggh!

The man was groaning in pain, and Alpha smelled blood, figuratively speaking. He picked up the pace and Hayden scrambled to keep up. Thirty seconds later, they entered a clearing and found the partially dressed man lying on his back, writhing in pain.

Hayden dashed past Alpha and circled behind the man, quickly surveilling the area to ensure they were alone. With his weapon pointed at the man's chest, Alpha moved closer to investigate.

He looked up and saw where the tree branch had snapped from the trunk. "I guess this is one branch we won't need to cut down."

"Help me." The man was barely able to speak, as the breath had been knocked out of him.

"Screw you, pal," said Alpha as he kicked the man's legs apart and felt his pants for weapons.

"There's the machete," said Hayden, nodding toward the base of the tree. Then she glanced back over her shoulder toward the river. "I guess he decided not to fight his way through the razor wire."

Ryan and Alpha had installed concertina wire stretching from the end of the block and brick wall into the Henry River, where it was affixed to an old fence post. Priced at only a hundred dollars per roll on Amazon, it had become one of their most used security tools. Any unsuspecting intruder would try to wade around the wall through the water, only to be sliced up by the razor-sharp wire.

"That's a shame. He'd really be torn up. Much worse than what I'm about to do to him." Alpha shouldered his rifle and reached for the man's arm to pull him upright. "Time to talk, buddy. No more foolin' around."

Alpha drew his fist back and was about to land the first blow to the man's face when the sound of a drone hovering overhead stopped him. He looked up, and within seconds, another drone appeared.

"Crap! And to think those things were my idea."

"Alpha, this is Ryan. Over."

Alpha pushed the man back onto the wet ground and hissed, "Don't move."

"Are you gonna answer him?" asked Hayden.

Alpha looked into the sky and shook his head. "I don't think I have a choice. If I beat the crap out of this guy, Ryan'll be pissed. Blair, on the other hand, will give me an award."

"I like her," said Hayden. "Tough as nails, which is exactly what we need right now."

"Ryan's tough, too. He's just less impulsive than I am. Probably better that way."

Alpha reached for his radio and looked up toward the drones. He waved to make sure they could see their recaptured prisoner.

Ryan's voice came across the radio. "I see. Good job, y'all. I'm on my way and I'll send Tyler with the medical cart."

"Roger that," said Alpha, who placed the radio back into his utility belt. He grabbed the man by the arms and hoisted him off the ground. "On your feet."

Hayden shouldered her rifle and quickly cuffed the man, giving the Safariland zip-tie handcuffs an extra-snug fit, much to the chagrin of the recaptured prisoner.

"Let's go," said Alpha with a gruff as he dragged the man along the path at the base of the wall. The drones had departed and Alpha grinned slightly as he gave the man a shove, causing him to plant his face on the rough cinder-block wall.

"Nooo!" The man begged for mercy as blood streamed down his forehead from a gash. "I just wanna go home."

"Yeah, I'm sure you do," snarled Alpha, who gave the guy another shove against the wall. This time, the man turned slightly to avoid hitting his face, but crashed into it with his back, which had been injured by the fall.

"I hear four-wheelers," warned Hayden, subtly suggesting to Alpha to stop the extracurricular brutality.

"Yeah, thanks." Alpha helped the man up and led him into a larger clearing where the main trail opened up at the Haven's northern perimeter.

Tyler was the first to arrive on the scene. He noticed the man's bloody face first. "Whoa, what happened to him?"

Alpha was curt in his response. "Resisting arrest."

Tyler furrowed his brow and pointed toward his medical cart. "Bring him over here and I'll patch him up."

"Nope. I want his buddy to see what he looks like first. He needs to know escaping is not a good idea."

"But—" Tyler began to protest.

"Not gonna happen. He's caused us enough trouble. I should've shot him like I wanted to."

Ryan arrived in his Ranger and jumped out before it came to a complete stop. "What happened to—?" He didn't complete the question, the look of recognition on his face indicating that he'd answered his own question.

"We got our man," said Hayden, attempting to take the heat off Alpha and reminding everyone that the manhunt was over.

Ryan sighed and pointed toward the medical cart. "Put him in the back and strap him to the rails. Alpha, stay with Tyler and make sure this guy's properly secured. Hayden, I'll need you to come—"

His sentence was interrupted by a radio call from the front gate. "Ryan, this is Main Gate. Over."

"Go ahead, Main Gate."

"Um, we have three women and a couple of kids approaching us on foot. Do you want us to deal with it?"

Ryan turned to Alpha, who said, "Go on. We've got this."

Ryan's eyes darted from Tyler to Alpha and then to the battered prisoner. "Okay. But, Alpha, I think the guy's got the message. Do we understand each other?"

Alpha grinned. "Yep, I think he got it loud and clear."

The radio crackled to life again. "Main gate to Ryan, over."

"Go ahead," Ryan responded.

"These people are missing their husbands. From the descriptions they gave us, it could be the guys we fished out of the water. Over."

Ryan looked at Alpha and Hayden. "Let's throw their fish back. Whadya say?"

CHAPTER 33

Across the Henry River
Near the Main Gate
The Haven

Chepe's men had taken up a position on a hillside overlooking the main gate of the Haven. They'd traveled around the river, using a route other than the one that ran parallel to the Haven's walls after their foot surveillance discovered that armed men were guarding the bridge near the main gate. They used sketch pads to create a general outline of the Haven's two-hundred-acre compound. Using various vantage points, they were able to identify buildings inside the property and likely uses.

They'd camped in the woods opposite the row of cabins on the Haven's easternmost boundary along the river. They saw the two men thrashing in a panic as they bobbed down the river until they became tangled up in the fallen trees. Earl, who was an experienced fisherman, warned of the treacherous waters in that part of North Carolina during the wet winter season. The Henry River in particular was known to be a calm, fairly muddy flowing tributary that easily became torrent-like during heavy rains.

Ollie, whose eyesight was better than his older partner's, adjusted the focus on the binoculars. He'd been watching the front gate ever since he saw the group of women and children approach from the road.

"Two women, three kids, and an old lady. They're arguing with the guards, and now a guy just showed up in a four-wheeler. It's kinda cool, almost like a small car."

"That's exciting," said Earl sarcastically. "What's the argument about?"

"I don't know. Wait. Here come a couple of other four-wheelers. One looks like those golf cart wagons they cart busted-up football players on. The other is just a regular all-terrain vehicle."

"Let me see." Earl, who'd grown increasingly frustrated with Ollie as their mission wore on, took the binoculars. Ollie wasn't interested in getting wet, dirty, or cold, opting instead for taking the easy way of surveilling the Haven. Earl, on the other hand, suspected this was going to be a target of Chepe's, and he wanted to provide a full and accurate report.

Earl studied the body language of everyone involved. "It's the two guys they pulled out of the river. One's beat up pretty bad and they're both in handcuffs. Heck, one of them can't even stand up on his own."

"What are the women doing there?" asked Ollie.

"Hang on."

Earl continued to watch as the two captured men tried to pull away from their captors. The women and children rushed the iron gates and were trying to reach through the bars. The guards were doing their best to push them back but were unsuccessful.

Ollie grew impatient. "Well? I wanna head back to Charlotte soon."

"I'm guessin' they're all family. They took the men through the small guardhouse and shoved them through another gate onto the ground. Looks like they've been released."

Earl watched for another minute and then handed the binoculars back to Ollie.

"Now can we go?" Ollie asked.

"No. Let's wait 'til around noon. I wanna study their drone activity. My guess is that these people will step up their surveillance after what happened with those two guys. I doubt that's what Chepe wants to hear."

Ollie began to study the skies over the Haven. "I just saw one lift off. It came from the middle of the property near that large barn we saw yesterday."

"I see it," added Earl.

"Here comes another one," said Ollie. "It's headed toward— quick. We've gotta take cover or it'll see us."

One of the Haven's quadcopters flew straight toward them and then took an abrupt turn toward the bridge crossing the river. It lowered its altitude and buzzed out of sight toward the south. The two men stayed hidden in the underbrush until they heard it returning at a high rate of speed.

"Wow! Look at that thing go," said Ollie.

The high-pitched sound of the drone grew louder as it approached their position on the hillside and then started to quieten as it passed. The men craned their neck to watch the drone sail past. Moments later, it flew past them toward the south again.

"They're gonna start sweeping the river," observed Earl.

Ollie thought for a moment. "Do you think they'll pull people from the wall?"

Earl stood and backed deeper into the woods. "I'd count on it."

CHAPTER 34

Little Red Schoolhouse
The Haven

Although the intruders were captured and subsequently expelled to their concerned families, the residents of the Haven were on edge as reality started to sink in. It was easy to forget about the dangers that lurked outside the protective walls that surrounded them. Most were not aware of the circumstances in cities and towns across America, where neighbor fought neighbor for scarce resources. The war of words waged behind the protective shields of avatars and made-up names on social media was replaced by the use of force, deadly at times, as people fought one another to survive.

Ryan and Blair agreed that everyone needed a day off to put the stress of the prior evening behind them. Alpha and his security team took the time to discuss what had happened and what breakdowns in security led to the intrusion, if any.

The rest of the Haven enjoyed a respite from their normal daily activities. It was an unusually warm day, which allowed the children to play outside rather than attend school. Some of the children practiced their quadcopter operations while others simply enjoyed an opportunity to be kids.

At the Little Red Schoolhouse, Meredith and Hannah were working on the lesson planning for when everyone returned. Meredith was just about to write the outline on the blackboard when she got a visitor.

"Knock, knock!" The man announced himself in a sheepish tone of voice. "Is anybody around today?"

"Sure!" replied Hannah cheerily, but her mother tamped down her enthusiasm.

"Wait, Hannah. Let me see who it is first."

Meredith walked out of the main classroom and carefully peered around the corner. X-Ray stood alone in the doorway, waiting for her invitation to come in.

"Oh, hi," she said hesitantly. "You're X-Ray, right? We saw each other at the main house one evening but never really got a chance to talk."

"Um, yes. My real name is Eugene, but everyone calls me by my nickname, X-Ray."

Meredith's eyes darted around the room and then past X-Ray toward the grassy area in front of the school. She smiled and waved him inside. "Come on, I'll show you around."

Hannah emerged from the classroom. "Hi, Mr. X-Ray. I like your name!"

X-Ray fidgeted, nervously kicking at the floor with his sneakers. "Um, thanks. My grandfather gave it to me. It's better than Eugene, I guess."

"Mom, I wanna cool nickname like his. I'm gonna talk to Daddy about it tonight."

Meredith and X-Ray shared a laugh.

"Come on, let's show our guest around," said Meredith. For the next ten minutes, the Cortland women walked X-Ray through the Haven's school, pointing out the thoughtful features incorporated into the curriculum by Blair and Ryan. After he'd received the nickel tour, X-Ray paused.

"Say, do you think your kids would like to learn more about computers? I have a couple of extra desktop PCs. You know, I could teach them the basics, depending on what they know already."

"That would be great, Mr. X-Ray. I had my own iPad at home, but I haven't been able to use it here because we don't have wireless."

X-Ray looked down at Hannah, who appeared to be anxious to learn. "Well, there's a whole lot more to a computer than the internet. I'd be glad to show you some things that will help you later in life."

X-Ray gulped and closed his eyes for a moment, an emotional reaction that caught Meredith's eye.

She patted him on the shoulder and smiled. "Don't worry. Things will settle down soon and we'll all be able to return home to our normal lives."

"That's right, Mr. X-Ray. My daddy promised that all of this will pass and we can go home to Mobile once it's over. You'll see."

X-Ray sighed. "You know, I think you're right. Meredith, Hannah, I'm gonna go back to my cabin and sort through some stuff. I'm anxious to help the kids out any way I can."

With that, Hanson Briscoe's inside man slipped out the door without another word.

CHAPTER 35

Schwartz Lodge
Off U.S. Route 222
Near Kutztown, Pennsylvania

Schwartz and Briscoe found they had more in common than once realized. Although they were from opposite ends of the political spectrum, their upbringing and family history followed similar paths. One thing they both agreed upon was the fact that a nation required a catalyst, a massive upheaval, in order to effectuate real change. Whether it be a continued lurch to the left and an adoption of European socialism tenets, or a retreat to the past, to the days of the nation's founding, the winds of change could only occur through an internal struggle. Call it a civil war or insurrection or a battle of ideologies, to Schwartz and Briscoe, it was necessary for one set of core beliefs or the other to take the lead.

The other thing the two men shared was their desire for revenge. Both of them lost sight of what had drawn the ire of George Trowbridge in the first place.

To be sure, Briscoe had attempted to assassinate Trowbridge's son-in-law. He'd begun to feel genuine remorse for his actions, even contemplating an apology.

Jonathan was not quite as contrite. On the contrary, he maintained that politics, and the ideological war being waged in America, was fair game to now use all manner of techniques to gain the upper hand. Jonathan maintained that Trowbridge had just as many financial and potentially criminal skeletons in his closet as his father, and therefore the extraordinary decision to take advantage of the martial law declaration to imprison him was beyond the pale of fair play. As a result, he was prepared to stick Trowbridge in the heart by taking away the Cortland family, just as the old man had taken away Jonathan's father.

The men were once again sharing a brandy on that cold evening, sitting by the fire and talking about successful political strategies they'd utilized. They both agreed the events since New Year's Eve would create a wholly new dynamic in the U.S., one in which the old rules and methods of operation would no longer apply. Whichever side won the battle to come, they faced the daunting task of bringing the nation back together and rebuilding the destruction resulting from the conflict.

By prior arrangement, Jonathan had instructed Chepe to call him precisely at eleven that evening, and they agreed to speak for less than one minute. Early in the day, Jonathan and Briscoe had driven into town on a Kawasaki Mule side-by-side four-wheeler, wearing camouflaged hunting gear stored at the Schwartz lodge. They'd purchased more brandy, some food supplies, and half a dozen Tracfones to be used for future calls with Chepe.

Tonight's call would be the last one between the two men utilizing Jonathan's old cell phone. They spoke for a moment and Jonathan advised Chepe he'd be calling back on the burner phone, after activating them through the satellite internet system at the lodge. Schwartz-affiliated operatives had tapped into the MegaFon internet service provider network in Russia.

Established as part of Russia's Digital Economy National Program, the system was designed to segregate Russia's own web from the rest of the world to prevent future cyber attacks. MegaFon, the third largest communications provider in Russia, was partially owned by Gazprombank, an international banking conglomerate controlled by Schwartz family interests.

Chepe, who'd grown frustrated with his inability to place cell phone calls to his operatives, had switched to satellite phones provided by Schwartz.

Jonathan placed the phone on speaker so Briscoe could engage in the conversation as well.

After Chepe had reported the details of his operatives' surveillance, Briscoe explained that he had a man on the inside who might be of assistance.

"This young man is one of hundreds of trusted operatives—insurance policies, as I call them—I employ around the country who are bought and paid for. Of course, as is almost always the case, I have some type of personal information on this young man that would be devastating to his future career paths or, at the very least, extremely embarrassing if it were to be made public."

"Is he a danger to my men once the operation begins?" asked Chepe.

"No, on the contrary, he comes across as meek and timid. The people who should be concerned about his presence within this compound are the families of teenage boys. In any event, that's not the issue at the moment. He's an asset and can be used as we see fit. I can message him. Is there anything in particular you'd like to know about the compound?"

Chepe was silent for a moment. "I mean no disrespect, but I don't know him, and trust is a factor with the type of attack I have in mind. I would rather that he not be told we're coming."

"I understand, but he does have value as a set of eyes inside the compound," countered Briscoe.

Chepe thought for a moment and then said, "Well, simply instruct him to advise you if the Cortlands leave. We've downloaded images from our people in Brussels who still have internet. Thank you, by the way, for the satphones in your last delivery."

"You are welcome," responded Jonathan. "When do you plan on moving on the compound?"

"Day after tomorrow," replied Chepe. "There is one more operation to undertake in the Wedgewood area of Charlotte, near the Northlake Mall."

"Are you going shopping?" Jonathan showed a rare jovial side. Perhaps it was a combination of the brandy soaking into his body coupled with the prospect of driving a dagger through the heart of George Trowbridge.

"Something like that," replied Chepe. "Unless there is something urgent, I suggest we not speak again until I report in following the attack."

"Agreed," replied Jonathan. He glanced over at Briscoe, who nodded.

Jonathan disconnected the call and raised his glass of brandy to Briscoe. "To revenge!"

Briscoe clinked the two glasses together. "Yes, to revenge."

Briscoe set his glass down and retrieved his phone from his pocket. He reinserted the SIM card for the sole purpose of sending this text to X-Ray.

Keep your eyes on the eagle and advise if he takes flight.
Godspeed, Patriot!
MM

Unfortunately for Briscoe, there were more sets of eagle eyes than just the ones that he employed.

CHAPTER 36

Main Gate
The Haven

"Main Gate to Alpha. Over."

The radio transmission interrupted the morning briefing as Alpha was discussing increasing the patrols along the river. Annoyed, he yanked the radio out of his belt. "Go ahead."

"We have a group approaching the gate in a vehicle. Our scouts along the road indicate it is a man, woman, and a teenage boy. Pennsylvania plates. Just wanted to give you a heads-up, as our residence roster shows as full."

Delta, who was standing at the rear of the room, as had been his practice, stepped forward slightly and addressed Alpha. "Did he say Pennsylvania?"

"Yes," said Alpha. "Why?"

"Would you ask the make and model of the vehicle?"

Alpha pressed the mic button on his radio. "Front gate, give me a description on the vehicle."

"Maroon. SUV. Dodge, I believe. It's slowly approaching now. Should I engage?"

Delta began to wave his arms. "I know who it is."

"Stand down, Main Gate, but stay on alert. We're on the way."

Alpha turned back to the group. "Bravo, will you finish this up for me? Ryan, Delta, let's go."

Alpha was all business as he shouldered his rifle and headed for the rear of the room. He glared at Delta as he walked past. Ryan spoke briefly to the group and then he hustled to catch up.

Once outside, Alpha waited by Ryan's Ranger for Delta to join

168

him. "Let me guess. It's the ex and your kid."

"I think so, and if there's a man with them, it's my former partner and the guy who took up with Karen. His name is Frankie."

"Is he dangerous?" asked Ryan.

"Not before this," Delta began to reply. "Truthfully, before the incident in Philly, and his subsequent taking of my wife, he was a pretty good partner. Now, of course, I've got no use for the guy."

Alpha exhaled and piled his large frame into the front seat of the Ranger. Ryan sped away, and within a couple of minutes, they arrived at the front gate, where Frankie and Karen stood in front of the SUV with their hands raised over their heads.

Ryan had barely brought his Ranger to a stop before Delta jumped out of the backseat and jogged up to the gate.

"Will, tell these people to lower their weapons," began Frankie. "We're unarmed and you know us."

"Doesn't matter," Alpha's voice boomed from behind Delta. "And it's not his call to make."

Karen tried to reason with Alpha. "I'm his ex-wife, and his son is in the backseat. He's badly injured and we shouldn't be treated this way."

"It doesn't matter," began Alpha before Ryan tapped him on the shoulder.

"Let me take it from here, big guy," whispered Ryan, who then turned to Delta. "I know this is family, but for your sake, and everyone else's, let me handle this per protocol. Okay?"

Delta stopped and nodded his agreement. He did move aside for Ryan to pass, and to create a little space between him and Alpha.

Alpha made eye contact with him, scowled, and shook his head side to side. Like Blair, he wasn't one for inserting unnecessary drama into the Haven.

"Hello, folks. My name is Ryan. I'm sorry for the weapons, but we have procedures to follow. Now, if you're in agreement, we need to search you and your vehicle for weapons. If there are any, please tell us now and turn them over. If you refuse, you'll need to leave immediately. Do you have a problem with that?"

Frankie spoke up for the group. "We're unarmed. You can search all you want."

Ryan bristled at the man's attitude but continued because this was Delta's family, dysfunctional as it was. He nodded toward the guards, who brought the German shepherd over to the SUV to conduct their search.

While Karen was being patted down by one of the female gate guards, she turned her head to the SUV. "Come on out of the truck, Ethan. Show your father what happened to you."

Ethan gingerly exited the truck, revealing his bruised face and arms.

When Delta saw his battered body, he rushed to the gate to get a closer look. "Son, what happened to you? Who did this?"

"Um, hey, Dad. I got into trouble at a gas station in Richmond. These dudes just decided to beat on me."

Karen was loaded for bear. "He's lucky he's alive, Will, and you should be ashamed for putting him in that position. Look at him! He was barely alive when that family found him."

"It wasn't like that, Mom," yelled Ethan. "All of that was on me, not Dad!"

"Enough!" shouted Alpha. "Let my people do their job without this soap opera or I'll send you all packin'."

Ryan turned and winked at Alpha. Then he leaned in to whisper to the no-nonsense head of security, "I need to get Blair down here. I suspect we're gonna need to make a decision."

Alpha turned his back to the new arrivals and walked briefly with Ryan, who made his way behind the Ranger. "You're not gonna let them in, are you? They can't even get along with the bars separating them. What's it gonna be like when they can actually slug it out?"

Ryan laughed. "It'll be like an episode of *Jerry Springer*. We could call it Friday Night Fights."

Alpha managed to laugh, as Ryan successfully eased the tension built up in his top security guy. "Okay, maybe that would be worth watching. Listen, boss, I'll do whatever you say. But this bunch has the potential to screw up a pretty good thing. You know?"

"I do. Let me get Blair down here so she can assess the situation with me."

Ryan raised Blair on the radio, and while he waited, Delta focused his attention on Ethan's injuries. The security team gave Alpha an all-clear after a thorough inspection, and the travelers were allowed to lower their arms. Frankie and Karen nervously kicked at the gravel, waiting to learn their fate.

Blair pulled up on her Kawasaki Prairie, her AR-15 resting in the gun clamps mounted to the front bracket. She quickly hopped off and spoke with Ryan behind the Ranger. She asked her signature question as she approached him.

"What kind of fresh hell is this?"

"This is the former Will Hightower family, plus one home-wrecker—the former SWAT partner."

"Fabulous. So why are they still standing there? Tell them to get the hell off our property or we'll shoot them."

Ryan spontaneously erupted in laughter. Of course, he knew Blair was serious in her statement, and he'd come to expect that level of blunt honesty from her. Because he loved her so much, he never tired of her delivery. He was certain that if he told the security people to get out of the way, Blair would march up to the front gate, pull the charging handle on her AR-15, and tell the trio of travelers they had three seconds to vacate the premises, or prepare to die.

"Okay, let's talk about it, shall we?" Ryan tried to calm her down, knowing that shooting them wasn't an option.

Blair was incensed. "No, Ryan. Why should we talk? We told Delta that we can't tolerate this soap-opera crap. We took in his kids because he's a valuable member of our security team and he had no other options for them other than to leave altogether. Then the older kid steals a car and takes off. Now he brings mommy and the home-wrecker, your words, to create an episode of *Modern Family* inside the Haven? No f'n way. Not gonna happen."

Ryan had a hard time arguing with her logic, but he had a weakness, a kind heart, and a constant desire to help others, even if it placed himself in peril. "Okay, let me say this first. The boyfriend,

171

Frankie, is persona non grata. He's got law enforcement skills that would most likely be used against us if he and Delta got into a serious disagreement. That's an easy decision. With respect to Ethan, we let him in once. Arguably, we could let—"

Blair raised her hand. "Hold up. He stole the old man's car off that farm to the north of us, bringing the sheriff and his posse right to our front gate. We should've kicked them all out for that reason alone."

"However, Delta stayed loyal to us and didn't chase after Ethan. Apparently, the kid got beaten up pretty badly for his efforts."

Blair was having none of it. "What's to keep him from pulling the same stunt again?"

"He might, or maybe he's learned his lesson. I believe in second chances."

Blair exhaled and looked around the Ranger at Karen. "What about her? Do you wanna let her in, too?"

"She's kinda mouthy," said Ryan. "She laid into Delta pretty good the first chance she got."

"Oh, let me guess," began Blair. "He lost his father-of-the-year award because his petulant brat teenager decided to steal a car and run off."

"Plus, he got the snot beat out of him in the process," added Ryan. "Yes, that was all Delta's fault and she let him know about it. Now, to Ethan's credit, he just took responsibility for what he did and defended Delta."

Blair rolled her head on her shoulders and wandered around the back of the Ranger for a moment. She closed her eyes and shook her head side to side. After exhaling, she returned to Ryan and delivered her opinion. "Okay, Frankie hits the road. I don't care how much everybody pisses and moans about it. He's not comin' in. Ethan can stay, but he doesn't get any more passes. First screwup, no matter how insignificant, and we're tossing him in the river. Got it?"

"Yup. What about the mom?"

"Well, mommy dearest needs to make a decision. Is she gonna stay at the Haven and take care of her kids, or is she gonna leave with her boy toy? If she stays, then I'm gonna read her the riot act. No arguments. No cold-shoulder attitude. She becomes a productive, good-natured, no-scrapping-with-ex-husband member of the Haven, or she'll get tossed in the Henry River, too."

Ryan smiled and reached to squeeze Blair's shoulder. "I'll let them know."

"Nope, you're too nice," said Blair. She immediately walked away and marched toward the gate, where Ethan, Karen, and Frankie moved closer to hear the Smarts' decision.

"Who are you?" asked Karen.

Immediately, Blair didn't like the woman's attitude, but she let it go. "My name is Blair and you've already met my husband, Ryan. Here's what we're gonna do." Blair paused and then turned to Ethan.

"Ethan, you can stay. But know this. One screwup and you're out of here. No arguments. We'll throw you out on your own, and trust me, the world is a far more dangerous place than it was a few days ago when you left. My guess is that you can't disagree. Am I right?"

"Yes, ma'am. I'll stay."

Blair turned to Frankie. "You're not family and we don't have room for anybody else. You have to leave."

"What? We drove all this way."

"Don't care," replied Blair. "Nobody told you to come here. Our decision is final. You have to go."

"What about me?" asked Karen, who wrapped her arm through Frankie's. "We're together."

"You gotta make a choice, Mrs. Hightower," said Blair with emphasis, drawing a glare from both Frankie and Karen. "Your children will be here and they're safe, assuming they don't run off like that one did."

"Yes, but I can't—" Karen's demeanor changed, and she'd become more humble.

"You *can* if you want to," Blair cut her off mid-sentence. "You have to make a choice. There is no way we can allow your friend inside. Delta, um, Will has been with us for some time, and I'll not subject him to living with the man who stole his wife."

"Hey, I didn't steal her," protested Frankie. "He drove her off."

"Well, that's not the way I've heard the story told, but it doesn't matter," said Blair matter-of-factly. "Either way, it doesn't matter. You're out. Now, Mrs. Hightower, are you staying, or are you going?"

"Well …" She hesitated.

"Let me say one more thing to you. No drama. Do you hear me? No arguments. No scraps. No yelling. If you two can't be civil to one another, then say nothing at all. The first sign of trouble brewing between you two, and you're gone. Understood?"

"I'll agree to that," said Delta, who'd been listening intently to the conversation.

"Um," began Karen, who looked over at Frankie. "I'm sorry, Frankie. I need to take care of my kids. I'm staying."

"Are you kidding me?"

Karen turned to Blair. "Thank you. I will stay and I totally understand where you're coming from."

Frankie reached for Karen's arm and squeezed it, causing her to recoil. "Seriously, Karen. You're picking that loser over me?"

"He's not a loser!" shouted Ethan.

"They're my kids, Frankie. I need to make sure they're safe."

Frankie was infuriated. "Then let's load them up and take them home."

Will inserted himself into the conversation. "Back to Philly? No power. Anarchy. No way. My kids stay here where they'll be safe."

"Shut up, loser!" Frankie rushed the gate and reached through it in an attempt to grab at Delta. The guards on both sides quickly moved in and pointed their rifles at his head.

Blair turned to Ryan and raised her voice for all to hear. "I don't know, Ryan. We're off to a bad start, don't you think?"

Karen pleaded with Blair. "No. Please let us in. Ethan and I will behave. Right, Ethan?"

"Yes, Miss Blair. Let me make it up to you, and to Dad."

Frankie was being pushed back toward the Durango. Karen, who made no effort to hug him or say goodbye, had made her decision and cut ties with her boyfriend.

"Frankie, you can have my car," she began as she turned her head toward Delta. "I won't be needing it anymore."

Alpha instructed the gate guards to retrieve her luggage out of the back of the truck and to escort Frankie off the Haven's driveway.

Karen and Ethan entered through the gatehouse entrance, where they were reunited with Delta. The former family had a tearful reunion, which included apologies and pledges to start over. It was a heartfelt moment that tugged on the Smarts' heartstrings.

As the gate was secured once again, the Hightowers prepared to join Skylar at the cabin. Blair spoke to them before they left.

"Y'all, don't make me regret this."

A tearful Karen replied, "I promise. I'll never forget how you brought us together again. This is my family. It always has been."

Ryan joined his wife's side. "Good. Then let's start over. My name is Ryan Smart. Welcome to the Haven."

Chapter 37

North of Charlotte, North Carolina

Frankie was out of his mind with anger as he raced away from the Haven at speeds approaching a hundred miles an hour. Driving out of control as if he had a death wish, he narrowly missed two people riding their bicycles toward Interstate 40. The near fatal accident shook the anger from Frankie long enough to regain some state of composure, so he pulled into the parking lot of a looted Burger King before he got onto I-40.

He exited Karen's Durango and walked around it for a moment, pausing to look skyward, and then buried his face in his hands. He wasn't completely in love with her. From the moment she fell into his bed during the media turmoil over Will, he enjoyed her enthusiasm and spontaneity. Their trysts were more physical for him than emotional. For Karen, they appeared to be designed as a way to get back at Will for the trouble that had been brought upon the Hightower family.

In the couple of years since he and Karen had gotten together, there was little talk of marriage. They became more like companions than a couple. Sure, they were intimate from time to time, but the newness and excitement soon wore off. It was replaced by the reality that any long-term commitment to Karen automatically included two nearly grown kids that weren't his.

She had no desire to have any more children, so Frankie had little choice but to foresee a future in which he would try to raise Skylar and Ethan as his own. Early on, it became apparent that was never going to happen. Skylar would always be enamored with her father, and she'd frequently given Frankie the cold shoulder when he tried to get close to her.

Ethan, who'd become rebellious and somewhat out of control after Will left for Atlanta, became more of a burden to Frankie than a potential son. Frankie was always there to bail Ethan out of trouble, but Ethan never seemed to fully accept him as a father figure.

As a result, there were many times that Frankie considered leaving to find another girlfriend. The cruise that cost him a month's salary was intended to rekindle the old sexual flame the couple had shared when they were sneaking around on Will. Other than a couple of alcohol-induced romps, the fire wasn't relit.

Despite the fact his relationship with Karen was likely doomed, Frankie was still furious that she chose Will over him. He'd lost sight of the fact that her children were involved, and his anger reappeared as he suddenly walked around her truck, kicking the door panels and fenders, leaving it full of dents.

He gritted his teeth and spoke aloud to an empty parking lot. "Ungrateful. Thankless. Selfish. Arrrrgh!"

Frankie reached down and grabbed a handful of gravel, then angrily pelted the small stones against the side of the SUV. He spun around and pounded his right fist into his other hand, emulating what he'd do to Will, Karen, or both, if he ever got the chance.

He made his way back inside the truck and slammed the door shut until he was engulfed in silence. He exhaled and looked around.

"Now what, Frankie, my man?" he asked aloud.

He started the car and checked his fuel gauge. He had less than half a tank that wouldn't get him back to Richmond, much less all the way to Philadelphia. He didn't have a map and the Durango wasn't equipped with a GPS option. He'd found his way to the Haven with Ethan's guidance.

He sat there for a moment and then thought about a friend he had in Charlotte. It was a guy who used to be on Philly SWAT with him before taking an administrative job with Mecklenburg County.

"Wedgewood," muttered Frankie. "Yeah, I remember now. North end of the city. He lived near a park. Um, Hornet's Nest Park, if I remember correctly." Frankie remembered how he and his pal had joked about leaving inner-city Philadelphia only to move to a neighborhood next to the Hornet's Nest.

Frankie shrugged, fired up the Durango, and headed east on I-40 toward Statesville and Interstate 77 southbound.

*****

He'd driven a little over two hours and the fuel gauge had dipped toward empty. He'd just crossed through the I-485 interchange when things began to look familiar to him. His buddy had picked him up from the airport and used the loop to get to the north part of the city.

Frankie recognized the Northlake Mall exit that would take him to his friend's house adjacent to the park. Frankie navigated down the ramp onto W.T. Harris Boulevard, a road named for the founder of the Harris Teeter grocery store chain.

Ordinarily, the mall would be bustling with shoppers loading up their cars with packages from Macy's or Belk. Others would be enjoying a late lunch at TGI Fridays or Olive Garden.

Today, the streets were practically deserted, and stores like Best Buy were boarded up. Frankie drove slowly down the once-bustling shopping district to observe what societal collapse looked like.

Damaged storefronts. Abandoned cars. Trash strewn about. Very little human activity.

He recognized the Lowe's Home Improvement store as the location where he was to turn left toward Hornet's Nest Park. He eased through the intersection because the traffic signal was not operating, and wound his way past a couple of crashed cars. He'd cleared the wreckage and turned onto Reames Road when suddenly a group of thugs ran out of the woods toward him.

One man smashed his windshield with a lead pipe while another tossed a gallon of white Valspar paint on the glass to obscure his view. Frankie reacted by pressing the gas pedal to the floor, causing the SUV to lurch forward.

As he did, he was unaware of the sheets of plywood lining the street in front of him, containing dozens of nails sticking up. Seconds later, all four tires on the Durango were flat and Frankie was creeping along on a tangled mess of mangled rubber and metal rims.

Dazed and confused, Frankie tried to make sense of it all. However, his attackers were on him too quickly. As he tried to exit the SUV to see what had happened, he was jumped from behind and dragged to the ground. He attempted to curl into a fetal position, seeking protection for his vital organs as several people kicked him, causing him to roll over and over until his back made contact with the nail-laden sheet of plywood.

He screamed in agony, much to the delight of the marauders. His eyes opened long enough for him to see one woman stomping on his chest, the force of the blows driving the nails deeper into his back.

Frankie mustered the strength to knock her leg away from him, and he escaped the bed of nails by rolling through them to the other side. Bloodied and in pain, he got to his feet, wobbly from the onslaught.

"Hold on!" a man's voice shouted from behind the attackers. "Yeah, just hold on one minute. I can't believe my eyes!"

Frankie was stunned by the attack, and with the warmer temperatures, sweat mixed with blood dripped into his eyes, obscuring his vision. He tried to wipe his face so he could make eye contact with the person who'd stopped the attack.

The man's voice was closer. "Scallone? Is that you? Well, isn't this a pleasant surprise. Ladies and gentlemen, I'd like you to meet Officer Frank Scallone with the Philly SWAT unit. You're a little lost, aren't you, Scallone?"

Frankie furiously wiped the fluids from his eyes and managed to get one eye free to focus on the man who recognized him.

He'd arrested a lot of people during his time on the force, and he couldn't necessarily remember every one of them. Joseph Jose Acuff, also known as Chepe, was not one of them. The famed Antifa leader had harassed some Marines and was a high-value target of the administration for his anarchist activities. In the moment, Frankie realized that Chepe hadn't changed his ways.

"Nice to see you, Acuff." It was an odd way to address the man whose cohorts had just begun to beat Frankie to death, but he thought he needed to do something to change the direction of the battle that he was sure to lose.

Chepe and his fellow anarchists laughed uproariously at the bloodied man's casual attitude. "Yeah, I guess it is, considering only one eye seems to be working." This drew more laughter.

"So, Chepe, did I make a wrong turn, or what?" Frankie continued to take a mollifying approach to the situation, hoping that if it worked, his life would be spared.

"Well, you ain't in Philly anymore, Toto," said Chepe, who was warming up to the playful banter. "Let's just say we're two lost souls who've crossed paths again."

"How do you know him, Chepe?" asked one of the men, who'd circled behind Frankie.

"Oh, we're old pals, right, Scallone? Why don't you answer that question for my friend?"

Frankie hesitated and then he quickly came up with a plan that most likely saved his life. *If you can't beat 'em, join 'em.*

"Well, when I was a cop, we got an order from Washington to arrest Chepe. I didn't wanna do it, but you know how it is with the feds. You can't tell *the man* no."

"You arrested Chepe?" asked a woman to Frankie's left.

"I think he deserves a beatdown for that!" shouted another.

Frankie's body stiffened as he prepared to be attacked. He wiped the blood and sweat off his face again, so he now had full vision. He was surrounded by a dozen people, some armed with guns and others carrying steel plumbing pipes. With his back in excruciating pain, he'd never get far if he tried to run.

"Seriously, Chepe. That's not me anymore. I left Philly SWAT. I couldn't stand to be associated with racist guys like that Will Hightower. Yeah, sure, he got reprimanded, but he kept his pension. I mean, what kind of justice is that? It sickened me so much that I joined the ACLU as a consultant. They needed to know how the Philly PD worked so they could do right by the people, you know what I mean?"

Frankie held his breath, as Chepe didn't respond immediately. "Yeah, I know those guys. How's Sharif doing. Is he still the ED?"

Frankie furrowed his brow but tried not to let on what he was thinking. Chepe was clearly referring to the executive director of the ACLU in Philadelphia, but the man's name was Reggie Stafford. Stafford had been in the news a lot recently as a spokesman for illegal immigrants seeking federal child welfare benefits.

"Um, I don't know anybody named Sharif. The fellow I work with is Reggie Stafford. He used to be one of their chief litigators and worked his way up. Who's Sharif?"

Frankie had successfully called Chepe's bluff and passed the test. "Oh yeah, wrong ACLU. Reggie's a good man."

"What do you want us to do with him, Chepe?" asked one of his men.

Frankie looked around at the people who surrounded him to see if they'd relaxed so that he'd have an opening. The sound of a vehicle approaching helped move the stalemate along.

"Nothing," replied Chepe. "You guys go hit that other car but try not to tear it up like this one. We need more transportation. I'll have a chat with Scallone."

One of Chepe's lieutenants took control of the group. "All right, everyone. Get into positions."

As they scurried off to ambush the next car, Chepe was left alone with Frankie. He approached him cautiously, holding his hand on the grip of his pistol, which was holstered in his belt. He reached into his pocket and pulled out one of his bandannas, which had a skull and crossbones screen printed on it.

"Here," he said as he tossed it to Frankie. "Clean yourself up and let's talk."

CHAPTER 38

The Varnadore Building
Uptown Charlotte, North Carolina

Frankie rode in the backseat of Chepe's vehicle as the anarchist army in Charlotte returned to their headquarters at the Varnadore Building. Fortunately for Frankie, Chepe didn't press him further about his make-believe position with the ACLU. Instead, Chepe chose to brag about how he'd beaten the rap laid on him by the Department of Justice. Chepe lit up a marijuana cigarette and shared it with Frankie, creating a bond that neither man ever envisioned occurring. Somehow, in a world turned upside down, even former adversaries could set aside the past simply because they were familiar with one another.

After the caravan of newly stolen vehicles returned to the Varnadore Building, Chepe introduced Frankie to a young woman who was the group's nurse. That evening, she worked her magic on Frankie's back, making him forget the pain endured by being punctured with dozens of nails. Later, she also made him forget Karen Hightower.

Frankie emerged from the office-turned-bedroom after the woman fell asleep. He overheard Chepe talking with his top lieutenants in a small conference room down the hall. He eased down the hallway to hear better, being careful not to get caught lurking about.

Chepe was leading the conversation. "From what Ollie and Earl have relayed to us, crossing the river, even in the darkness, would be a mistake. There are fallen trees everywhere, and the current is swift this time of year. If just one of our canoes tips over, their sentries could be alerted."

Another man spoke up. "I don't think a full-frontal assault will work either. The iron gates appear to be ten feet tall and firmly strapped together with heavy-duty chain. The only way to bust through them with one of our trucks is to hit it full steam. Earl said their security people man the gate twenty-four seven. He thinks the guards carry AKs or, for sure, AR-15s."

Frankie leaned against the wall and held his breath. It was obvious to him that Chepe was planning an assault on a gated community. However, the descriptions were starting to sound familiar. He considered their words carefully when Chepe continued to speak, interrupting his thoughts.

"That's why our little trip to Northlake paid off today. We've managed to load up all of their extension ladders. That wall is ten feet and spans the entire west and north side of the compound. We'll take their little castle just like they did in the old days. Drop a ladder onto the wall. Pull one over the other side. And sneak in and conduct our business."

"The guys said the place is full of women and children, too. Plus, their people are armed. Are we gonna go in there with our guns blazin', killing everything in sight like that dude did on that island in Norway ten years ago?"

Another man spoke up. "Nah, come on, man. We're not child murderers. We've just got a job to do, right, Chepe?"

"That's right. We've got our own firepower, courtesy of our benefactors. If someone gets in our way, then we cut them down. Earl and Ollie have given us several possible locations within the compound where this guy Cortland is staying. We'll hit them first. If we don't find him right away, we'll scare the hell out of their people until they give him up."

Frankie took a chance. He was convinced, based upon the cursory description and his recollection of the names Ethan had given him during the ride to the Haven from Richmond, that a guy named Cort lived there.

Frankie steadied his nerves and cleared his throat so he could be heard down the hallway. He casually strolled toward the partially opened conference room door, where he was greeted by one of Chepe's men.

"Sorry, man. Private meeting."

Frankie responded loud enough for Chepe to hear him. "Um, yeah. I figured that."

"That's okay," said Chepe. "Come on in, Frankie."

Chepe's lieutenant opened the door and Frankie entered the room. The smell of marijuana filled the air, and several remnants of smoked joints occupied an ashtray in the middle of the table.

"Hey, sorry to interrupt. I needed a little break from *Nurse Goodlove*. Man, she really knows how to fix a guy up."

The men, and a young woman, all enjoyed a laugh. "Oh yeah, we've all been treated by Nurse Goodlove, except Maggie here."

"Yeah, no thanks," the woman mumbled.

Chepe gestured toward an empty chair across from him. "Sit down, Frankie. We're just winding it up and I thought we'd burn one before we got some rest. My people have a big day tomorrow."

"Sure. I hadn't smoked weed for a long time. You know, bein' a cop and all. We were constantly pee-tested. But after a quit the force, I found myself partaking of the herb, as they say."

Chepe laughed as he lit the end of a rolled joint. "Man, this stuff is all-natural and legal in most states with a doctor's script. I don't know what the big deal is." He took a deep draw on the marijuana cigarette and handed it to Maggie.

The joint made its way around the table and Frankie took a toke. With all of the marijuana in his system from earlier that evening, taking a deep draw immediately relaxed him and gave him confidence. He decided to speak up. "Chepe, I wanna apologize for something, but I also feel the need to say something."

"About what?" he asked.

"Well, when I stepped into the hallway to get some air, I overheard you guys talking about what you have planned."

Two of Chepe's lieutenants straightened in their chairs and looked at one another and then over at Chepe. He caught their glance and then raised both hands, indicating they should relax.

"Go ahead," said Chepe.

"I'm gonna go out on a limb here and tell you something. Before I came to Charlotte today, I was at a place northwest of here, just south of I-40. They call it the Haven. Now, before you say anything, let me describe what I know about it. It's a big parcel of property, maybe a couple of hundred acres. It has ten-foot walls on one side and a long stretch of river on the other. The single entrance is off the road down a long tree-lined driveway, where an iron gate is located in a slight clearing."

The room grew silent, but the looks exchanged between Chepe and his people spoke volumes. He took a deep breath and exhaled before reaching for the joint. Everyone stayed silent as Chepe took another draw and filled his lungs with marijuana smoke. Finally, he spoke.

"Frankie, what were you doing there?"

Frankie was past the point of no return. His opportunity to escape was gone, and he had to make a decision as to whether he was all in with these anarchists. He closed his eyes momentarily, and all of the good times he'd shared with Karen flashed through his memory. When he opened them, his nose caught the scent of Nurse Goodlove and the feelings of pleasure he'd experienced that evening as he was taken in by Chepe.

The words spilled out of him as he relayed to Chepe everything he knew about the Haven and its residents, knowing full well that he might have just sentenced Karen and her kids to death.

PART FOUR

CHAPTER 39

Haven Barn
The Haven

It was early on Saturday morning and HB1 was abuzz with activity. In addition to the morning meeting, Tyler was meeting with the patrols, the drone kids were beginning their first full day on the job, and Echo was organizing a team to fortify their barriers at the points where the ten-foot security walls met the Henry River.

Tyler was handing out emergency trauma kits to be shared by the patrol units. Each day, just before the morning meeting of the top security personnel of the Haven, the night shift came off duty and turned their gear over to the morning shift. Tyler had created fanny packs with essential trauma supplies in the event someone was badly injured in the farthest reaches of the compound's perimeter.

Each kit contained certain basics like gloves, bandages, and methods to clean wounds. Using the Haven's vast supply of medical supplies, and the camouflage-pattern fanny packs purchased by Ryan at Big Lots, Tyler added several trauma essentials. Each bag contained a CAT tourniquet, Israeli bandages, a HALO chest seal, padded aluminum splints, ammonia inhalants, and instant ice compress packs. All of these items were designed to provide the injured person immediate treatment until he could arrive to provide medical assistance.

At the Haven, the security team worked in teams of two. Each carried an AR-15 rifle and a sidearm of choice. They also carried chest rigs with backup ammunition, a compact sidearm if they had one, and other tactical gear like pepper spray or a police baton.

While Tyler was giving the evening and morning teams a basic tutorial on how to use the trauma supplies, Alpha was addressing his new charges, who made up his drone Air Force brigade.

During the midnight to morning shift, the drone operators were limited by the number of infrared cameras at their disposal. After the shift change, the number of drones placed into operation usually numbered four at a time, so the compound was divided into quadrants. As the batteries were used up on these four units, the other four would be charging and swapped out as necessary. With this schedule, the Haven was almost always provided air surveillance except during shift change.

This morning, Alpha was going to deploy four drones so that he could train the kids who'd be handling weekend and after-school shifts. He towered over his weekend team as they stared up at him, hungry for knowledge and excited about the prospect of contributing to the Haven's security.

"I see two unexpected faces this morning," he began, staring down at Skylar and Hannah.

Meredith stood close behind them and smiled. "We talked about it, Alpha. All of our kids are prepared to make the sacrifices necessary to protect us. After you spoke with Ethan and his dad last night and agreed to give this young man another chance, we decided Hannah should do her part as well."

Alpha knelt down in front of Hannah and Skylar. "I have to ask you two a question. Are you doing this because you want to? Or are you joining the drone brigade because you think it's the right thing to do?"

The two preteen girls answered simultaneously.

"Both!" Then they looked at one another and exchanged high fives, coupled with a giggle.

Alpha smiled at their enthusiasm. "Okay, welcome to the drone team. Here's the thing, kids. What you will be doing for the Haven is very important. It requires discipline, patience, and focus.

"The discipline requires you to stay in your assigned quadrant. Patience requires you to fly the drone slowly, keeping in mind that you need to watch the grounds and that someone back at Haven House needs to monitor four of these at once. Finally, focus. Don't get distracted by each other. This is not a game. You're not down at the video arcade or on the comfort of your sofa back home. Lives are depending on you doing your job properly."

"Can everybody commit to this?" asked Meredith.

"Yeah!" shouted J.C., who was chomping at the bit to get started.

The others responded positively.

"Good," said Alpha. "For starters, I'm going to put Ethan in charge. There are five of you and we'll only be operating four drones at a time. At first, Ethan will bounce around, touching base with each of you to answer questions or to check your technique. He was pretty good at it until he went off the reservation."

"What's that mean?" asked J.C.

"It means I screwed up," said Ethan. He looked directly into Alpha's eyes. "It won't happen again."

Alpha nodded and continued. "Throughout the day, we'll change it up. There will always be a fifth operator who acts as a rover. The rover will check with the other operators continuously to see if they need anything, or to monitor when their batteries have almost lost their charge. This is very important. Before the battery dies, the rover needs to come to the barn and retrieve a fully charged quadcopter and controller. Take these to the drone operator and exchange them out. Okay?"

All the kids voiced their acknowledgment. Alpha gave them a tutorial and enlisted Ethan's help to show the kids how to connect the devices to the charging stations.

While he did, Meredith pulled Hannah aside. "Honey, I'm very proud of you for stepping up."

"Thanks, Mom, I wanted to, but I was afraid you'd say no."

Meredith frowned and shed a tear. "I know. I can be a protective mother hen sometimes. We live in a new world now, Hannah, and it's time for you to grow up. I guess I wanted to keep you as my darling little princess forever."

Hannah hugged her mom and then looked up to her. "It doesn't work like that, Mom. At some point you have to kick the little bird out of the nest."

Meredith laughed through the tears and hugged her daughter again. Then she reached behind her neck and unclasped her silver, double-cross pendant necklace. She pulled Hannah's hair to the side and lovingly hooked it around her neck. Hannah reached up and touched the larger cross that was accompanied by a smaller one connected to the chain.

"This was your grandmother's. She told me that the larger cross was to protect her as my mom, and the smaller one was to protect me, as her daughter. My mom told me that one day, I'd pass this on to my daughter. I think today is that day."

Hannah smiled and hugged her mom for a third time. The two Cortland women shared a rite of passage in which Meredith acknowledged it was time for her daughter to grow up. She'd symbolically kicked her little bird out of the nest.

CHAPTER 40

Outside the Haven

The surveillance intelligence received by Chepe was excellent. Ollie and Earl had carefully recorded their observations of activity at the Haven and kept meticulous notes. Frankie had supplemented their findings, confirming some things while adding additional information about their hierarchy and security procedures at the front gate.

Chepe surmised that the residents of the compound had experienced prior difficulties when outsiders approached their main entrance. Both his operatives and Frankie were of the opinion that the head security personnel and the couple running the community were likely to be called to the entrance in the event someone threatened to breach their entry gate.

This was just one of the distractions Chepe planned to deploy to pull people away from the massive wall that surrounded the Haven. The other, based upon the increased drone activity from the day before, was to play on their existing fears and concerns.

With constant drone flyovers along the Henry River's banks, Chepe suspected that the security team at the Haven would be overly preoccupied with further intrusions coming from the river side of the compound. He planned on giving them what they feared most, although it would turn out to be a false alarm.

His group had arrived outside the Haven in the early morning hours before dawn. He didn't like it, but they necessarily had to split into two groups. One was on the river side of the compound, and the other, the larger attack squad, was on the walled side of the Haven.

Using two-way radios they stole from a sporting goods store in Charlotte, he was able to communicate with each team to coordinate their efforts. Ollie and Earl identified a window of opportunity of approximately fifteen minutes in the morning when the security teams traded shifts and the drones temporarily stopped flying along the perimeter of the compound. This was the point when they'd make their move.

Counting on the cover created by the distraction, perfect timing, and the deployment of his most athletic people to scale the walls in order to man the ladders, his handpicked team of ten ruthless anarchists, plus Frankie and himself, would storm the compound in search of Michael Cortland and his family. Once inside, circumstances would dictate who lived and died.

He looked at his watch. It had been ten minutes since the drones stopped flying. He checked in with his team on the east side of the Henry River. They confirmed they were in place and also had eyes on the clearing around the front gate.

He touched base with two female members of his group who were prepared to approach the guards at the bridge, and another two who'd walk up to the front gate seeking shelter. They would provide a distraction for both sets of guards and lock them in place while his people scaled the wall at various points around the compound.

He'd circulated a single sheet of paper with images obtained of the Cortland family off the internet. Although the web was down in the U.S., Jonathan had instructed Chepe on how to access the Russian internet using his satellite phone and the Bluetooth link to a printer. It was a tedious process and involved several conversations with Russian hackers, but they got the information they needed.

Everyone committed the names and faces to memory and prepared their gear. If everything went according to plan, they'd be able to slip into the compound quietly, infiltrate the housing and other buildings in search of their targets, and eliminate them without being detected.

They had the element of surprise and a viable plan. Everyone knew their jobs, and all were willing to both kill and die for the cause. When Chepe told his group who the target was and why, he had to tamp down their enthusiasm. Nobody knew the Cortlands, but they all were familiar with George Trowbridge.

After Chepe told them what Trowbridge had done to Schwartz, and that Jonathan had been forced into hiding, their angry voices built to a crescendo.

He checked his watch again. It was time.

CHAPTER 41

Haven House
The Haven

Ryan and Blair stood on the front porch, enjoying a coffee drink and the warm morning sun. "Are you not going to the morning meeting today?" Blair asked as she took a sip of her Couples Coffee mixed with a few squirts of caramel for flavor. Ryan gurgled the last of his iced coffee through his straw and studied the bottom of the cup, hoping that a refill would magically appear.

"Nah, I wanted to stay out of Alpha's way today. He's teaching the kids about the drone program, and Tyler's got some medical kits to include with the security patrol's gear. I thought it would be nice to hang out with you this morning."

"Oh."

"Whadya mean, *oh?*"

"I mean—"

"Does your boyfriend come over and play while the big cat's away?" asked Ryan teasingly.

"Lol. The *big cat* has a tendency to leave a messy litter box," replied Blair as she playfully shoved Ryan toward the steps. "I haven't straightened the house since all of this started. We've had people traipsing in and out all day long. Lord knows how many germs are inside."

"Yeah, but they're our germs," countered Ryan.

"Not necessarily. You know I've never been the same since I read those pandemic books. It just takes one cough or sneeze, you know."

Ryan pouted. He genuinely wanted a day of peace and quiet with Blair and the girls. In the end, he'd take any amount of time together with them, regardless of what they were doing.

"I can help," he offered.

"Okay. The girls need bubble baths. We'll start there and then …" Blair stopped as she saw X-Ray walking toward them. She was still skeptical of the newcomer and tried not to share more than she had to when he was nearby.

"Good morning," he greeted as he arrived at the foot of Haven House's front steps. "I hope I'm not interrupting."

"Not at all," said Ryan. "We've got a pot of coffee that's still warm. Can I get you some?"

X-Ray smiled shyly and declined. "No, thanks. Have you got a minute?"

Blair patted Ryan on the shoulder and turned toward the door. "I'll get started inside. Join me if you can."

"Actually, Blair," X-Ray began, causing her to stop. He pulled his flip phone out of his pocket and twirled it in his hand nervously. "I really need to speak to you both."

Blair glanced at Ryan and then motioned for the guys to follow her inside. The two guys settled at the dining table and she poured herself another cup of coffee.

"I need to get right to the point, and when I'm done, I'm prepared for whatever consequences you consider to be appropriate," continued X-Ray.

"Well, that sounds ominous," Blair said in a serious tone as she sat next to her husband. "What's going on?"

X-Ray set the phone on the dining table and rubbed his face with the palms of both hands. He'd begun to sweat despite the fact that the temperature in Haven House had dropped to the low sixties without a fire burning. The mild temperatures had prompted Ryan to save firewood that day.

"There is some backstory, and I'll go into it if you want me to, but I need to just tell you both something because I'm not sure what it means."

"We're listening," said Ryan as he leaned forward and placed both elbows on the table.

"I have a side job, sort of, working for a group of people I consider to be real patriots. I help them with cyber intrusions during major election cycles, do opposition research, and even manipulate election results when necessary."

"Patriots?" asked Blair.

"I believed them to be the good guys," he explained. "Face it, both the left and the right employ dirty tactics and underhanded means of influencing elections. My job was to make sure the right side of the aisle could keep up with the left side. There are dozens of us around the country, if not more."

"Okay, fine," said Blair. "I'm aware of your political leanings, and I assumed that you didn't just use your talent to play casino games online or surf teen porn sites."

X-Ray became more nervous. "What?"

"Eugene O'Reilly, aka X-Ray, aka ..." Blair paused for effect. "X-Ray, need I continue? I know more than you think."

"Blair, what are you—?" Ryan tried to get Blair to explain, but she cut him off.

"Ryan, I suspect that will be a conversation for another time. I'm not concerned with this man's sexual preferences. I wanna know why he's here to see us."

X-Ray fidgeted in his seat and then got to the point. "My contacts with this patriot group sent out a text on the morning of New Year's Eve. I assume everyone on the distribution list got it and not just me. Anyway, the text identified Michael Cortland and instructed us to notify him, or her, or whoever it is, if he's spotted. We were to refer to him as the *eagle*."

Ryan emitted a heavy sigh. "Why are you just now telling us this?"

"Well, at first, I didn't think it was a big deal, especially since it was coming from the people who had paid for all of my equipment, and then some. Also, they're like us, you know. I didn't think it would put him in any danger."

"Danger? What would put him in danger?" Blair was becoming angry.

"After Ryan and Cort came by my place that night, I replied to the text to let them know Cort was here. I didn't know what else to do, so I followed instructions."

"You should've come to us immediately, that's what you should have done!" shouted Blair. Ryan tried to calm her down, but she had fire coming out of her ears now.

"There's more."

Ryan and Blair stared at the young man in disbelief.

"Talk. Now!" Blair demanded.

"I received a text last night, but I didn't see it until this morning. It instructed me to advise them if the *eagle*, that's Cort, left the Haven."

"They used the word *Haven?*" asked Ryan.

"No, sorry," replied X-Ray. He opened the flip phone and navigated to the text message he'd received.

He read it aloud. "Keep your eyes on the eagle and advise if he takes flight. Godspeed, Patriot! MM."

Blair reached for the phone and scrolled through the other messages. "They use the same sign-off as the others—Godspeed, Patriot, followed by the letters *MM*."

"You guys received the messages, too?" asked X-Ray.

"Some of us." Blair's response was curt. She thought for a moment and then looked to Ryan. "What about this message that came in thirty minutes ago? How is your phone working?"

"Text messages only. Blair, I just saw it and that's why I'm here. I'm afraid something is about to happen and it's all my fault."

"Let me see," said Ryan, who took the phone from Blair. He read the text.

It's always safer to keep your head down, but your eyes wide open.
Fare thee well,
Godspeed, Patriot.
MM

"I think that message was intended only for me, and not the group of hackers I'm affiliated with," said X-Ray.

Ryan stood and began to pace the room. He threw the phone on the dining table, and it slid to a stop in front of X-Ray. Nobody said a word as he angrily paced back and forth, stopping once to pick up a pillow off the couch only to toss it into a chair on the other side of the living area.

Blair stood and joined her husband. She was about to speak when X-Ray offered to leave.

Ryan shouted his response. "No! Stay where you are. Let me think."

"Cort's in danger," whispered Blair.

"Darling, we all are now. I've got to alert Alpha, and we need to be prepared."

"For what?" asked Blair.

"I don't know, but we can't take anything for granted, nor can we assume this guy's admissions can be trusted. Who knows whether he's trying to manipulate us or warn us?"

Blair reached for Ryan's hand and gave it a squeeze. "Either way, we need to lock him away until we figure it out. Right?"

Before Ryan could respond, his radio sprang to life.

"Bridge to Haven House, do you copy?"

Ryan pulled his two-way off his belt and replied, "Go ahead, Bridge."

"Front Gate to Ryan. Over."

Ryan pulled the radio away from his mouth and stared at it, looking for answers.

"Ryan, this is Alpha. We've got reports of two loud splashes hitting the river across from the cabins. I'm en route."

X-Ray slid his chair away from the table and spoke. "I think they're coming."

CHAPTER 42

The Haven

Chepe and his people had made their way to the Haven's wall during the shift change. Each team consisted of three people, one to handle the ladders and the other two to search for the Cortland family. The diversionary tactics were deployed, which included rolling two large boulders into the Henry River to create the illusion that two people had either fallen in or were attempting to breach the Haven's perimeter. Coupled with the approaches on the bridge and at the gate, the diversions were designed to draw the Haven's security resources away from the wall.

"Hit it," Chepe ordered into the radio. Along the wall, extension ladders were hoisted up, and the teams began their ascent to the top. Once there, a second ladder was handed up to them to provide a quick and safe landing inside the compound.

This was where speed and luck came into play. Although every member of his team was armed, he preferred not to raise alarms by firing their weapons. He'd hand-selected the people to enter the compound based upon their ability to kill with knives or their bare hands if necessary. These select few were known for their commitment to the cause.

He expected one-on-one fighting as they moved through the Haven, and that women and children would fall victim to their assault. He couldn't have any members of his teams become squeamish or uncertain, as that would jeopardize their entire mission.

Chepe was teamed with Frankie, who knew the most about the inner layout of the Haven from his conversations with Ethan. He was aware that the main house, where the Smarts resided, was centered within the Haven and not that far from the front gate. The day Frankie had tried to gain entry, he'd observed Ryan calling for Blair on the radio, and he'd heard her four-wheeler start up and head down the gravel road toward the gate. This seemed to confirm what Ethan had told him.

Further, Frankie knew that the large barn located toward the northern end of the Haven was a center of activity. It was the site of daily meetings and housed the quadcopters that Ethan had used the day he ran away. Through casual conversation, and due to the fact that Ethan was unaware that the cop was using his police interrogation skills to learn more about the new place where he hoped to live, Frankie had a pretty good idea of where to start looking for Cort and his family.

He and Chepe dropped to the ground and got their bearings. Using a compass taken from the sporting goods store, they headed due east through the woods until they approached a clearing where the Haven's gravel road split the property in half.

Frankie, who'd been trained through Philly SWAT on techniques to avoid detection during a raid, led the way, and Chepe dutifully followed his directions.

Chepe had turned down the volume of his radio and instructed all of his fellow anarchists to do the same. When the time came to extract, Chepe had an air horn that he'd sound, at which time everyone would make their way back to the wall where they came in. The members of the ladder team were responsible for keeping them hidden from view, taking out any patrols who threatened their position, and to be ready when the extraction alarm was raised.

"Drones," said Frankie under his breath. "Listen to the pitch. Can you hear them take off?"

"Yeah, to our left," replied Chepe. The two men held their breath as they focused on the sounds. Chepe then counted aloud. "One, two, three, four."

"Makes sense," whispered Frankie. "Ethan said there were eight. Four on. Four off."

They ducked into the underbrush and hid as a four-wheeler raced down the road past them toward the barn. They could hear shouting coming from their right.

"Already?" questioned Frankie. He couldn't imagine that their operation could've been blown so quickly.

Chepe shrugged. "Maybe they're responding to the diversions at the river."

"You've got your best shooters up there?" asked Frankie.

"Yeah. Both were hunters. If Cortland shows his face along that riverbank, he'll be dead."

"What about his family? We'll lose the element of surprise."

Chepe ducked as a drone sped over their head. "We'll take the big prize and go. I'm sure my people will be satisfied with his head on a pike."

The drones were now buzzing all over the property, and the sounds of four-wheelers filled the air. Then the first crack of staccato gunfire could be heard.

"Dammit!" said Frankie in frustration.

"Do you think that's our guys across the river?" asked Chepe.

"No way. That was rapid fire. This operation has just turned into a gunfight. Listen, we're gonna need to split up. I'll take the main house and you take the barn."

"What about the cabins?" asked Chepe. "That's where you think Cortland lives."

"Ethan wasn't totally sure about that, and we've got the shooters on the hill plus the two end teams who are responsible for taking the cabin. We need to stick to our plan and move. Now!"

Chepe nodded and began to step out onto the road.

Frankie rolled his eyes and shouted to him, "Stay under the tree canopy. The drones will see you in the open."

Chepe backtracked and began to work his way through the underbrush, darting from tree to tree as he went.

Frankie looked for a trail that carried him toward the main house, where he expected to find the women and children. He didn't care much about Cortland or fighting any political battles on behalf of someone he didn't know. He was interested in getting revenge against Will Hightower, and the way to do that was to draw him out in the open by snatching Karen or one of his kids.

CHAPTER 43

The Haven

Ryan grabbed his AR-10 rifle and put on his chest rig. He had purchased his tactical vest online at a law enforcement supply store. It allowed him to carry extra rounds of ammunition and a compact nine-millimeter handgun to supplement his regular sidearm. He gave instructions to Alpha over the two-way radio, completely disregarding normal communications protocols due to the circumstances.

"You get your security personnel in place and the drones in the air. I'll head to the front gate and see if this is related to what X-Ray has told us. Who's got the riverbank?"

"Tom and Cort," replied Alpha. "Bravo and Charlie will meet you at the gate, and then I think we should send them to patrol the outside perimeter, including the bridge. I'll put my two seasoned vets up against anybody who wants to get into this place."

"Okay. What about you?"

"I'm with Foxy. We'll be focused on the interior perimeter. If someone comes across that wall, we'll put 'em down. I'm out."

Ryan signed off and turned to Blair. "Gather them all back to the house. Keep X-Ray in cuffs and tied to the post in the holding cell out back. He understands why and shouldn't give you any trouble."

"Ryan, I'll shoot him if he does. Without hesitation."

"I know. I'm assigning Delta to handle security here."

"But—" began Blair before Ryan raised his hand to stop her.

"No arguments. I don't want anything to happen to you."

"Where are you headed?" she asked.

"I'm gonna check the front gate and then I'm going to retrieve

Cort. I'd feel better if he was here, under your protection, with Delta's help. I'll work with Tom to watch the river activity and then bounce around as needed."

Blair kissed Ryan. "It's gonna be okay. I love you."

His brow furrowed as he spoke. "We're gonna have our hands full today. I love you with all my heart."

Blair pointed her finger into his chest rig. "Don't talk to me like you might not come back. Go out there, watch your six, and take care of business."

This drew a laugh from Ryan. "I love it when you talk dirty to me."

"Go!" she ordered and backed on to the front porch, her eyes scanning the grounds in front of Haven House.

*****

Alpha bellowed as he entered Haven Barn. "Let's go, Foxtrot! We're goin' huntin'!"

"Hunting for what?"

"I don't know yet, just a gut feel," he replied. While she hurriedly went through her security locker and donned her gear, he explained X-Ray's revelation and the sudden occurrence of events at their main gate, the bridge, and along the river. She reached the same conclusion.

"They're trying to draw our attention away from the wall."

Alpha helped her adjust her gear while he spoke. "That's what I think, too. If that's the case, we've overreacted by sending so many people to the river and the gate."

"So send them back to their assigned posts," she suggested.

The sounds of the drones from outside Haven Barn grabbed their attention as they simultaneously looked outside to see them lift off.

"I can't, just in case I'm overthinking it," replied Alpha.

Hayden studied Ethan as he gave the kids instructions. "Are you sure we can rely upon him?"

"I don't have a choice. I've got all of the adults either working security to guard our buildings or assigned outside of their normal responsibilities to act as warm bodies if we need backup somewhere."

"What about Haven House?"

"Blair and Delta have that covered, along with Echo and Charlotte."

Hayden checked her weapon and confirmed that her rig was full of extra magazines. "Then it's just you and me, big guy," she said with a chuckle.

"Just the way I planned it," he added. "Listen, stay frosty. I've got a bad feeling about this."

"Let's roll, then."

Hayden and Alpha took off in a slow trot down one of the trails leading away from Haven Barn. Just as they entered the woods, they heard the first rounds of gunfire.

Alpha immediately stopped. "Looks like we've got ourselves a hot war." He reached for his radio, and before he could call for a situation report from his assigned posts, Ryan contacted him.

"Alpha, this is Ryan. Over."

"Go ahead."

"We've got a breach on the southernmost end of the wall. We've got a man down, and two hostiles are dead."

"Roger that."

Ryan added another piece of information. "They were armed with AKs and had a ladder to scale the wall."

"Have you advised Blair? We're gonna need the eyes in the sky."

Ryan replied quickly, "It's my next call. She'll advise us both. Out."

Alpha looked to Hayden. "There's gonna be more. Are you ready for this?"

"Hey, I've gotta lot of built-up frustration. I've got no problem hunting bad guys. Let's go!"

The two of them separated slightly and moved more deliberately down the trail, walking heel to toe in a low crouch. After a couple of hundred yards, Alpha dropped to one knee and raised his fist, causing Hayden to stop.

She immediately lowered herself and turned to monitor the trail behind them. Satisfied that no one had snuck up behind them, she turned her attention back to Alpha, who held up two fingers and pointed off to his left. That was when Hayden heard the crunching sound of feet shuffling through the woods. The intruders were not experienced hunters or military. Their heavy feet gave away their position.

Alpha inched forward and kept his rifle trained on the location where the sound emanated from. A cross-trail cut through the woods, giving him a clear line of sight if they attempted to go through the clearing barely wide enough to accommodate a four-wheeler. He steadied his aim on a spot in the center of the trail. He intended to wait until all of the intruders were visible in his sights.

Several tense seconds later, the first and then a second man walked across the trail, headed toward Haven Barn. Alpha didn't hesitate as he squeezed the trigger. Unlike the other AR-platform weapons in the Haven, Alpha had installed a bump stock on his before they were banned by the government. The rapid fire generated by the weapon recoiling off his shoulder sounded like a machine gun and was just as effective.

The two men's bodies exploded in blood, parts of their chest and neck shredding into ribbons of goo. Alpha inched forward, looking for any kind of movement from the two men. He relaxed slightly as he rose out of his crouch.

"Two dead guys," he said proudly before his words were muted by the sound of Hayden's rifle.

"Make that three," she said. Another man, one of Chepe's ladder team, had snuck down the trail, carrying a lead pipe, and had planned on attacking Alpha. Despite his close proximity to her partner, Hayden had confidence in her aim and quickly dispatched the attacker.

"Thanks, Foxy. I think we're just getting started."

CHAPTER 44

The Haven

Tom and Cort were patrolling along the banks of the Henry River, discussing X-Ray's statements to Ryan. Cort tried to shrug it off as most likely being his father-in-law keeping tabs on his family. Tom wasn't so sure, especially in light of the activity at the gate and bridge. Cort countered that it was probably the people who were here before, looking for a way in to steal food. Both men stopped their debate when they heard the rapid gunfire emanating from the southern end of the Haven.

"Cort, we've got to get you to safety," implored Tom.

Cort was about to respond when a reflection of light caught Tom's eye from the hill across the river. He didn't hesitate, using remarkably fast reflexes for his age. He shoved Cort toward an old decorative wishing well, and just as he did, two gunshots rang out.

The first shot caught Tom in the back of his right shoulder and spun him around. The second bullet whizzed by his head and embedded in the wet ground.

Tom screamed in pain as he tried to roll his body toward the well. Cort rose on one knee and returned fire, shooting wildly in the direction where he thought the shots came from. With two more three-round spurts fired toward the hill, he broke cover and helped Tom crawl to the well.

Within seconds, other residents of the security team who'd been patrolling up and down the riverbank came racing toward them. They took up positions near the well, using boulders and four-wheelers for protection.

"The shot came from the hill!" shouted Cort.

He fumbled for his radio and tried to gain his composure to contact the hospital. Tom was covered in blood and his eyes were beginning to shut. Finally, he called out to the other residents surrounding him.

"Call medical! Tell them we need Tyler for a gunshot victim!"

He purposefully didn't say that it was Tom who'd been shot, because he knew Donna was at the hospital. She'd insist upon joining Tyler, and there were still snipers across the river who could begin to open fire at any time.

Cort turned his attention to Tom. "Tom, hang in there. I've got help coming. Can you hear me?"

Tom nodded.

"Okay, good. I need you to sit up against the well. There's still a gunman over there and—"

"Two. There's two."

"Okay, two. Come on, let me help you. We need to raise the wound above your heart."

As Cort helped Tom sit up so that he was propped against the brick structure, he checked for an exit wound. "Good, Tom. The bullet went in and out again."

Cort removed his Yale sweatshirt and began to apply pressure to both the entrance and exit wounds. Tom grimaced as the pain began to overtake him. "Tell Donna I love her," he said breathlessly.

"You're gonna tell her your—" Cort wasn't able to finish his sentence as gunfire erupted from the woods up the bank. They were being fired upon and found themselves caught in a crossfire.

Cort scrambled to all fours and looked around. His only hope was to get the four-wheeler parked forty feet away. With his tall, lanky frame he made for a bigger target than most men, but he had to create some additional cover between Tom and the shooters in the woods.

Without further hesitation, Cort bolted for the four-wheeler as a trail of bullets tore up the turf at his feet. He slid to a stop on the river side of the John Deere Gator and crawled into the seat, keeping his head as low as possible. He started the engine, and using his hands to press the gas pedal, he drove the Gator next to Tom.

More bullets rained down on them, blowing out the left side tires and ripping into the machine's fenders. But the green-and-yellow utility vehicle provided them added protection.

"Cort, this is Tyler. Over."

"Go ahead, Tyler."

"I'm at the trail opening just to your left. Can you see the front of my cart?"

Cort replied, "Yeah, but, Tyler, they're in the woods. You can't come out here."

"I know. Just hang in there. Help's on the way."

Neither man was able to speak again as gunfire exploded in the trees. The sounds of men screaming in pain filled the air as the relentless onslaught of bullets ripped through tree branches and bodies. After a minute, the deep baritone voice of Alpha came across the radio.

"Hold tight, buddy. We've gotta mop up and then we'll get your partner to the hospital."

Cort realized that Alpha didn't use their names, something a seasoned military veteran would know, but Tyler would not.

"Roger," replied Cort.

The drones flew overhead, and one hovered for a moment above his position. Cort looked up and gave a slight wave as single gunshots could be heard coming from the woods. He presumed the words *mopping up* could be equated with *finishing off*.

Seconds later, Tyler came racing down the hill, his cart bouncing off the bumpy terrain of the riverbank until he reached their position. He and Cort placed Tom on the stretcher and began to load him onto the medical cart when he noticed Alpha and Hayden slowly backing out of the woods with their weapons, scanning the trees for any signs of movement.

The gunshot wound gave Tyler a sense of urgency. "Come on, Cort, we need to get Tom treated."

Cort grabbed his rifle and joined Tyler. He tried to snap out of the shock of seeing the man whom he'd been told to trust with his life gunned down by a bullet meant for him. When he heard more gunfire off in the distance, he sensed it wasn't over.

CHAPTER 45

The Haven

Ethan heard the gunfire first. "Did you guys hear that?" he asked as he flew his drone along the northwestern quadrant of the Haven, which covered the area that included Haven House.

"Hear what?" asked Kaycee, who was still trying to learn the operation of the quadcopter. "These things are pretty loud."

The last drone, operated by J.C., lifted off the ground and headed north toward the area where the wall runs into the river. He and his sister were responsible for the entire riverbank and also the bridge, although it was outside the Haven's property.

Hannah had volunteered to be the rover, the person responsible for replacing drones as their batteries began to die down. She and Skylar had recently swapped positions, with Skylar taking the controls for the area above the main gate.

Suddenly, the two armed guards assigned to watch over the drone brigade and Haven Barn closed ranks around the kids. Almost simultaneously, their radios exploded in chatter, as did Meredith's, who had elected to hang around the barn rather than join the others at Haven House.

"We've got gunfire in the southwest quadrant," a man shouted into the radio. "We need eyes!"

"Who has the southwest quadrant, near the front gate?" asked one of the security people.

"Me," replied Skylar. "Ask them if they're near the river."

Skylar used the motion of her body to simulate flying the drone in a cockpit seat. As she turned the drone to the right, her whole body, together with the controller, would lean right with it. The determined look on her face indicated that the technique worked for her.

"Meredith, can you read?"

"Hey, that's Mom!" exclaimed Kaycee.

"Go ahead, Angela."

"We've got two injured men coming our way from just past the front gate. When they get here, Donna and I could use an extra set of hands."

Meredith didn't immediately respond, choosing instead to study Hannah and the other kids. She thought for a moment, but Angela interrupted her.

"Meredith, are you there?"

"Hannah," Meredith said as her daughter ran to her side.

"Mom, we've got this. The guys need me, and these men will protect us."

"Honey, I don't know ..." Meredith's voice trailed off.

"Meredith!" Angela shouted into the radio as more gunfire pierced the air, except much closer this time.

"Go, Mom."

Meredith nodded. She bent down to kiss her daughter and climbed onto her four-wheeler. Seconds later she was out of sight, about the time that Alpha and Hayden opened fire on the intruders at the back side of the barn.

The gunshots drew the attention of the armed guards, who cautiously approached the barn and separated. They began to investigate, leaving the children alone. Ethan was the first to notice.

"Okay, you guys. We've got this. We know what to do. Our job is to give Blair or whoever is watching in the main house the best view we can of what's going on."

"Yeah, let's roll!" shouted Kaycee enthusiastically. The kids came together as a team and followed Alpha's instructions. *Discipline. Patience. Focus.*

Barely a word was spoken between them as they flew the drones within their quadrants, periodically stopping in order to get a better look at something of interest. The high-resolution cameras enabled the kid to determine if movement on the ground was a resident of the Haven or one of the intruders.

J.C. was operating the drone that covered the riverbank near the cabins. "Oh no! One of our guys got shot!"

Ethan quickly attempted to calm him down. "Okay, okay, J.C. Slow down above him and give Blair a good view of what is happening around where he's located. Turn your camera angle around slowly so that she can get a good view. Maybe she'll see where the shooter is."

"I understand." J.C. furrowed his brow and concentrated as he slowly lowered his quadcopter to provide a better perspective of the woods and the hills across the river.

"Good," said Ethan. He provided J.C. some additional direction. "Stay with it for a little longer and then make a quick sweep of your quadrant before coming back."

J.C. nodded and Ethan looked around. When he noticed that the two guards hadn't returned, he assumed they were responding to the shooting by the river, so he shook it off. He turned his attention back to his own quadrant, although so far, he hadn't seen any activity. All of the action was along the riverfront.

Until now.

"Huh?" he mumbled to himself. He swung his drone around and returned to the spot where he thought he saw a person running through the woods with a rifle in his hands. Ethan, who'd become well-versed in the drone's maneuvering capabilities the day he left the Haven, swung the machine back toward the main house and looked for a clearing to spot the man running toward the house.

There! he shouted to himself. *I see you again.* That was when Ethan's mouth fell open. It was Frankie.

He spun around, looking for the guards who'd wandered behind the barn. He didn't have a radio and had to rely upon someone in Haven House to see Frankie's approach.

He couldn't trust that. His mom and dad were there.

"Hannah! I need your help."

"What is it? Is your battery almost dead?"

Ethan glanced down at the controller, and he was on his last quarter of battery life. He didn't want Frankie to get away, but he didn't want the drone to die either. "Um, yeah. Hurry, get me another one. Run!"

Hannah bolted for the barn and Ethan continued to follow Frankie's progress. He'd slowed down as he got closer to the house and then moved toward the backyard.

"Here you go," said Hannah.

"Come here, Hannah. We need to keep this one up while I fly the other one down there too."

"Both at once?" she asked. "They said to bring one—"

Ethan shoved the controller in her hand. "I know what they said, but this is different. Keep the drone focused on the backyard."

"Yeah, sure."

Ethan quickly powered up the controller of the fifth quadcopter, and within half a minute, it was screaming down the gravel road, covering the three-quarters of a mile to Haven House in very little time.

Once he had it positioned over the house with a good look at the backyard, he exchanged controllers with Hannah.

"Okay, same thing. Do not move from this position, understand? Somebody is going after them and I need to make sure they know."

Ethan flew the other quadcopter back and hastily landed it near the entrance of the barn. Without another word, he dropped the controller and ran toward Haven House as fast as his sore ribs would allow.

CHAPTER 46

Haven House
The Haven

Frankie ran from tree to tree, trying to avoid being detected by Will, who was pacing back and forth through the backyard with his rifle swinging back and forth. Overhead, a pesky drone had tracked him part of the way but apparently lost him, because it had hovered for a while and then suddenly disappeared, only to be replace by another one. Sporadic gunfire was taking place all around him, but he kept his eyes on the prize. First, he'd kill Will, and then he'd take back Karen. *Or not,* he said to himself with a devious grin on his face.

Frankie moved around a small storage shed and found a trail that circled toward the back of the house. It seemed to lead to a small garage, just large enough to park the Smarts' two four-wheelers. Frankie eased into position and laid his eyes on Will, who was patrolling the back of the house.

Will glanced up at the drone. He'd become distracted by its presence. It didn't dawn on him that the drone might have been tracking someone. That was fine by Frankie, who wanted this fight to be mano a mano, allowing him to give Will what he deserved.

The drone dropped lower in the sky until it was hovering just above the roofline. The loud buzzing sound was beginning to annoy Will, who kept turning his head to see what it was doing. Frankie saw his chance.

He abandoned the idea of catching Will off guard and slitting his throat with the hunting knife he'd chosen from Chepe's weapons stash. At the end of the day, he thought, why not just kill the guy and get the heck out of dodge. *A kill is a kill.*

Frankie worked his way down the trail, keeping the trees between them, and focused on Will, who continued to glance upward. Finally, Frankie was in a position where he could crouch behind a couple of large landscape boulders and take a clean shot.

He steadied his weapon and was about to pull the trigger when he was knocked down from behind. The force of the blow tore his rifle from his grip, forcing it to the ground and sending him tumbling into the rock. The brutal contact with the rock caused the gash to be reopened on his forehead.

His vision was blurred from the blood that poured down his forehead. He reacted instinctively, swinging wildly at his assailant, who attempted to swing at his head.

Frankie couldn't see, raising his level of fear and causing him to defend himself like a cornered animal. He just kept fighting back, pummeling his attacker with blow after blow until their body crashed against the same rocks and went limp.

Frankie tried to regain his footing and groped his paddle holster for his pistol, but it had fallen out in the fracas.

"Don't move!" Will shouted at him. "Frankie? Dammit! What have you done?"

A blow to the temple courtesy of Will's buttstock turned out Frankie's lights.

*****

Will threw his rifle aside and fell to his knees. He crawled over to Ethan's lifeless body and gingerly lifted his son's head off the ground. A huge gash in his skull bled uncontrollably. Brain matter was smeared on the rock where Ethan's head had violently made contact.

Will began to sob uncontrollably. His hands were shaking so bad that he couldn't trust whether he was feeling Ethan's pulse or not.

"Ethan! Wake up, son. Please, God. Help him!"

Will hugged his child, begging for help, when Echo burst out of the back door of Haven House followed by Blair. They both arrived at the boulders together and found Will rocking his son's body in his lap.

"Oh, Jesus," groaned Echo as he slowly walked up and placed his hand on Will's shoulder.

Blair held her rifle in one hand, pointed at Frankie's torso, and felt his pulse with the other. "He's still alive. I'm tired of fooling with this jackass!"

Blair shouldered her rifle and pulled out her handgun. She cocked the hammer on the more powerful .45-caliber weapon and was about to put a round in Frankie's head when Karen came running out of the house screaming.

Blair turned to slow her progress. No mother should see her son like this, but it was too late. She fell to Will's side and hugged her only son in a frenzied combination of sobbing and begging God to save Ethan.

Will tried to comfort her, but she pushed him away. He finally relented and sat to the side, allowing her to grieve with Ethan alone.

Blair stepped away from the family and turned to Echo. "I wanna kill this guy myself, but now's not the time. We need to let these two mourn their son without another gunshot echoing through their minds."

"I'll cuff him and drag him around front. Should I have Tyler come tend to his wounds?"

"No! Are you kidding me? Find some salt to pour in them."

"It'll be my pleasure."

CHAPTER 47

The Armageddon Hospital
The Haven

"Okay, Tom. Not to be cliché, but you dodged a bullet, sort of," said Angela with a slight laugh. She was trying to lighten the mood because Donna had been so distraught, she was unable to function, requiring Angela to frantically call for Meredith's help as her stand-in trauma nurse.

"It hurts like hell," he said. Then he added, "It's a good hurt, though. You know, the kind you can only feel if you're alive."

"Well said, Commander," said Angela. "You're a pretty tough old bird. Your wing was clipped, but the good news is the bullet went through the exit wound cleanly. Meredith and I irrigated it extensively, and neither one of us could spot any indication that the bullet fragmented."

Tom explained, "The shooter must've been a hunter because he used a heavy-grain bullet. It spun me around, yet it was a good clean shot. Nobody wants their deer meat full of lead fragments."

Angela smiled and gently patted him on the chest. "Okay, Tom. You rest up and I'm sure Donna will come get us if your condition changes. I've got a couple more guys to attend to. Flesh wounds, mostly, nothing like the cannon that hit you."

The sound of a four-wheeler approaching caught their attention, and Tyler, who'd had a busy day of his own, went onto the front porch to investigate. She noticed it was Blair with a body draped over the front of her four-wheeler. Angela's curiosity caused her to join Tyler outside.

Blair roared toward the cabin and squeezed her brake levers on the handlebars, bringing the Prairie to an abrupt stop. Her forward momentum threw Frankie's limp body onto the porch of the hospital.

"Who's this?" asked Angela. "He's not one of ours, is he?"

"Nope. His name is Frankie. He's Will's ex-wife's ex-boyfriend."

"Huh?" asked Tyler as he rolled Frankie over to take a look at his head, which was now bleeding more after being slammed against the porch.

Blair allowed the Prairie to idle. "It's a long story. Listen, I don't care if you keep him alive or not. Throw him in the river for all I care. I just wanted him off my front lawn."

"Angela?" Meredith had suddenly appeared in the doorway and glanced down at Frankie, who was bleeding all over the deck. She waved the trauma doctor back in to look at one of the perimeter guards who'd received a blow to the back of the head. He was concussed but started to awaken.

The two applied some wet cloths to the man's neck and forehead. Angela was going through her routine for patients with concussions when they heard screaming.

"Now what?" she asked, immediately stopping her examination before quickly moving to the front door. The high-pitched squeal sounded like children, and it was coming from the direction of the barn.

"Meredith, it's the kids!"

Meredith pushed past Angela and ran into the front of the hospital. Tyler had already begun to run in the direction of the voices, and Blair hopped on her four-wheeler. She slung gravel all over Frankie as she chased after the concerned dad. She pulled her sidearm and held it as she drove. She and Tyler arrived at the screaming kids simultaneously.

J.C. was covered with blood.

Tyler fell to his knees and held his son with both hands. "Where are you bleeding from? What happened?"

"I'm fine, Dad. It's not my blood."

"It was from one of the guards," said Skylar. "They went to check on a noise behind the barn and only one came back. His face was all bloody and the back of his head had a hole in it. He fell on top of J.C."

"Then he started twitching on the ground," added Kaycee. "It scared us, so we all started running away."

Meredith arrived with Angela close behind. Angela hugged J.C. and frantically searched his body for a wound.

"I'm okay, Mom. It's just, um, sticky."

Meredith took a few steps toward the barn and then spun around.

"Where's Hannah? Hannah!" She turned around again and looked at the three children. "Kids, where's Hannah?"

"She got scared, too, and ran into the barn," replied Kaycee.

Suddenly, the group was startled by the piercing sound of an air horn. They looked at one another, not sure what it meant.

Finally, Blair spoke up. "That's not one of our procedures. Tyler, please raise Ryan on the radio. I'm taking Meredith to the barn to fetch Hannah. Hop on."

Meredith ran around to the back and climbed onto the seat. Tyler called Ryan but didn't immediately receive a response. As Blair took off for the barn, the Rankins hugged their children and comforted Skylar, who was completely unaware that her brother lay dead in the arms of her mother.

CHAPTER 48

Haven Barn
The Haven

Blair stopped just short of the barn and pulled the Prairie into the woods. She patted Meredith's leg and motioned for her to get off the back of the seat.

"Why are we stopping here?" asked Meredith as she swung her leg over the back.

Blair held her index finger to her lips. She whispered her response. "You see that guy's face down in the gravel? He's probably dead because his head's been bashed in. I need to check things out until we get some backup."

"I'll back you up. Let's go." Meredith began to walk toward the barn; however, Blair grabbed her by the arm and pulled her back to the four-wheeler.

"There is no *let's*, and lower your voice," ordered Blair. "I'll go in, but you have to wait here."

"No way, Blair. My baby's in there somewhere. Frightened, or maybe hurt."

Blair sighed and ripped her sidearm out of its holster. She thrust it at Meredith, butt-end first. "Do you know how to use this?"

"Um, no. But I'm going with you." Meredith pulled the gun out of Blair's hands and began to walk toward the barn.

Blair shook her head and caught up with her. "Don't shoot me." Blair moved past and raised her rifle, crouching as she walked, swinging the barrel from side to side in search of a target.

They entered the barn together. Blair pointed Meredith to the right near the conference room and she took the left side, which was full of equipment and boxes. It was a likely hiding place for Hannah, or one of the intruders.

As Blair methodically conducted her sweep of the barn, she listened for the slightest sound. Heavy breathing. The shifting of feet. Even the quiet cries of a frightened child.

Nothing. After a few minutes, she and Meredith met toward the back of the barn where the quadcopters were parked.

"Stay out here and check the lockers," Blair instructed. "They're a little small for a man, but Hannah might be too frightened to come out. I'll clear the conference room and then we'll get help to search around the woods."

"Okay."

The women split up and Blair entered the conference room. She immediately dropped to a knee and pointed her rifle under the table in the center of the room. Then she cleared the corners. When she didn't see anyone, she noticed the couch was slightly askew by the window overlooking the front of the barn. The blinds had been turned as if someone had been looking outside.

Blair kept her rifle trained on the sofa, prepared to shoot through the padded back in order to take down one of the attackers. She eased up to its side and then quickly stepped forward to get a clear look behind it.

Still nothing.

She peered through the blinds and saw Ryan's Ranger streaking toward the barn. To her left, Alpha and Hayden emerged from the woods and were inspecting her Prairie with their weapons drawn.

"Did you find anything?" asked Meredith, startling Blair, who reactively swung around and pointed her gun at her.

After lowering her weapon, she replied, "No, not a trace. Ryan's on his way. Let me have my gun back."

Meredith began to tear up and her arm went limp. Blair approached her slowly and reached out to take the handgun, and she slid it back into its holster.

"Come on, Meredith. Hannah's just scared and she probably went into the woods because—"

Ryan interrupted her. "Blair! Are you in here?"

"Yeah. Meredith, too." The two women emerged from the conference room. They were greeted in the barn by Ryan, Alpha, and Hayden. Cort was running toward them from the gravel road. The group walked back into the midday sun to greet him.

"They said Hannah is missing?" asked Ryan.

"Yeah," replied Blair, who lowered her weapon for the first time. Meredith began to cry in earnest as she ran toward Cort. Blair watched the couple crash into one another, allowing their emotions to pour out to one another. Blair turned her attention back to the guys. "Is the Haven secure?"

"We think so. When they sounded an air horn, several of our teams caught their people trying to climb over the wall. Quite a few got away, but we killed several of them in the process."

Cort shouted for Ryan. "We've got to find our daughter!"

Ryan broke away from Blair and approached the distraught couple. "We will. She can't go far, Cort. She's probably scared and hiding in the woods. We've got all of our people scouring the woods and underbrush to make sure all of the attackers are either gone or dead."

"What about Hannah?" begged Meredith through her sobs.

"They'll find her," replied Ryan. "She's probably frightened. She's not sure who she can trust. I think what we need to do is split into groups and start working the area behind the barn."

"Yeah," interjected Alpha. "Foxy and I just came from the river's edge. We would've seen her if she ran down toward the cabins."

Blair walked away from the group and began to look around. Something was not quite right. Then she heard it. The buzzing sound of a drone coming toward them. The sound grew louder as it approached.

The others heard it too. They wandered around the gravel area in front of the barn, looking skyward in all directions for the drone. Both Hayden and Alpha fanned out, scanning the woods in search of any threats.

The high-pitched sound emanating from the four motors of the quadcopter grew even louder, until it suddenly sailed over the roof of the barn and down the gravel road toward Haven House. Then it suddenly stopped and swung back around.

Slowly now, the quadcopter returned to the barn. Moving painstakingly slow, it inched closer and lowered its altitude as if it were an airplane preparing for landing.

The group stared at the device. Some were confused; others pointed their weapon at it, anticipating that the machine might attack them in some way.

Cort hesitated, and then he began to walk toward the drone. Meredith quickly caught up to them until they stopped. The operator smoothly set the drone a few feet away from them and the motors suddenly shut off.

The rest of the group gathered around as the four propellers stopped, leaving them in complete silence.

Meredith began to wail as she pointed at one of the arms of the drone. Tears poured out of Cort's eyes as he lowered himself to pick it up. Attached to the arm was the double-cross pendant necklace Meredith had given Hannah earlier that day for protection.

Also wrapped around the arm was a note affixed with one of Hannah's colorful hair ribbons. Cort wiped the tears and sweat out of his eyes. He tried to regain his composure long enough to read and comprehend the words.

"The King needs to come to the Queen City and we will turn over his Princess. Frankie knows where to find me. Come alone."

THANK YOU FOR READING
DOOMSDAY: MINUTEMEN!

If you enjoyed it, I'd be grateful if you'd take a moment to write a short review (just a few words are needed) and post it on Amazon. Amazon uses complicated algorithms to determine what books are recommended to readers. Sales are, of course, a factor, but so are the quantities of reviews my books get. By taking a few seconds to leave a review, you help me out and also help new readers learn about my work.

And before you go …

SIGN UP for Bobby Akart's mailing list to receive special offers, bonus content, and you'll be the first to receive news about new releases in the Doomsday series. Visit: www.BobbyAkart.com

VISIT Amazon.com/BobbyAkart for more information on the Doomsday series, the Yellowstone series, the Lone Star series, the Pandemic series, the Blackout series, the Boston Brahmin series and the Prepping for Tomorrow series, totaling thirty-plus novels, including over twenty Amazon #1 Bestsellers in forty-plus fiction and nonfiction genres. Visit Bobby Akart's website for informative blog entries on preparedness, writing, and a behind-the-scenes look into his novels.

Made in the USA
Columbia, SC
09 October 2021

46982792R00159